MW01518134

I hope
you are having
a good year!
Enjoy!

I. L.

Mary

LITTLE NAT

T.L. May

authorHOUSE®

AuthorHouse™
1663 Liberty Drive
Bloomington, IN 47403
www.authorhouse.com
Phone: 1-800-839-8640

First published by AuthorHouse 10/7/2009

ISBN: 978-1-4490-3002-5 (e)
ISBN: 978-1-4490-3001-8 (sc)

Library of Congress Control Number: 2009909795

Printed in the United States of America
Bloomington, Indiana

This book is printed on acid-free paper.

"The Lord is my light and my salvation;
Whom shall I fear?
The Lord is the defense of my life:
Whom shall I dread?
When evildoers came upon me to devour my flesh,
My adversaries and my enemies, they stumbled and
fell.
Though a host encamps against me,
My heart will not fear;
Though war rise against me,
In spite of this I shall be confident."

(Psalms 27:1-3)

I would like to dedicate the inspiration for this book to God, the only source for all creativity and beauty in this world.

I would also like to dedicate this book to my immediate and extended family in New Brunswick and beyond, my sis, Bridget, my best friend, Jackie L. ("to the beat of our own drum"), my husband Ben, and to my mother, Judy Anne Bovaird Coughlan.
I miss you mom but I know I will see you again.

1

The wind was blowing gently that autumn afternoon as the old man made his way down Main Street for his usual afternoon stroll. Residing in the small town of Hampton, New Brunswick most of his life, walking had become more difficult as time wore on.

Yet, today was a special day. It was to visit his love…a love he had lost many years ago.

Reaching Cemetery Road, the man continued up its gentle hill towards the old cemetery's entrance. Walking past original sites from its earliest Loyalist days, it still appeared the same after all these years. Nothing was foreboding at all as all was as it should be.

Peaceful.

At one point in time, when he was young, this same field contained few tombstones. Only townspeople, whom after living their whole life in the village, were laid to permanent rest.

A natural death.

Only after the Second World War's aftermath, did this particular burial site become the resting place for some of its casualties. An era passed but not forgotten. Remembrance Day ceremonies had concluded the day before on Memorial Hill close to School Street, where spirits that had come and gone before were honored. The memory of who they were as people, now asleep to the present world that has moved on without them.

With his walking cane in tow, further up the hill he went until he reached a solitary tombstone he knew all too well. Holding a singular, white rose clasped tightly in his left hand, an ache began in his heart as it always did, remembering her...

An untimely death.

What was this? Flowers?

How interesting that people who never knew her brought her flowers. How kind and thoughtful.

"Hi...It's me again."

The tombstone remained silent.

"I just happened to be strolling by and I thought I would stop and bring a rose for my girl," he boyishly grinned. At the age of eighty-one, time had been good. Despite thinning gray hair, the wrinkled face that stared down at her tombstone could not disguise the handsome man of the past. "I know it has been awhile. I've been busy I suppose....I've been doing a lot of thinking actually. I guess retirement does that. You have more time to just.... think..."

Deafening silence.

"You are still my girl you know....Maybe not physically," he sighed, "but in my heart....always...and that is what counts, right? The heart?"

Once again the grave remained silent to him. The only voice heard was the whisper of a soothing wind, as the leaves gently blew past him.

If only she could hear him."If I could, what I would give just to have more time with you...Lately for some reason, it's almost as hard as it was in the beginning. I feel it all over again."

"Would you believe me if I told you that sixty years later, I *still* think about you, almost daily, in some way?" he asked painfully. "I don't understand why and I don't pretend to know why. Only thing I do know is that you haunt me, and nothing I do seem to shake me free of that. I know that we can't change our past, as God knows best. We make the most of our time, and God knows I have done my time." Then he thought long and hard for a moment."I know God is not punishing me. I understand that we must be grateful for the time given, and I am. I just wish you could have been around a little longer.

Then he began to chuckle, a quiet chuckle of a memory only he knew of.

"Those were good years!" he resigned. "Lord knows that meeting you felt like I had just been hit by a train…"

The day he first saw her flashed in his mind. Her perfect, pale complexion glistening under the August sun. She was a sight to see in her cotton white dress! Guarded by a fierce mane of long, black, Irish hair, that face and those mysterious hazel eyes were forever sketched within his mind's eye. A man could get lost in eyes like those. Eyes that spoke so much, revealing such a depth of soul he never knew existed.

"If only I had known……" he spoke, looking wistfully at the large oak tree across the field.

A peaceful warmth was in the air as the wind gently blew leaves off the large oak tree that stood in the centre yard of St. Joseph's Orphanage. On this cool but sunny day in late August, 1931, over a hundred children came running outside its large, castle-like, oak doors upon hearing the school bell ring. In Halifax, Nova Scotia, the school year had begun and the children were delighted to finally go outside and play. Dressed in the standard two-piece, blue uniforms, boys and girls ran to its swings and fields to play their childish games. As the laughter and excitement filled the air, one child meekly remained inside the orphanage. Peering out from her window pane, she looked wistfully up into the sky from her windowsill. An emaciated, pale nine year old girl, Natalie decisively withdrew to do what she knew she had to. Hurrying past the various small cots in the room to make her way to her own bed residing in the corner, the little girl's black hair was unmistakable. Natalie, referred by others merely as 'Nat,' rested herself down on the plank flooring so as to open the bird cage one last time. With intense, green eyes, she reached in to take hold of the young dove who was now her best and only friend in the orphanage.

"I looked outside. It's nice today. Everything is perfect," Nat said, rising up on both feet. "Little Nat?" she said holding the bird up to her face so as to get its attention. "You won't have any problems flying, I promise! I am going to be there to help you," Nat reassured. Then, putting Little Nat to her cheek to hug her, Nat whispered earnestly, "We're best friends forever. I know you need my help today because you are flying alone, but I'm going to be there...And I know you'll be there to help me when I need you. Friends are always together. You would never let me fly alone."

"I guess we have to get going. I have chores to do soon," Nat said, breaking free from her hug. "Little Nat, can you make me a promise?" she asked fearfully, hesitant to head out the door. The bird simply cooed back at her.

"Promise me you will come back to see me? Don't leave me here alone," Nat pleaded. "I'll be waiting for you to come back and get me. When the spring comes, I will still be here." Little Nat cooed once more and Nat smiled in relief. Little Nat would come back for her.

With her tiny bird in tow, Natalie headed down the stairs, racing excitedly down the hallway to rush out the front doors to the playground. Holding Little Nat gently in her two small hands, she discovered that Sister Marie and some of her classmates were already waiting patiently to see Little Nat fly.

"Well?" Sister Marie smiled. "Is she ready?" Nat looked downwards doubtfully, nodding slowly. "Well then. Let's see." Nat took a moment to think. Something in her did not want to let go. Turning her back to her peers, Nat walked away to have some time in the field alone.

"Children, wait here. We'll be right back," Sister Marie assured.

"Is something wrong Natalie?"

Nat looked up with troubled eyes. "Sister Marie, can I talk to you alone?"

"Of course. No one can hear us now," Sister Marie said walking over towards her. Nat was very quiet. Finally.

"I can't do it," she confessed sheepishly.

"Why?" Sister Marie asked, gently knowing.

"Little Nat! I can't let her go! I didn't think it was going to be this hard."

Sister Marie gave a knowing smile.

"Can't she just stay with me?" Nat asked. "I would take care of her. Why would she want to leave me? I'm her best friend."

"Nat, I understand how you feel. It is hard to let a friend go," Sister Marie comforted, kneeling down. "Let me ask you this. Does she belong here?"

Nat thought hard before finally shaking her head.

"Little Nat was hurt at one time, and she did lose her way, but you changed all that Natalie. You helped her, and that is a wonderful thing. Yet, she does not belong to us. Little Nat belongs to God, like all of us. Her time has come to fly on her own journey, as we all must do. Even little animals. She has to be free to do that.....Little Nat has to be free to fly higher than she ever flown before, like all of us are meant to do. Do you understand?" Sister Marie asked.

Natalie nodded. "She doesn't belong to me."

"The sky is where Little Nat belongs. That is her home, her life. Not in some room where she is left alone most of the day. She will never be able to live that way. No one can live unless they are free."

"Yes," Nat whispered, her eyes becoming watery. "We all need to be free so that we can live and be as God wants us to."

"Yes. That is what life is all about. We are God's instruments. Little Nat knows what her purpose is, as will you someday. I know you love Little Nat, but know that when you truly love someone, you set them free."

"I'll be by the swings if you need me, okay?"

Nat nodded once more as Sister Marie slowly rose to her feet, walking away. Looking down at the tiny animal that was encompassed in her two hands, Nat pulled the bird close to her cheek again, as a tear fell and tapped Little Nat gently on the head.

"I do love you Little Nat," she whispered. With that, Nat held the dove high above her head, and opened the palms of her hands to let her go. Little Nat's wings fluttered violently as she took flight to the sky.

"Sister Marie, look!" Nat cried out in wonder. Sister Marie looked up to the sky, as the other children did the same. "She's flying Sister Marie! She did it! She's really flying!!!" Nat exclaimed with pride.

Little Nat flew magnificently, heading straight up into the clouds. She was soaring higher than she had ever flown before. Looking as if she were about to touch Heaven, the dove suddenly planed out to take flight across the playground. Watching her go, Nat could not contain herself and with abandon, took off running to fly with Little Nat following her from below. Running past the girls who were skipping on their ropes and the other children that were playing, Natalie excitedly raised both her arms to the sky, as if embracing the sun with her own wings, to fly alongside Little Nat across the field. It was as if at that particular moment in time, the two were one.

Yet such moments do not last.

The closed gates of the orphanage remained locked, and as Natalie's flight came to a halt, Little Nat continued on without her, past its barred gates. Natalie's arms reached through the bars, out to the small bird that was disappearing out of sight. "No Little Nat. Wait for me! Let me fly with you!" Natalie cried out desperately.

On she flew.

"Wait–"

Onwards.

"Please. Wait…"

Becoming smaller.

Until Little Nat was gone.

School had continued on the next day as usual, but something was different. In the room that night as the other girls lay fast asleep, Natalie remained awake, staring out her window into the darkness. Staring at the barred gates that Little Nat had surpassed, as the rain continued its endless tapping against her window pane. All Nat could see was the gate and how outside those same gates was a world happening that she knew nothing of and could not participate in because she was stuck inside.

She wasn't going anywhere.

As the weeks passed, the days seemed to be getting longer. Natalie continued to do well in school, but her tenth birthday was fast approaching. Soon she would have to leave the orphanage for another where children were older. That was unless someone wanted to adopt her before she turned ten.

Although she hoped and prayed, Nat knew.

No one was coming for her.

"Natalie Bovaird?" Mother Superior asked somewhat surprised.

"Mother Superior, with all respect, this child needs a home," Sister Marie spoke plainly. That was their working relationship, and a respect was there.

"I have many children that need homes. Why are we merely discussing one child?" Mother Superior replied sharply, continuing on with her daily office work.

"We discuss this one child because she turns ten in two months time. She will have to leave this orphanage for another one in Nova Scotia. I am all that she has. The move will be devastating."

"Please Sister," Mother Superior responded, dismissing her concerns. "Children surprise us all the time. Miss Bovaird will be fine. She will learn to adapt. She has thus far demonstrated incredible resiliency." Continuing on with her work, Mother Superior looked up to see Sister Marie still looking down at her, unsatisfied.

"What would you suggest I do?" Mother Superior finally asked, peering up from her reading glasses. "Sister Marie, you know as well as I do that to find this child a home is next to impossible. The country's economy has fallen as unemployment is high. People are losing their farms. You honestly believe that a family would want the burden of providing food and shelter to an extra child? I have more children than I can even begin to deal with, and I am not alone. Especially with the number of Home Children from Britain taking so much space, all across the country, other orphanages are facing this similar dilemma. The number of children far outweighs our resources. Factor in her age with most people preferring to adopt children when they are younger and the fact she is a girl, unable to help with a farm, does not help," Mother Superior concluded.

"Mother, I understand what position you are in, but Natalie has a good chance of making something out of herself. I believe very much in this child. She is bright, imaginative, independent, and very determined. I just want her to grow, not fade away. Natalie is losing hope that she will never see life outside of any orphanage, let alone fulfill God's purpose for her in this world," Sister Marie confessed sadly.

Mother Superior thought for a moment to think of how best to address Sister Marie's concerns. "I do have eyes," she acknowledged. "However, to simply look through her file is not enough." Standing up, Mother Superior walked over to her closet door to pull out a large file box. Resting its contents on her desk, she sifted through many papers before coming to Nat's file. "Everything there is to know about this child is in her file," she stated, pulling out a thick folder and reading its contents. "Some basic facts are clear. There was no father, no relatives to speak of, and her mother, Elsie Bovaird passed away of cancer two and a half years ago. She was sent directly to a foster home at the age of seven to live with a family for over a year, before coming here to stay permanently with us until she reached a proper age. Guardianship was supposed to be given to a Mr. Robert Shaw, a military man. We are still trying to locate his whereabouts. When Natalie's mother passed, he was stationed somewhere in Europe. Only in the last year did he move to Canada, but it was B.C., then Manitoba, then Ottawa. The Ward has always been one step behind. One month ago he had been tracked down to the Maritimes. Still, where is the question? With that being said, even once he is contacted, who can tell definitively that he will accept guardianship, let alone consider legal adoption after the first two years? This man is not the father, he has no relations, and he's not even a family friend. He has no connection to the child at all. Unfortunately, there is nothing else new to tell. Only time will tell. The Ward will let us know when they have made contact."

Mother Superior sat back down at her desk. "I do sympathize with your concerns, but Natalie will just have to learn to deal with what life has ahead for her, as all of us must do. She does have a purpose, and we must have faith in God that He alone will help her find it."

"Yes Mother," Sister Marie acknowledged. "I do have faith. I also believe that it is up to us to meet God halfway. This man's name is Robert Shaw? Very well then," Sister Marie said, getting up to leave. If she had to talk to the man himself, she would.

"Sister?"

"Yes Mother."

"I wanted to discuss another matter with you since you are here." Sister Marie nodded respectfully, waiting at the door. "With my workload," she explained, "I could use an assistant. Would you be interested?"

"Of course Mother," Sister Marie answered dutifully.

"Good. I have this folder that needs to be reevaluated. To my knowledge it is the complete file of an orphan girl within our care, Natalie Anne Bovaird. This file is strictly confidential, as no one must hear or read from its contents except for you and me, because you are my 'Assistant.' Understood?" Sister Marie smiled, taken back. "This child needs a home. If anything new turns up I am sure you will let me know."

"Yes," Sister Marie gratefully answered, graciously taking the file.

"Good," Mother Superior replied with a smile before recomposing herself. "That is all," she replied sternly, returning to her administrative work.

"Thank you Mother!" Sister Marie exclaimed, turning to leave the room. "You have a good day!"

"Thank you," Mother Superior nodded, "and the same to you!"

2

"Natalie!" Elsie greeted from outside their small home in Cornerbrook, Newfoundland. Kneeling down, the single-working mother extended both arms to her six year old daughter, who came running from down the road to jump into them. At five foot six, Elsie was a thin, but striking young woman. With pale green eyes and black, Irish hair, the two were unmistakably connected.

"Did you have fun at school today?"

Natalie broke away from her mother.

"Yes mummy, I know my A, B, and C's. Listen," Nat announced proudly, beginning to sing. Elsie began laughing.

"That is wonderful! I am so proud of you!"

Nat smiled back, happy.

"You are so smart."

"I like school mommy." As Nat began to recount all she had done and learned that day, Elsie smiled encouragingly. Attempting her best to listen, another dizzy spell was beginning to overtake her unexpectedly. Clasping onto Natalie's tiny frame to keep her balance, Elsie fell awkwardly to the ground.

"Mommy? What's wrong?" Natalie asked, immediately dropping her schoolbooks to aid her mother. Elsie suddenly felt so nauseous; she was unable to give her daughter an answer.

"Mommy?"

Then, as quickly as it came, her dizzy spell had passed and Elsie regained her balance and composure.

"Mommy?" Natalie cried, visibly upset, grabbing her mother's waist to help support her. Elsie rested her right hand on Natalie's head, and with an assuring smile said, "Mommy is fine. I am just very tired, that's all. Being a nurse is a tough job," she said finally, standing up. "It takes a lot of hard work."

"I am sorry I make you tired Mommy," Natalie's voice quivered, as she picked up her school scribblers.

"Oh Natalie," Elsie explained, wrapping her arms around her scared little girl. "Nothing you do could *ever* hurt me."

"Really?"

"Yes, really! I love you so much," Elsie whispered, looking deep into Natalie's eyes. "I'll always love you," she promised. "Even when I am not there to love you, you will feel as if I am."

Natalie smiled back at her mom, reassured. They would always be together. "Now, let's go inside so you can tell me all about your day."

Natalie nodded. "Yes mommy....Mommy?"

"Yes?"

"You shouldn't work so hard." Elsie agreed. Fatigued and cold, the two hurried inside. In the fall of 1928, there was a definite chill in the air.

"Happy Birthday dear Natalie, happy birthday to you!" Elsie sang with two other children, placing the homemade cake down in front of Natalie. "Now make a wish!"

Natalie closed her eyes and thought hard before blowing out the candles in one single puff.

"Good Natalie!" tiny, five year old Cindy cried out clapping. Natalie was not quite sure if it was her, or the thought of getting cake soon that excited the girl more. Needless to say, Cindy lived down the road and was fun to play games with.

"How does it feel to be seven?" Elsie asked, beginning to cut the cake.

Natalie looked up into her mother's eyes. "Special. Thank you mommy." Elsie hugged her daughter.

"You are very welcome sweetie. Now it's time for your presents." Elsie reached across the table and grabbed the first of three. Nat opened the small present excitedly. It was the Holy Bible.

"Oh thank you mommy! I needed one for Sunday school."

"I know you did, but you need to make sure you read it and keep up with your prayers," Elsie warned.

"Oh mommy I will. I like Jesus a lot. He was very nice to people, especially children."

"Yes, he was. If there is anything you do not understand, ask me or Mrs. Ketchum, okay?"

Nat nodded, as Elsie handed over her second present. Ripping it apart with glee, Natalie happily found herself looking into the black button eyes of a stuffed animal. The white teddy resembled a tiny polar bear with its black paws. Nat gave her new furry friend a hug, and decided at that moment, "I'm going to name him Fluffy, because that's what he is!"

"Sounds fitting," Elsie nodded handing Natalie her final present.

As Natalie opened it, she was a bit confused as to what it was. "Why did you give me a box mommy?"

"Not just any box." Elsie answered softly. "Open it." Unhooking its small, tiny hinge, Nat found herself looking upon a beautiful, young girl twirling in one spot to a sweet melody. The girl was smiling as she danced and she was beautiful.

"Oh mommy, thank you," Natalie swooned, not taking her eyes off the beautiful figurine.

"You are most welcome sweetie." Elsie was happy. Worried that Natalie might be disappointed at having few presents this year; there obviously had been no need. Natalie loved her musical box.

Attending church service the next day, Natalie could not help but look toward Mrs. Barnes, who was kneeling in the pew across from her. Mrs. Barnes' eyes were black again as she sat next to her husband and their two small children. Younger than Natalie, Chris was five and Tanya was three.

Mrs. Barnes was the nicest lady she knew in Cornerbrook, second to her mom of course! Every time Natalie came over to play with Chris and Tanya, she was always greeted with a big chocolate chip cookie from Mrs. B. Sometimes two! Those were a treat.

As everyone repeated the Catholic prayers of Father Fitzpatrick, even if she did not know what was going on, Natalie always followed suit. When verses and stories from the Bible were read in church, Natalie had a hard time understanding. Yet, when Mrs. Sheppard explained

Jesus in Sunday school, then it was all good. That is why Natalie spent most of her time during mass looking at the sad statue of Jesus, hung up on the wall above the altar. Crucified on the cross, he was crying. Yet, she was distracted today. Mrs. Barnes' eyes were too dark this time. Natalie had to know why.

"Mrs. Barnes, why are your eyes black?" Nat asked when outside the church, interrupting a conversation Mrs. Barnes' was having with two other women.

"Why Natalie," she responded shaken and flustered. "Where's your mother?"

"Over there," Nat pointed, as Elsie was busy talking with the Father about the day's service. "Did you hit something?"

"Yes," she responded awkwardly, and then with a reassuring smile, "I keep falling down our stairs." The other two women slowly walked away in silence.

"Why?" Nat prodded.

"Well see, ah, our stairs are broken, so I sometimes trip, and fall down them, and hit my face."

"Can you fix those stairs?" Nat asked pragmatically.

"Someday maybe…It costs money, so we'll see," she explained gently.

"You should Mrs. Barnes. Then you can get your pretty eyes back. I mean your regular eyes."

Just then, Natalie heard her mother call her. "Bye Mrs. Barnes!" she waved before running off.

"Bye Natalie," she smiled back, waiting patiently for her husband and children to join up with her.

"Okay, let's go get your doll," Elsie smiled but Natalie stood still. "What? What is it?"

Natalie suddenly had a wonderful idea! Something that Jesus would do! Natalie took her small, glass, piggybank out from under her mother's left arm and began walking over to Mrs. Barnes who remained standing alone.

"Here," Nat offered. Mrs. Barnes looked at Elsie who had followed and was now standing behind her daughter. "It's my piggybank," Natalie explained, placing it into her unsuspecting hands. "Now you have the money to fix those stairs so that you won't fall down on them anymore and hurt your face." Mrs. Barnes looked down immediately in shame.

It was then that Mr. Barnes finally approached, and Elsie sensed his anger. It was an anger he always carried with him. His demeanor was intimidating.

"Come along Natalie," Elsie spoke firmly. "Goodbye Enid."

"Goodbye Elsie," Mrs. Barnes offered meekly, feeling the presence of her husband behind her.

As Natalie began walking away, hand in hand with her mother, she turned around to wave goodbye, only Mrs. Barnes did not wave.

She was gone.

Playing with her toys on the living room floor, Natalie pretended not to notice that her bedtime on Christmas day had been missed. Elsie entered the room from the kitchen with an apron on and a towel in hand. "Natalie, it's time to go to bed."

"Oh mom," Nat moaned, beginning to whine.

"None of that," Elsie wearily but firmly warned. "You'll have plenty of time tomorrow to play with your toys, now off you go."

"I know, but I want to play with them tonight," Nat argued, putting up a fight.

"Natalie, I said now. This is your bedtime and you know it. Christmas day or not. You need your sleep." Nat then reluctantly got up to begin her nighttime ritual of washing up. Elsie gave a knowing smile. Natalie never was very difficult to manage. With explanation, her daughter knew that her mommy knew what's best for her.

Feeling quite sick, work had been getting the best of Elsie lately. It was either that or some recurring stomach flu that made her increasingly tired and suffering from abdominal pain.

Returning to her walk-in kitchen, Elsie found herself struggling to just finish drying the dishes so that she could go to bed and get some sleep herself. After a couple of minutes, she had had enough. Tossing the towel on the counter, she sat down to rest at the small table exhausted. There she fell asleep almost immediately. That is until Natalie called her.

"Mommy?"

"Coming," Elsie called back. Taking a sigh, she pulled herself out of the chair and went into Natalie's room. "What is it sweetie?"

"I keep seeing a dark monster," Nat answered hesitantly.

"Oh? Where is this creature of the night? I'll knock his block off," Elsie said playfully.

"He only comes out when I am alone. He tells me terrible things-"

"What things?" Elsie gently prodded, walking over to Natalie's bed.

"He says that you are going to leave me, or that I am going to leave you somehow-"

"Well then, you have nothing to fear, because I have no intention of leaving you. Nothing is going to happen to us. Trust me Natalie. I will fight to keep such a thing from happening," Elsie promised.

"I believe you mommy," Nat concluded after a moment of thinking, "but can you sing me a song, because I'm still a little scared?"

"Of course I can." Elsie held Natalie close to her bosom.

> "Hush little baby, don't say a word,
> Momma's gonna buy you a mockingbird,
> If that Mockingbird can't sing,
> Momma's gonna buy you a diamond ring,
> If that diamond ring turns to brass,
> Momma's gonna buy you a looking glass,
> If that looking glass gets broke,
> Momma's gonna buy you a Billy goat,
> If that Billy goat runs away,
> Momma's gonna buy you another todaaay."

By the time Elsie had finished, Natalie had drifted off into a peaceful sleep.

Months later, deathly pale and breathing erratically, Elsie lay motionless in her hospital bed.

God? Would the pain ever go away? It was relentless, aching all over her entire body.

Unknown to Elsie, in the cold hallway corridors outside her room, two doctors spoke in hushed tones.

"The patient is not improving," Dr. Malory agreed. "If anything, she is dramatically deteriorating day by day."

"Her cancer is too far spread to try preventative measures," Dr. Wilson concluded. "Even with treatments, all she would be doing is buying time…The pain would be the same, only extended for a longer period. You should suggest that she notify the proper authorities regarding her daughter. She will need to appoint a guardian or find proper placement of some sort……Aside from that, I think the time has come to tell your patient the reality of her condition," Dr. Wilson urged, knowing that this news would come best from her own treating physician, Dr. Malory.

"I understand-I've just never had to do this before. Not on my own. How do you tell someone that they are going to die?" Dr. Malory asked.

"You just do. Your job is to help your patient die **well**, with as little pain as possible. God willing, it will be quick," Dr. Wilson said, patting him gently on the back before walking away. Dr. Wilson had seen many people die over the course of his career. Dying, although difficult and tragic as it was, was just a natural part of life.

Taking a moment, Dr. Malory slowly headed down the hallway to give his patient, Elsie Bovaird the bad news.

Natalie had not seen her mother since late January, 1930, when she became so sick at work that she had to stay at the hospital permanently. It was now late May, and Natalie had a lot to tell her! How Mrs. Ketchum let her stay with their five children. How a sixth child was expected to come by summer. That she was doing really well in grade one, and that she had just learned how to read and write. Mommy would be so proud of her! Besides, she missed her mom, and she wanted to know when she was coming home. Then they would be a family again.

Usually reserved solely for Sunday School, Natalie insisted on wearing her best dress. Natalie excitedly grasped Mrs. Ketchum's hand as the two walked down the hallway together. Mrs. Ketchum knew the way, as she had visited Elsie many times over the last four months. Making sure the bow in her ponytail was set just right, Natalie sat down on a chair as Mrs. Ketchum instructed. "You wait right here, okay?"

"Yes Mrs. Ketchum."

"I'll be back soon," she said, heading down the hallway to talk with Elsie's doctor. Nat sat alone, waiting patiently.

cre her, was her mother! How she wanted to peek but she promised to sit still. Finally Mrs. Ketchum returned, and Natalie jumped up off her chair.

"Natalie, I want to talk to you for a minute, before you go see your mother," she said shakily, sitting Natalie back down on the chair. Something was wrong. Natalie could tell.

Not quite sure what to say, the words managed to come out. "Natalie, your Mother has been gone for a long time because she has been very sick. You might be a little scared when you see her because she looks very tired, but you must not be. She is very eager to see you."

Natalie listened intently. "She can't talk very much, so you have to really listen to what she has to say, okay? You have all of today to be with her, so enjoy the time you two have together, okay?"

"Okay Mrs. Ketchum," Nat answered earnestly.

"She is waiting for you behind that door," Mrs. Ketchum guided, standing up off her chair. "I'll be right here if you need me," she added.

Natalie nodded. Turning slowly away, she walked up to her mother's door and knocked. No answer. Turning back, Mrs. Ketchum urged her to just walk in.

Natalie then came up with a great idea. How she would surprise her mother! Opening the door just wide enough to slip her little hand through, Natalie held out a white rose.

"Excuse me Miss Bovaird," Natalie giggled, "I have a flower to bring you from your daughter." Bursting into laughter at her own silliness, Natalie ran through the door and cried out with open arms, "Surprise!!!"

The surprise was suspended as the door closed itself slowly behind her. Natalie's smile dissipated when her eyes rested across the dark room on the gaunt, emaciated figure of her mother lying under her bed's sterile sheets.

"Mommy?"

Elsie had heard her daughter, but was unable to lift her head. The pain was too much. This would require all the strength she has to keep focused on controlling the pain.

Natalie's arms slowly came down. Was she sleeping? That's when Natalie saw her mother's left index finger slowly rise up to gesture hello back. Her mom wasn't asleep!

"Mommy, it's me!" Natalie laughed, running over to her bedside. "Don't you recognize your own daughter?"

Slowly, Elsie's eyes that stared aimlessly up at the ceiling, rolled over to the side, so that she could see her little girl.

"Hi Mommy," Nat smiled down at her. "It's so good to see you again!" Elsie's pale face cast a weak grin.

"Hi my Little Nat. How's my little girl been?" Elsie hoarsely whispered, barely able to speak.

"Oh I have been really good," she reassured her mother." Well, I didn't feed Itchy, Mrs. Ketchum's dog for a few days, and he got sick, but it wasn't my fault because I forgot," Nat explained. Elsie could only open her right eye.

"School?"

"It is a lot of fun. I have learned how to read and write! Before I forget, this is for you," Nat offered, showing the white rose to her mother. "Do you want to smell?" she asked, pulling the flower up to her mother's nose. "It smells very nice, doesn't it? You can keep it here with you." Nat then turned to place the rose in her mother's hand, but they were fists. Nat tried to open her palm, but it was no good.

"I'll put it here at the window so that you can see it every day," Nat said, walking over to the windowsill.

"Nat, I have to talk-" Elsie said in slow, irregular breaths. Nat came back to her bedside and listened carefully, as Mrs. Ketchum had instructed. This would take everything Elsie had left.

"Something has happened to mommy. It is something that makes me sick, and the doctors know that I cannot get better."

"I thought that you were going to be coming back home. They are wrong," Nat stuttered, shaking her head in confusion.

"No Nat. They are right. That is why I need to talk to you. I want you to know that I love you with all my heart. You are the most precious gift that God has ever blessed me with," Elsie whispered in great physical and emotional pain....I have to go away. I have to say goodbye-"

"Well, where do you have to go mommy? Can I go too?" Nat asked, a tear rolling down her cheek.

"No Nat. You can't. I have to go alone," Elsie answered softly, holding back her own tears.

Natalie burst into crying, "No mommy, I want to come, I want to go with you! Don't leave me mommy, PLEASE don't go without meee."

"Shhh. Listen. Shhh," Elsie struggled. Nat quieted. "I will not be able to be there when you need me. You have to be strong. I need you to be. Promise me that you will be strong? That you will never give up?" Unable to speak because of the lump in her throat, Nat simply nodded, crying silently.

"That's my girl. I know that you will be just fine. A man I knew from the war, before you were born, is going to look after you. He will take good care of you. You need someone strong to develop your character and faith. Don't forget what I have taught you," Elsie said choking back her own tears.

"I won't mommy."

"Nat, I love you so much...Please forgive me for having to go."

"I love you too mommy..."

Elsie was quiet.

"Is it time to go now?"

"Soon...If I had a say in it, I would stay here with you forever, Nat, but I can't fight it anymore. Mommy is too tired. God and I will always be watching over you, always…Always. You did not make me sick. This is not your fault. It is no one's fault. It's just my time to be with God. Understand?"

"Yes mommy….I love you."

"I know."

Nat hugged her mother so tight that Elsie could feel Nat's love warm her ailing body. "Now go with Mrs. Ketchum, okay? Be good…Bye my Little Nat," she whispered.

"Bye mommy," Nat couldn't stop crying. Devastated, she turned away from the bed to leave the room as her mother had wanted. It was only then, at that moment, that Elsie allowed herself to cry quietly, her right eye struggling to stay open.

How she just wanted to die already to end the pain.

Nat turned around one last time to look at her mother, and that's when she saw. Her soul peered into the depth that was her mother's soul, and she saw her mother's great pain. Terrible pain that had been endured for five long months. Pain that her mother did not want her to see. Nat had people looking after her, but who was looking after her mother?

No one.

Her mom would not die alone. When Nat was scared or alone, her mom had always been there. Mommy must be scared, Nat thought to herself, as she slowly walked back to her mother's bed. That's when Elsie saw her daughter look deep into her right eye that was yellow. Nat reached out and gently wiped her mother's tears away. Stroking her face, Elsie calmed. She was completely helpless.

Nat then crawled softly unto the bed and snuggled up next to her dying mother. Kissing her mom on the cheek, Nat began to stroke her mother's hair and sing to her as she had been sung to.

> "Hush little baby, don't say a word,
> Momma's gonna buy you a mockingbird,
> If that mockingbird can't sing,
> Momma's gonna buy you a diamond ring..."

Elsie awkwardly opened her fist to hold her daughter's hand. Nat took it. How tight her mother held. How scared and sad she was.

> "If that diamond ring turns to brass,
> Momma's gonna buy you a looking glass
> If that looking glass gets broke,
> Momma's gonna buy you a billy goat"

As the pain faded, Elsie sensed a peace take over her entire being. Elsie began to let go of her life that was now ending.

> "If that Billy goat runs away, momma's gonna buy you another today...."

As the two rested together, side by side, Natalie continued to lie next to and hold onto her mother's hand as the daylight hours passed. As Elsie closed her eyes and drifted off into her eternal sleep, Nat stayed with her.

Until the very end.

3

Dressed in black, Nat was the last one to leave her mother's burial. Staring down at the wooden casket before her, it was hard to believe that her mom was really gone.

Forever.

Yet, she was in Heaven, where angels would take care of her. In a better place where there was no more pain.

Still, Nat missed her already.

"I have to go mommy. I don't know if they will let me come back, but I want to say that I love you mommy, and I won't forget you," Nat cried softly, looking down. "Ever."

Nat kissed her mother's coffin.

"Goodbye mommy," Nat whispered resting a white rose on her coffin. Alone, Nat headed back down the hill to the dirt road where Mrs. Ketchum stood waiting.

Nat did not know where she was going. The only thing she did understand was that a new life without her mother was awaiting her...

"Hurry up girl! How many times do I have to scream at you before you start doing as you're told!?"

What a shriek!

Dumbfounded, Nat looked at her new foster mother with terror. How she was a harsh, moody woman. Unattractive, the woman's plump, short physique and chubby face resembled that of a pig's, Nat thought. Nat did not mean to think such bad thoughts, but the woman's dark, beady eyes appeared delighted by their own capacity for cruelty.

Already after two months, Nat could not find one nice thing to like about this woman. In fact, Nat found that she was growing to hate her with every passing day.

"Here," Nat defensively said, placing the three bags of groceries down on the floor.

"That is not what I'm talking about. Mary needs her bath sometime today. Instead she waits for you because you take your diddley-squat time doing your errands!"

Must she always be yelling?

"I can only do so much," Nat said stubbornly, trying not to let the old woman make her cry.

"Right missy. Well don't just stand there. Take Mary and give her a bath!" she barked.

Nat looked at Mary standing fearfully next to her mother. Even though she was only four years of age and deaf, Mary could physically see what was going on by her mother's face and Nat's body language. Nat offered her hand and Mary gladly took it, just so she could get out of the room. Walking into the bathroom, Nat looked down at the water in the modestly full tub. It was partially dirty. Nat knew then that the eldest had already bathed and that she would be last to bathe in the cold, dirty water. Nat thought maybe she could empty the tub, and start boiling new water, pot by pot to fill the tub. Nat also knew that she would get screamed at for doing so. Not wanting to put up a fight today, because any fighting she did always seemed useless, Nat did as she was told.

Nat turned to Mary, and in sign language told her to get undressed for her bath. Mary looked back at Nat distressed signing, 'Do I have to?' Nat simply nodded and signed, "Sorry." Mary, not wanting to get Nat in any more trouble, took off her summer dress and got into the tub.

Coming out of the bathroom in a towel, Nat followed Mary past the living room to the bedroom. Pulling out fresh, clean clothes, Nat handed them over to Mary.

"What about you girl?" a dry voice came from the doorway.

"What about me?" Nat snapped back, choosing to dress Mary rather than look up.

"Don't give me your lip. You have to take a bath too. School is tomorrow. I don't want someone saying I don't clean or take care of you."

"I'm not dirty," Nat said looking her in the eye. Nat was standing her ground and stubbornly refused to budge.

"Really?"

Oh no-here she comes…Staggering over, the woman grabbed Nat's right hand forcefully. "Looks like filthy hands to me." Nat could smell it. The same stink. Every time the old woman started up, she always had the same smelly breath.

"I can wash my hands but that doesn't mean that I need a bath," Nat yelled back vehemently. With lightning speed, Nat was slapped across the face so hard that she flew back into the closet door behind her.

Mary screamed.

"How dare you talk to me like that? Who do you think you are?" the drunken woman screamed, punching and slapping Nat. "I feed you-I clothe you-and I get no respect in return! Everything is a battle with you! Maybe that will teach you!" she reasoned, finally ending her abuse without remorse.

"There, that will teach you," she repeated backing away, only to have her legs give out on her. Back she fell, hitting her head hard on the floor.

The old, drunken woman had knocked herself unconscious.

The room was silent. Breaking free from her sheltered cocoon, Nat slowly started to move. The storm had passed once more, and she had survived its trauma. Battered and bruised, Nat slowly crawled over to Mary who had curled up in the corner. Feeling a tiny hand touch hers, Mary knew it was Nat.

"Are you okay?" Mary signed. Nat nodded with a smile, wiping away the blood from her lip.

"You?" Nat asked, signing back. Mary nodded.

"Good," Nat said, hugging Mary. "We're good."

That night at the supper table, no one in the family said a word. Nat had made it to dinner that night, only no one acknowledged the blatant evidence of her physical beating that day. Nat's face had a black eye, swollen lip, and bruises on her arms from where she had been kicked. The woman's own children were too afraid of her to say anything.

There was no father. Mary told Nat that her daddy left to go find work. That way he could send money back home until he had enough to come back for them. The thing was he never came back. Maybe that is why she was so mean, Nat thought to herself. She missed her husband.

Still, Nat could understand why a man would leave her, as she didn't want to live with such a mean woman either. That's when Nat began devising a plan. Eating her porridge, she watched the woman across the table and knew she could get out of this. If Nat continued to be a pain over the next few weeks, the woman would send her back to the orphanage because she was sick of her.

That would mean being as difficult as possible.

Nat could do that! If the woman saw that she was useless to her, unable to keep up with her chores say, then she wouldn't want to keep Nat no more.

How Nat had prayed to God to get her out of this house. She had thought about running away, but there was nowhere to go. This was her only answer.

So it would begin.

Nat was going to drive the old woman crazy.

As Sister Marie read through Nat's medical record, the reported physical abuse under the care of her foster mother was a difficult read. Malnourished and inflicted with bruises and broken bones, Sister Marie was shocked to learn the extent of Nat's injuries. One could only imagine how an eight year old had the resilience to endure, despite such viciousness inflicted upon her over the duration of a year.

This is why when Nat arrived that cold, October morning last year, Sister Marie made it her mission to help Nat. She had been informed that there was abuse, but was not aware of how extensive it was. Little Nat, she had determined, would need extra, special care. Certainly she sensed what Nat was feeling.

That a part of her was dying. As the gates closed shut behind her, Nat sat in the back of the police vehicle without saying a word. Driving up to the large, cherry-stoned colored, brick building, Nat felt a sense of gloom take over her world. That's when she saw the engraving above the crumbling building's front doors.

'St. Joseph's Orphanage.'

The vehicle door opened and Nat was unable to move. Why was she here?

"Come now child," a gentle voice spoke.

It was the policeman offering his hand. Defeated, Nat dutifully obliged. He took her one bag of belongings from out of the backseat. Closing the door, the policeman guided Nat up the building's overwhelming steps. As they stepped through the entrance way together, Nat felt another door closed shut behind her. Like an animal being sent back into its cage, Nat knew she was being locked up.

Why did you have to leave me mommy?

As the policeman handed over her singular bag of belongings to Sister Marie, Nat realized that she was on her own again. Although this is what Nat wanted initially, it still would be a new place to survive in. As Nat watched the policeman leave, how she wanted to go with him.

Why didn't anyone want her?

Sister Marie reached out her hand gently to touch Nat's mane of black hair, but Nat instantly retreated.

Nat did not want to be touched by a stranger.

Not by anyone.

Sister Marie looked down at the delicate creature she saw before her, knowing her story.

"Natalie is such a beautiful name, for a beautiful girl."

Nat looked down, choosing to remain in her own safe world. A world where she did not have to trust adults.

"I know this must all seem overwhelming right now, but you will get used to it over time. We have a lot of good children here, children your age, whom you can meet and make friends with. My name is Sister Marie."

Nat gave no expression to her kind face.

"I have a feeling that over time Natalie, we shall become good friends. Come. Let's take your bag to your new room." This time Sister Marie did not reach out, but merely led the way. Nat followed her slowly up the oak staircase to her cot that lay in a room amongst nineteen others. How the wooden floors creaked and smelled of wet mildew. Nat had her own bed which would be nice, but as she walked next to her assigned mattress, something began to stir within her.

"Breakfast will be downstairs in the Main Hall at nine. I will be back shortly Natalie to show you every room. There is nothing to be afraid of dear. You are safe here," Sister Marie assured before walking away. Nat scanned her new surroundings.

Although the sun shone its rays through the room's three windows, the darkness was creeping in on her, as everything was becoming clear. Nat did not know where she was because she was lost. There would be no rescuing her from a life that was so far from the home that she once knew.

Nat would never be going home again. Her mother was dead and was waiting in heaven for her.

This is it. The only one in this world who still loved her was Jesus, but even then she was not so sure anymore if he was still watching her. Nat had been bad at her foster home on purpose. Did Jesus still care about her? Did he still look her way even?

So many questions with no answers. The only answer Nat was sure about was that no one was coming for her. If it was meant to be otherwise, it would have happened by now.

As the weeks wore on, and winter turned to spring, Nat carried out her daily chores, and attended her classes as taught by the nuns at the orphanage. Nat's favorite class was Language Arts, where Sister Marie taught. Encouraging and praising Nat for her reading, writing, and verbal aptitudes, Sister Marie would often give Nat higher level books to read so as to keep her keen mind engaged. Nat did not mind, as she became aware and enthralled by the lives of the great historical figures she read about. Incredible people such as Napoleon, Mozart, and her favorite Saint Joan of Arc.

Joan of Arc was an inspiring girl. God loved her so much that he chose HER to lead the armies! Only fifteen, Joan was chosen to be part of something grander than herself-this great adventure alongside men! Nat had no idea that women had ever attempted such great things before.

This was the power of God. If he decided to give Joan, an ordinary girl, that gift for his purpose, maybe God had something amazing planned for her!

Although months had passed, Sister Marie had noticed great improvement within Natalie. In particular, how Nat had the uncanny ability to adapt rather quickly to any given situation. It was as if the child possessed great survival instincts and needed little guidance from anyone. Nat verbally asked questions one on one, never in front of the class, and excelled not only in Language Arts, but all subjects offered.

Nat attended Sunday Mass and Sunday school, working especially hard to receive her First Communion. The life of Christ had always fascinated Nat.

"Why is he on a cross?" Nat had asked her mother one time when she was six.

"He is on there for us. Jesus was killed for us because he loved people so much. God, his Father, sent him down from Heaven to earth to bring his light and love to this world, so that all who believe in him will not perish. That way we can go up to Heaven and be with God forever," Elsie explained, staring up at the church's statue alongside Nat. "Those are nails in his hands and feet Natalie. He went through great pain to save us. We must be thankful always. Be thankful to God for sending his only Son."

Kneeling at the pew, Nat once again observed the orphanage's statue of Christ crucified, and wondered what her end would be. Nat had learned that death was a part of life, but when would her time come? Would it be as painful as Christ or her mother? All that Jesus had sacrificed, the miracles he had done for people, was what she wanted to follow and do. Nat knew she could never be Jesus, but did want to try and help people like he did. Live by what he taught. Try to be a good person and do the right thing always. Jesus loves everyone, even if they are sinners.

Would God forgive her for her sins? Would he still love her when she's dead?

If Jesus was sent by God, then Nat wanted to commit herself fully to being faithful to His instruction, just like Saint Joan. No one else would get in her way of His purpose for her life. Only then could she be reunited with her mother again.

"I will do my best God to honor you always and follow only your direction. You are my Father, and I promise that if you give me a chance Lord, I will not disappoint you. I will do great things someday with the second chance you give me," Nat vowed. At the tender age of nine, Nat was developing character that would be hard to break later on down the road.

Gesturing the holy trinity before rising, time was too slow for Nat. Newly possessed of the Holy Spirit from her First Communion, Nat had accepted the bread and the body of Christ and now was His.

What was becoming more apparent, besides Nat's unwavering faith, was her emerging intellect that surpassed any other child's in the orphanage. Sister Marie worried that Nat, preoccupied with her school work, was not developing socially. Nat demonstrated no interest in interacting with other children. Sitting in the back of the classroom, Nat often was either lost in her school work or a new book she happened to be reading that day. Preferring to work alone and do her own thing, Nat would politely decline working with others when suggested.

How could she get Nat to open up to others, so as to connect on an emotional level?

God would see to that. Sitting alone under a tree, Nat's daydreaming was disturbed by something she saw in the distance. A shining white light flickered, catching her eye. Nat suspiciously looked about to see if someone was playing a trick on her, but no one was nearby. Ever inquisitive, Nat had to find out what it was.

As she neared closer to investigate, Nat was surprised to find a baby dove fluttering its one wing frantically as she neared. Nat had never seen a bird up close before, but it did appear to be in trouble.

"Hi little one," Nat greeted gently, walking over.

Helping a child tie her shoelaces, Sister Marie could not help but notice that Nat was not in her usual spot under the tree.

Nat soothingly stroked the bird's head, and looked deep into its tiny eyes. "It's okay. Did you lose your mommy?" The dove instantly calmed under Nat's nurturance. "I did too. Don't worry…I can take care of you and be your mommy."

As Nat slid her one hand under the bird's frail body, Sister Marie witnessed for the first time in months, Nat open up completely. Not allowing anyone to come close to her physically, Nat had never before displayed any affection towards anything.

Cusped within her two palms, Nat closed her eyes and kissed the baby dove sweetly on its head. This was the loving child Sister Marie knew existed underneath Nat's guarded, obtuse and aloof exterior.

"I see you've made a new friend!"

For the first time, Nat smiled a toothy grin. "I think she likes me Sister Marie."

"Well, can you blame her? God put her in perfect hands."

"I think her wing is broken…Can I keep her until she gets better?"

"Yes, of course. She looks like she needs your help," Sister Marie reassured, stepping towards Nat so as to inspect the dove closer.

"She needs a mother. She is too tiny to be on her own," Nat determined. Yet, what to call her? Everyone has a name. It can't just be baby dove. Nat thought long and hard.

"Little Nat," Nat whispered.

"What was that?"

"Her name will be Little Nat because she is with me"

"Little Nat it is," Sister Mary beamed. "Come. Let us try wrapping up her wing, so it can heal."

Happier and feeling lighter these last few weeks, Nat would often hurry from the classroom during recess and after school to take care of her Little Nat. For hours Nat would talk to the bird, telling about her day, reading familiar stories, and taking the little dove along with her for walks. Always in the birdcage, Little Nat did not seem to mind this newfound, doting friend. In fact, Little Nat was often the center of attention for most of the children there, as they would routinely gather around her cage just to hear her coo. The children would then join in, laughing at their own silliness.

Sister Marie stood at the dorm's doorway to watch Nat, who was now laughing and interacting with the other children. Summer had arrived, and with it, so had a different child from the one she met a year ago. Somehow, with God's patience and love, this tiny bird had been the key to unlocking the soul of a child who had become emotionally inaccessible.

Little Nat was the miracle that Sister Marie had prayed for.

Closing her file that night, Sister Marie resolved that Nat's destiny was truly in God's hands now.

Only in God's perfect time, would he let Nat fly.

4

Standing tall at six foot five, the General's two hundred and twenty pound frame was both strong and defiant. With dark brown, curly, thick hair and a somber face, surprisingly it was his eyes that stood out the most. Dark and weary, his gaze had an edge and hardness that only forty two years of living can do to a man. A man who had seen and experienced war on and off the battlefield throughout his lifetime.

As a General, he turned boys into men, and watched friends pass throughout his military career. Very few challenged him any longer, because his strength and intellect would defeat even the most worthy opponent. What was unknown to most people, even to the General himself, was that beneath his icy veneer, the greatest battle he fought resided within.

Every day.

As the Drill Sergeant barked out the orders, a regiment of young men took to the field. Testing out their capabilities, an early morning exercise on the obstacle course proved to be a painful experience to witness. Of all days for the General to stroll on by, this was not one of them. Apparent was how ill-trained they were. This was the worst the General had seen yet.

"Jesus, Holy Mary, Mother of God," the General could not help but mutter aloud to himself. Known for being forthright and direct, the Commanding Officers nervously eyed his reaction. The thing to remember most about the General is his stillness. Always thinking well before he spoke, words were always selective. Unanimated physically, the General was a rock.

The men were in bad shape. Lacking cohesion as a group, their personalities were at odds with one another and it showed. The result was a regiment that was not a team. The General's disapproval was called for. Still, it was the General's temperament, his most uncompromising trait, which intimidated the men.

"These boys are horrible," he said after a moment, shaking his head.

"They are raw General Shaw," Sergeant MacDonald admitted.

"Damn straight."

The men fell silent.

"Jesus, this wasn't even worth the walk. Christ, did they all come straight from the soup kitchen?"

The General demanded an answer.

"Well?"

"Give it time sir," Sergeant MacDonald acknowledged. Emaciated and weak, the General was right in his brief estimation, as physical conditioning would need to be intense.

Now the General knew how to be more tactful. After all, he did not get to his position without being politically strategic. Quite simply his hangover made him sluggish, permitting little patience with anyone. To be quite frank, the General simply was not in the mood to mince words today. Not on the field. It was this very quality that the men respected.

The General was the kind of man who was charismatic enough to get respect both on and off the field. He knew how to run and maneuver his way through both worlds. Ensuring that the training at Aldershot, Nova Scotia remained consistent, and at a high level, the General made his rounds to all commanding officers from time to time. When the situation called for it, the General knew when and how to throw his weight around to ensure that the job got done. That is why he was a leader. Standing alone did not seem to bother him too much.

"See you next week," the General said, residing that it was still too early into the training. The General had made his point and the men knew that the next time around, he would expect much more.

"We'll be better next week. Thank you sir," Sergeant MacDonald said relieved, as the General walked away. Demanding but fair, the General was always a reasonable man.

Continuing on with his morning walk, the General inspected various platoons that day training. Always met with salutes by everyone on base, the men would step aside to clear a path for him.

Entering the military's main office doors to see his secretary typing away, he gruffly greeted, "Morning Jeanie."

"Good morning General." Before he could say another word, Jeanie cut him off. "The mail is on your desk sir, and I'll make you a fresh cup of coffee."

"Thank you."

Rising up to start his morning coffee, the General entered his office, closing the door behind him. As part of his daily ritual, the first thing he would do would be to hang up his coat and remove his handkerchief to wipe away the sweat from his forehead. Sifting through his pockets to find his morning cigar, the General sat back in his chair, lighting and savoring its first puff. How sweet it tasted.

Finally.

His morning could now officially begin. A moment of quiet before the storm. Before other matters would press against him, as they always did. Political bullshit.

After taking three tokes, he reached for his morning mail. Nothing was of any significance. One letter from General Porter, which he would definitely reply to. A few invitations to various functions. He was always being invited to everything, having such a wide berth of acquaintances. Most were professional, but occasionally some were of a personal nature.

Nothing new.

Wait. What's this?

A letter from the provincial ward, regarding St. Joseph's Orphanage. Probably wanting a charitable donation of some sort, he smirked. The General swiftly tossed the envelope aside. He had more important matters to attend to. Many other things that demanded his money and time.

One of those things being drinking every night at the local Irish Pub, Monty's. At the end of each day, he would walk through the place, making his way to the boys.

The General's drinking buddies that is. Chaps he had known forever.

Of course he would wink at the pretty women as he strolled by. The General was handsome and he knew it. Not that he was vain. It was only that meeting women had never been very difficult for him. Women were everywhere he went, and they were attracted to his physique and status. Financially secure, the General could take care of any woman if he had the desire to.

That was the thing though. He had never had that strong of a desire for any woman to imagine being with her for any extended amount of time. Besides, trying to make one woman happy seemed a daunting task. Something beyond his ability.

With the amount of moving and relocating that his job required, no woman would be happy with such an existence anyway. Not any women that he knew of. The General's strongest objection to being married had to be that marriage and having a family never really appealed to him. The General never desired that kind of responsibility. After all, his own family life had been so chaotic, that he liked the comfort and security that being on his own gave him. It was simpler that way. He was happy enough with just himself.

Still, he loved women though, and as he passed them in the pub, smiling their way, perhaps one would make him a lucky man tonight!

As he sat down with the boys who were waiting at their regular table, they all took a swig of their pints and told jokes. Drinking the night away, the boys retold old, familiar tales, and sang aloud their favorite Celtic melodies. The boys, as always, had another great, but predictable night.

The morning would prove to be another story.

It often was.

The General did not take anyone home that night, as he had been too drunk to do so, even if the opportunity had arisen. Stumbling all the way home that night, the General could not remember a thing. As he sat up on his living room floor the next morning, the General's appearance looked as trashed as his home. Dishes, clothes, and boxes were sprawled about everywhere, as the house was dusty, dirty, and dark.

No wonder he was cold! He had left the damn front door open. Kicking it shut with his foot, the General then grabbed his head in pain. The slam had made his headache throb all that much more. One thing was clear. He had to get to the kitchen and get some water to drink.

As the General crawled his way across the living room floor, he finally got a glimpse of the clock. He was late for work.

Really late.

Shit!

Pulling himself up fast, he had to hurry, but it was too fast. Running into the bathroom, the General began vomiting loudly.

Staggering into his office later that morning, the General, disheveled and unshaven, was in rough shape.

Again.

Loudly coughing up phlegm, the sound startled Jeanie away from her typing.

"Good morning General," she tried to smile, despite wincing.

"Morning," he mustered, hurrying into his office, shutting the door quietly behind him. Collapsing into his chair, the General amazed himself at the fact that he had made it to work at all. The General's exhaustion showed itself in his heavy breathing. Hell of a morning he thought to himself. If he could crawl up into a tiny ball that morning and hide, how he would.

Jeannie came in with his morning coffee.

"Any mail?" he asked looking down, trying to conceal from her that anything was wrong.

Jeanie knew about his drinking. "No General Shaw."

"Jeannie?"

"Yes, sir?"

"No calls for a bit."

"Yes, General," Jeannie answered respectfully, closing the door quietly.

Leaning back in his chair in much pain, the General reached over with his right arm to push open the one window. He needed air. Anything would be helpful at this point to ease his nausea. He had really gone overboard last night.

As the sun gently glistened through the window, the General felt its warmth touch the right side of his face. It made him squint, but it did feel nice. The morning had dawned, and a new day was upon him.

As he sat there, the only question he had rolling around in his head was whether there was anything new to look forward to?

Not particularly as every day seemed always the same. He used to like the routine and structure, but most days now, it all seemed so monotonous and boring.

Trivial. That was his life the last few years. Trivial.

Most of the time, the General felt everything was pointless. He had worked hard all his life, rising up through the ranks, to achieve everything he had ever wanted. Yet, the prize at the end of his ascension seemed so empty and dissatisfying.

Grateful to have such a good stable job, the General couldn't help the fact that he felt cheated in some way.

Disappointed.

Where was the reward promised?

The General remained as trapped and lonely just as much today as he had back in his childhood. How little things had changed over the years.

No matter what you do, it doesn't matter. We are all just cogs in a wheel, he snickered aloud to himself.

As the sun continued to pour in through the open window, the General noticed its tiny rays rest upon a letter.

It was an envelope waiting to be opened.

It was a letter resting on his desk from where he left it a week ago.

Reaching, he read its contents again.

Right. The orphanage.

Why not read it?

He had time. It's not like he had much to do this morning. Rubbing his eyes one last time so as to see clearly, the General weakly opened the envelope.

As he began reading, transparent was his change in attitude. With every passing sentence, he slowly sat up, the letter capturing his full attention. When the General had finally finished, he had to lean back in his chair again to sort out his thoughts.

Elsie Bovaird…A name he hadn't heard of in years.

Not since the war.

He did remember her. She had been a nurse in the year seventeen when he met her. With no other doctors on hand, she was the only one there. At the age of thirty one, he was at that time as scared and helpless as a child. Wounded, Elsie had told him that everything would be all right.

Dead.

He was shocked. Elsie was so young.

A very decent woman.

What perplexed him more was that she remembered him.

Why him?

They had spoken some as he recuperated in the hospital, daily sharing some stories about their lives, but it was such a brief moment in time that the General didn't understand why he had made that much of an impression. Yet, she wanted him to raise her child. Did she not know that he knew nothing about raising children? Training young men was not the same thing. Or was it? Soldiers saw him as their Dad, and he believed it was his responsibility to mold and shape them into young men. Certainly a nine year old child, Natalie Bovaird, would be no different. After all, Elsie had thought he could do it. He knew he certainly had the financial capability to do so.

The General would have to mull it over longer.

All day he sat alone in his office, until the answer became clear to him.

If it was Elsie's dying wish that he alone receive sole guardianship, then he would honor that wish. After all, she had saved his life that night, removing the bullet from his back, so as to bandage the wound and prevent him from bleeding to death. The General could not save her life in return. It was too late for that, but he could do this.

"Jeannie!" he called gruffly.

"Yes General," she said, opening the door.

"Cancel all appointments for the next three days," he said, placing the letter in his coat pocket. "I'm leaving on a personal matter."

"Certainly General," Jeannie said surprised, as he hurried past her. Steadfast, he would phone immediately to confirm with the orphanage of his impending arrival, before heading out tomorrow morning. From Kentville, the General was only two hours away from Halifax.

To be guardian of Elsie's daughter, Natalie, only one question permeated in his mind.

How hard could it be?

Waiting patiently by the bedroom window, Nat saw a figure in the distance. Could it be him? Intensely, she followed the vehicle as it entered the gates, kicking up a dirt cloud behind it as the jeep blazed its way up the road. Looking down, the vehicle stopped at the entrance below. A man got out, but all she could see of him was his hat. Racing out of her room, Nat looked from the staircase to sneak a peek.

Nothing!

Stepping out, the General looked around. How foreign it felt to be around children. They were so loud, with all their screaming, laughing, and talking. This was a big step for him, and a part of him wanted to leave. His presence was felt, as many children stopped playing to stare back at him.

"Don't they know it's not polite to stare?" he muttered, a bit annoyed. What manners were they teaching kids nowadays anyway? Putting on his hat, the General began his walk towards the building's front doors, escorted by two military soldiers. With an air of authority and confidence he entered, and many stood aside. That's when Sister Marie approached within the hall's corridors.

"General Shaw?"

"Yes," he answered briskly, removing his hat out of respect.

"It's very nice to meet you at last. I am Sister Marie," she smiled. "I can't tell you enough how wonderful it is to meet you finally." The General felt her warmth and kindness was too disarming to reciprocate. Looking closer, Sister Marie saw a tiny bead of sweat roll down his forehead. Instinctively she knew that something was amiss.

Why was she looking at him like that? She was a better looking nun than he had ever seen growing up, but nuns always made him feel uneasy. Every time he saw anyone in the robe and habit, all he thought about was how long it had been since his last confession.

Years ago!

"Come this way General. All the paperwork is ready for you to sign," Sister Marie offered, sensing his discomfort. Despite his best efforts to remain cool and in control, he was clearly a man out of his element.

The muffled sounds below were driving Nat crazy. It had to be him! She had been told to wait until she was called and that was exactly what she was going to do.

As the General signed the necessary paperwork, Sister Marie continued to chatter his ear off.

"Nat-you are going to love her!"

That's when the General sensed someone watching him. As he slowly turned, the General found himself face to face with a little girl who was staring at him from the open doorway. She was looking up at him with eyes that were in awe.

He was a giant.

A man of strength and greatness.

He was her new dad.

As Nat bravely walked towards him, he gave her a knowing smile to put her at ease. Evident to all was the fact that it was the General who needed to be put at ease.

Walking right up to him, Nat was unafraid. "You're big," she finally said after close inspection. The General paused a moment to decipher his own uncomfortable response.

"That's the army girl," he said with a half-smile.

Nat lifted up his left hand.

"Does all the food go into your hands?"

He felt like pulling away, but something made him resist this natural impulse. "No," he answered firmly.

"Your hand is as big as my face," Nat said. "What? You don't believe me? See," she said, putting his hand over her entire face. She was right. Sister Marie stood back and watched, knowing not to interfere. Such introductions were magical to watch. Nat put his hand down and looked back up at him.

Boy she was tiny. So small. She looked so fragile physically, like a twig that could be snapped in two. Too tiny and vulnerable for his liking.

Nat let go of his hand. "My name is Nat," she smiled up at him, offering her hand excitedly. Finally he was here! The man her mother had promised and chosen for her was finally here.

He had come for her...to *save* her.

The General felt himself being drawn in, as he took her hand a bit reluctantly and shook it. "My name is General Robert Shaw."

"What would you like me to call you?" Nat asked smiling.

So direct was she that it threw him off guard. He had not considered it as a thought. The General was silent.

"Nat," Sister Marie interjected, sensing his awkwardness. "Why don't you give the General a tour of our orphanage? Take him to your favorite spot outside. This will give you time to get better acquainted."

"Yes Sister," Nat complied, leading the way, but the General just stood there. Nat peeked her head back in through the office doorway. "Are you coming?"

"Yes," he smiled. "I'm coming," he spoke gently, following her out. As the two went outside, Sister Marie watched them from her window. The General was a guarded man, which explained the spatial distance he maintained as he walked alongside Nat. As the time passed though, and Nat shared her stories about the orphanage, Little Nat, her favorite spot under the tree, and her mother, the General finally began to move in closer. What was apparent was that the General was beginning to *see* who Nat was and all that she was.

Looking around at the other children, the General knew that Nat did not belong here. She was such an interesting, bright, beautiful little girl, that she deserved much better. He finally patted her gently on the head.

"Nat? "

"Yes General?"

"Let's go get your stuff," he said resolutely. "It's time to go. You're coming home to live with me." Nat's eyes began to fill up with tears. Ever impulsive, she hugged his waist tight.

"All right now," the General said removing her arms. That was unexpectedly too much. It made him feel uneasy again. "Straighten up now. No tears," he ordered, pushing her back.

"Yes General," Nat said, wiping her tears of joy away.

As the two headed back indoors, the General signed the remaining papers and the two headed out of the orphanage's doors for the last time. As they walked out, Nat did something that both startled and surprised him. He stopped for a moment to look down at someone who would be his new 'buddy.' Nat had taken hold of his hand so that they could walk out together. There was something about him that she trusted immediately. He would be the one who would protect her from now on. He would love and teach her, and Nat knew that all she wanted was to be the best daughter for him so that he would be pleased with her always!

As the General lifted Nat into the jeep, Sister Marie waited patiently. It would be hard to say goodbye, but she knew that there were bigger and better things waiting for Nat.

"This it?" the General asked.

"Yep. I only have one bag of belongings," Nat answered promptly, nodding.

"I think you are all set," Sister Marie smiled, stepping out from behind the General's shadow. "Have you washed up because it will be a long ride?" Nat gave a forced smile so that Sister Marie could inspect the cleanliness of her teeth. "Very clean."

"You will be in my prayers and heart always," Sister Marie whispered to Nat, as she hugged her goodbye. Sister Marie could tell that Nat was struggling to say something, but it was difficult. "Yes Nat?"

Looking down, Nat hated saying goodbye. She did not want to cry.

"I'll miss you Sister."

"I'll miss you too."

"Goodbye," Nat finally said.

"For now. I will see you again someday, I'm sure."

Nat nodded. In sign language, Nat signed, 'I love you,' something she had learned from Mary. Sister Marie understood its meaning and signed it back, as the General stepped into the driver's side.

As the jeep took off, Nat was leaving for good. Once again, for a new life that awaited her.

As the jeep came through the gates of the military base, the men as far as the eye could see, could not help but stop and stare at the sight before them. The General was driving with a little girl in his passenger seat.

A child.

She had a likeness to him with the black, Irish hair. Still, it seemed foreign to see.

Nat felt their gazes pierce through her. She was now entering a world unlike any other she had ever seen and experienced before. Nat had entered the unfamiliar world of men.

The military.

Where guns were carried.

Where everything is physical and active.

Where there would be no quiet space to read and imagine. No Christmas concerts filled with singing and plays. No dresses and women about to cling onto.

As the marching men chanted, Nat watched them in their quick step hustle by. How strange they were to her. Nat would have to work hard to understand how this new world worked and where she would fit into it all. After all, Nat was her mother's daughter in the beginning. Then, a foster child in a home and family that was not her own. As an orphan, she belonged to no one. Now, she was an adopted daughter to a man that she did not know. The question unknown to Nat, but ultimately that she sought an answer to, was what role would she be playing now?

Alert, observing every detail, Nat began unconsciously 'reading' her new environment. An innate talent that helped her survive. Strong-willed, Nat was incredibly resilient, despite her young age.

The General had noticed Nat's silence. How could he not? She had talked the whole drive up. It was a relief to have her quiet for a bit. No doubt she was feeling a little overwhelmed.

Fear had begun to take over Nat. The General was nice, but with all the men about, yelling out orders, and guns firing off in the distance in practice drills, this new world felt very unsafe. Still, as the General looked down at her, Nat looked up at him and smiled back. Nat did not want to go back to the orphanage. Something that she had learned early on was how to hide her fear.

Smile, even when you are afraid.

So as the jeep continued to kick up dust along the dirt road, Nat as an outsider resisted her impulse to look behind, jump and run. Instead, she bravely looked forward with anticipation into the unknown road which lied ahead of her. This is where God had chosen her to be, whether she felt belonged here or not. All Nat knew was that she would do her best to be a good girl and do as she was told.

As the General unlocked the front door, he allowed Nat to step in first. His home was as dark, messy, and cluttered as he had left it three days earlier. Nat was surprised to see that there were actual cobwebs on the wall, and the sound of flies buzzing about.

Where was that coming from?

As the General stepped in behind her to set down her bag, Nat saw the flies finally. They were flying around a half-eaten sandwich left on the General's living room couch. Since all the curtains were drawn, the General turned on the lights, which to Nat's shock only made things worse. The dust in the air was clearly visible, and something rotten smelled!

Somewhere.

Perhaps buried under the piles of papers and clothes strewn about the cherry, hardwood floors. Nat would be in so much trouble if her room at the orphanage was even slightly dirty! The poor General needs her help.

Nat looked up at him and smiled. "It's very nice General," she said sweetly.

The General nodded. It was probably a little dirty, but Nat, like himself, didn't seem to mind. As he led her upstairs to her room, Nat scanned her white room. There was a bed next to the window, which overlooked the forested field down below. It was a pretty sight to have such a large 'playground.' Nat would make herself right at home in no time at all.

5

The first thing that Nat would do is clean the house from top to bottom. It was the least she could do as this was Nat doing her part. Not an easy feat to accomplish those first few days, but Nat did eventually. Nat could tell that the General was impressed because he kept asking her where everything was when he needed something. The General knew that Nat was in charge of the house.

Living with the General was interesting as Nat thought he was funny to watch. Like the time when she made him breakfast and he didn't know what to do with it. He just played with his plate. Once he started eating, he liked it.

Maybe he had never had French toast before. It couldn't be because he doesn't eat in the morning. Everybody needs their breakfast.

What was strange was when the General prepared dinner because he would always cook such big meat. Sitting down at the dinner table one time, the barbequed meat he grilled for Nat was huge! It took up her whole plate. Yet, the General was oblivious to her dismay, as he anxiously cut into his own deer steak. Nat watched him, following his lead, cutting in with her own big dinner knife. How hard it was to cut through.

"What?" he asked with his mouth half full.

Nat was quiet for a moment.

"You can't cut it?"

"What is it?" Nat asked meekly.

"Steak. It's good. You cut it into small pieces," the General explained, "so that you can chew it, like this," he said, demonstrating. Nat let out a sigh of relief.

"Really?"

The General nodded, cutting her first piece and placing it in her mouth. "Chew," he instructed after observing that Nat was savoring its taste, but not moving her teeth.

"It's good," she smiled, a small drop of blood from the cooked meat escaping out of the side of her mouth as she spoke. The General nodded, getting back to his meal. Like two peas in a pod, Nat made her chewing in sync with the General. When both were done, the two of them leaned back in their chairs satisfied.

"That was good," Nat said her stomach full.

The General showed his affirmation by letting out a thunderous belch. Nat's eyes went wide, as it startled her! Then she started laughing.

"What? It was good," he smiled.

Nat couldn't stop laughing. "What do you say!?"

The General shook his head.

"You're supposed to say 'excuse me'," she giggled, continuing to laugh.

"Excuse meee," he teased. "There," he said, getting up. Walking out, he was tired now. Time to go sit out on the porch. Nat dutifully cleaned up.

How life with the General was like that.

Interesting.

Every day.

Putting Nat in school was another thing the General did. "Education is paramount to developing oneself," he told her. "It is something to be taken seriously." Nat would do anything he said, because she knew that the General was a very smart man. He knew many things, which is why everybody listened to him when he spoke. Nat would follow him anywhere and do whatever he told her.

As Nat sat down at her school desk for the first time, many of the girls came over to welcome her. Any worries Nat had were immediately put to rest that day.

At home though, Nat felt a little on the outside. How she wanted so desperately to get to know the General better, as he was the first and only Dad she had ever known.

How much she wanted to get his approval! To be the perfect daughter. To hear some of his stories, or what happens during the day when he works. The life of a General must be so exciting, filled with constant adventure and courage.

Nat knew this because he had taken her to a ceremony before. The soldiers marched beautifully as the General gave his salute. It was a moment of awe being Nat's first real taste of what it meant to be a part of something so grand. Something so much bigger than herself. It was a feeling she yearned to have repeated.

Nat wanted someone to come home to. Someone whom she could share her own day with, the way she used to with her mother.

Yet, the General seemed a quiet man at home, as he never really asked Nat much of anything. Nat would do her chores faithfully, but every Saturday morning, the General would be gone. Waking up to a teenager named

Martha, Nat would wait all day for her Dad to come home.

He never would.

Not until very late, after dark, when she was up in bed. Nat intrinsically knew that she was well cared for. How she was extremely lucky to be adopted by a man who provided her with food, a good home, nice dresses, and a good education. Still, something was missing. Nat needed something from him, so much, that it made her sad.

What Nat really wanted, more than anything, was to just be around her Dad. Nat wanted to see and share in all that he did every day and to be his friend.

That's why Nat decided one day to take the initiative. Surely if the General were to see her enthusiasm for what he does, then of course he would want to take her with him! As Nat scurried down the staircase, she skidded across the hardwood floors to pick up off the wall hook the General's winter coat. Scrambling to put his clothes on, she would have to be quick. The General was rumbling about upstairs, having just woken up. One by one, she began to look like the smaller version of the General, dressed in everything from his orange toque to his rubber boots.

What is that racket downstairs?

Sounds like mice.

Not a morning person by nature, the General was his natural grumpy self. However, he was taken by surprise when he found Nat standing at the bottom of his staircase, buried underneath his clothes that far exceeded her tiny frame.

"What are you doing in my clothes girl?" he asked, slightly annoyed. Obviously Nat was playing games, but he was hardly in the mood. It was his hunting day, and no one interfered with that.

"I want to come with you hunting," Nat answered.

"No," the General said swiftly, gently pushing his way past her. Reaching for his camouflage coat, he turned to find Nat standing defiantly between him and the door.

"I'm going with you." Unrelenting in her tone, Nat was putting up a fight. How frustrating for him. Why of all mornings did she have to be difficult today? She was making him late for his morning hunt.

He's not leaving me behind anymore, Nat determined. She would be a part of his life, whether he liked it or not.

"Natalie, I will be killing a deer today, if I see one. Are you prepared to see that?"

"Is that what we eat?"

"Yes."

"The deer is food. We need food. Yes, I can see that. I would like to help bring home food too."

The General could not help but give her the strangest look. How peculiar she could be. No girl wants to go hunting.

Still, if she wanted to come, what harm would she do, really? Maybe if Nat came this one time, she would realize that it was not for her and never again would she pester him about coming along with.

"Well, you have to keep up if I take you with. No slowing me down, understand?"

"Yes sir," Nat answered.

"Go pack some fruit," he said reluctantly. "We'll need it for later. I'll get my rifle."

"Can I shoot too?" Nat asked excitedly.

"Let's just see how well you do today first. Then maybe I'll teach you how to shoot safely. You're a bit young."

"Yes sir," Nat smiled, hurrying off to the kitchen, only to trip over her big clothing.

"Nat?"

"Yes sir?" Nat called, struggling to get back up on her feet as she kept slipping. The General knew that his clothes would never do. Helping her up, the General thought for a moment as Nat stood patiently looking up at him. Maybe if he got her other clothes, but there was none that he could think of that would work. She was simply too small. Nat needed clothes that would protect her from the elements.

Then the idea came to him.

Heading out the back door, the General grabbed some rope from the back shed. Nat worried that maybe he was leaving, angry with her for slowing him down, but the General came back. Rolling up her clothes, he used the rope to tie her clothes into place. This way Nat could be both mobile and safe. He did not want her falling again. When the General was done, Nat looked to him for approval.

"Well? Am I ready to hunt?"

Nat looked ridiculous, but the General smiled and nodded.

"Yep."

Nat was so proud of herself.

"I'll get the food!" she said, running like a fat penguin into the kitchen.

Leaving, the General lifted Nat into the jeep and was taken back by how happy she looked. He didn't know that it would be such a big deal to her. Nat was so excited to be going.

Now Nat could see what he does and learn why the General loved hunting so much!

As the two of them began trekking through the forested bush, the General turned back to find that Nat was indeed falling behind. Constantly…If she was not getting caught up in the trail's branches, her footsteps sounded like an elephant moving behind him. Must she make such a racket everywhere she stepped?

"Shhhhh!" he scolded, annoyed. "Walk quieter! You're scaring all the deer away," he whispered tersely.

Quieter? How was she supposed to be quieter? There were twigs everywhere! He was so fast, she was hurrying just to keep up with him! Oh no…No, no, no…Now the General was *really* going to be mad with her. Not paying attention, Nat had stepped knee deep into the mud. As she struggled to quickly get herself out, Nat helplessly watched the General go on without her. Yet, she did not call. Nat could figure out a way to get out before he came back.

Nat had fallen behind again, the General thought to himself impatiently. He would have to backtrack. As Nat caught sight of him again down the trail, her plight was hopeless. He would be mad. The General was about to start yelling, but when he saw Nat look down embarrassed, he found himself not having the heart.

"I'm stuck," Nat said, frustrated.

"That's all right," he sighed, resting his rifle against a nearby tree. Reaching out, he grabbed the back collar of her coat.

Plop.

With a little pull, he had lifted her up and out of the mud, gently setting her down next to him on dry ground.

"You okay?"

Nat nodded, looking down. "Sorry."

"It's no big deal. It's your first time out here. You'll learn to recognize the mud patches and not get stuck in them."

"Okay," Nat nodded, looking up. Suddenly she was not so embarrassed any more. The General determined that he would wait for her, even if she did slow him down. Wherever he goes, Nat would be right by his side.

As they continued walking on, on occasion when Nat would get tired, the General would sling her over his shoulder to give her a rest. Feeling like she was a wounded soldier on the battlefield, how Nat laughed because she was having so much fun. "Hurry, or you'll be shot too Dad!" she yelled, playing out the war scene in her imagination. The General played along.

"No, I'm not leaving you behind," he said, running along the trail.

"Save yourself Daddy!" Nat screamed laughing.

As the General tired, he set Nat down, so that they could continue on with their hunt. Fully rested and ready to go, Nat would see two squirrels, a bunny, and a mommy and baby deer that morning. Nat would also be relieved to learn that the General did not shoot women and children animals.

"Only male deer," he said, "because they are old." Since Nat was asking so many questions, the General had to explain how to hunt. Initially annoyed, he soon began to enjoy answering her many diverse questions.

"Why don't the deer come to us?"

"Well, because I will shoot them. They know how to protect themselves from anyone who is not them."

"So, how do we get to see them? Without them seeing us first?"

"We do it by being quiet, by hiding, by sneaking in closer to make that shot, and patience. You need patience to wait for it. Timing is everything."

"How do you shoot?" As the General began to demonstrate, Nat piped in, "Can I try?" Surprised but pleased, the General removed the bullets and relinquished his weapon. Something he had never done for anyone before. Nat lifted it up, but it was really heavy, so the General held up the barrel end.

"Better?" he asked, looking down at his little soldier. Nat nodded. "Hold it tight right to your shoulder. If you don't, it will kick and that hurts. See this tip at the end?"

"Yes."

"That's your aim, where your sights are. When you see a deer, you want the deer in the middle there. You also want a steady arm. Shaking, or one little move right before you shoot, may cost you the buck. That's why you need to focus and be calm." Nat squinted to peer through its sights. "The only time you raise your weapon is to shoot. Otherwise, you point it down to the ground. Safety first, understand?"

"Yes."

"At all times. Safety is the most important thing when you're hunting-"

"And in battle?"

Surprised again was he by Nat's keen intelligence and inquisitive nature.

"Yes, in terms of how to keep yourself and your men safe."

Nat smiled. She had learned so much today. "That's about it," he finished, taking the rifle back.

"Could we practice at home?"

"What do you mean?"

"Shooting, so that I can get better and catch a deer myself?"

Strange. The General had never encountered any girl before who wanted to learn how to hunt for herself.

"All right," he shrugged, his tone reflecting his puzzlement.

"Where do we go next?"

"There's a valley," he said, turning to his compass before pointing, "that way, where the bucks may be."

"Okay," Nat said, walking in front of him in anticipation.

Nat's very first time out hunting would prove to be a successful one that afternoon. A clean shot, the two of them tracked the blood trail of her Dad's fallen buck several yards away. Grabbing its hooves, they dragged the deer's body back to the vehicle, where the General lifted it up into the back of his jeep.

Stopping into town to fill up on gas, the General asked the owner if he could take a picture. Happy to oblige, the General brought Nat into the picture frame. The General included her in his glory, as they had both gotten the deer together. As the General raised the deer's head by its antlers, Nat could not contain her smile. A perfect picture for their fireplace mantel at home. What a buck they *both* got that day!

So it would be the next few weeks, out in the backyard that Nat would learn to shoot under the General's guidance. He would also teach her how to fish both in the summer and winter. However, as spring came, the General was increasingly being called away for work, either out of town, or for long hours. Martha was nice, but Nat wanted to see her Dad when she came home.

Sometimes, late at night, when Nat would be waiting for the General, a woman's voice would be heard downstairs. Disappointing not only because she was waiting for him, Nat was also disappointed because it was never the same woman's voice twice. Maybe Dad wants a wife, Nat thought, but if he did, why would he never ask any of them to stay? The thing that bothered Nat the most was why her Dad chose to spend time with these women, or work, rather than come home and spend time with her? Obviously she was not as important, as Dad gave his time to them and not her.

To women who were not his wife, and not her mom.

As the new school year started up, Nat at eleven was beginning to experience growing pains in her relationship with the General.

Standing on the playground, Nat saw grade six student, Tommy Hill, run by her and purposely smash Peter on the head with his lunchbox. Falling to the ground instantly, Nat looked down at her helpless classmate, extending her hand.

"Are you all right?"

Peter would not take her hand, choosing instead to remain lying on the ground until his head stopped paining. Nat looked up to see Tommy making his usual rounds, this time pushing a kid to fight who was only half his size. It was little Kenny Smith who had his head down and hands firmly in his pockets.

"What's the matter? You going to cry ya' little baby? Huh? Gonna cry?" Tommy taunted. Nat looked to Mrs. Gardner, a grade two teacher, standing at the main exit door watching. She had to see what was going on, Nat determined. Yet, no sooner had she thought this very thought, Mrs. Gardner intentionally turned her back and went inside the school.

"If you don't fight me now, I'm going to pound ya' anyway." Scanning the playground to see if any other teachers were around, Nat saw there were none. Looking back to Tommy, Nat began to get how angry. Tommy was a waste of human air and nothing more than a bully. All any kid ever did was stand by and let it happen, fear paralyzing them. Could they not see that Tommy was nothing? Could they not see he would be a coward if anyone stood up to him?

Kenny appeared to be on his own but not this time.

A small hand reached out to pick up a random plank of wood that had been resting against the school wall for quite some time. Three feet in length, it was weathered but in excellent shape.

"What? Are you going to cry?" Tommy laughed, slapping Kenny on the head. The children silently stepped aside as Nat came through the crowd. In awe and disbelief, they hoped Nat would be the one to stop Tommy. As Kenny looked up crying, he saw Nat fast approaching from behind Tommy, her index finger pressed to her lips, urging his silence. Kenny complied and looked back to Tommy.

"You're so stupid," Tommy laughed.

Raising the plank up above her head, Nat picked up her pace, sprinting towards her unsuspecting target with a speed and fury that was frightening.

"You're dead," Tommy said, raising his fists. Kenny timidly kept his gaze at Tommy, and watched in both horror and relief as Nat smashed the right side of Tommy's head with the plank, so hard that he went flying to the ground.

The children broke into a unanimous cheer. Seeing him struggle to get back up, Nat swiftly smashed a blow to Tommy's back to knock him down entirely. Kenny could not contain his smile, but Nat was not finished. As Tommy rolled about on the ground, finally residing on his back, Nat now stood directly over Tommy whose eyes were closed.

Nat thought she could just leave him and that would be lesson enough. Certainly Tommy would not be able to identify who had hit him. Still, Tommy did not deserve mercy, as he had hurt too many kids already. It was time to get his. Tommy was never going to bully another kid ever again.

The plank came down hard, as Nat smashed Tommy in the face, knocking him unconscious.

The teachers hearing the cheers of the children began hurrying towards the exits to see what was going on outside. Nat quickly raised herself up and threw the plank away, as far away from herself as she could. A few kids took their coats off to cover the wood plank from view entirely, as Nat's friend Christina, wrapped her sweater around Nat to cover Tommy's blood that was now on her dress.

By the time Principal Gilliam came, recess seemed surreally back in swing. The children had resumed playing as if nothing had happened.

That's when he saw Tommy lying on the ground, with Nat and Christina playing close by. "Tommy!" Principal Gilliam rushed, running to his side. The boy was still breathing. "Who DID THIS?!" he yelled, standing up. The children stopped what they were doing, stunned by his tone. "Who did this? One of you must know!"

The crowd was silent. Nat looked carefully about, but there was no denying the power of what she had done. The silence seemed to last an eternity. No one uttered a word. It was then that Principal Gilliam approached Nat. Raising up her head, Nat looked up at a man who appeared to be a giant.

"Nat, you were close in proximity. What did you see?"

One thing Nat had learned very early on was to hide her fear. If they see fear, they've got you. If she told the truth, she would get sent away for sure. Nat loved her Dad...There would be no going back to the orphanage. Holding on tightly to Christina's sweater wrapped around her, Nat hid her fear behind a smile. "I was playing with Christina sir. I didn't see a thing."

So convincing was she that Principal Gilliam never questioned her again about the incident. Nat knew that no one would ever suspect her of being the culprit. Nat was a girl after all, and girls don't do that.

As Principal Gilliam walked away to take Tommy inside to see the school's nurse, Nat knew that this would not be the end of it. Certainly parents were concerned, Tommy's parents in particular, furious that no disciplinary action seemed to be happening. Principal Gilliam had to find out who did it first, before he could discipline. Over the next few weeks, he called students into his office to question, one by one, but every student said the same thing.

No one saw anything.

"Perhaps it was the school's ghost," scoffed Mr. Gilliam to grade one student, Mary, before dismissing her.

As the child left, Principal Gilliam determined that he would be watching more closely to see the 'new' one in charge of the playground. Boys will be boys with their ways of proving who's the toughest. This new kid would reveal himself soon enough, and watching, Mr. Gilliam would be ready.

At the age of twelve, Nat had discovered by accident the General's secret. Cleaning out the hallway closet, she had found a dozen whiskey bottles, both empty and half full, hidden purposely under some clothes. Spring cleaning, Nat could not believe how much was here. It made her sick to her stomach. Although the General had never been mean to her, Nat despised alcohol because of her foster mother.

How could she make him stop? Could she even?

All Nat knew was that life without the General was becoming increasingly difficult to do alone, which is how she felt.

Alone.

Certainly she relied heavily upon God, asking through prayer every night that He would help her to be a good girl, get good marks in school, and above all, help her Dad. Nat was beginning to figure it all out. The late nights 'working,' Dad was out drinking at the army bar. That's why he was not home a lot. That's also why when he did come home, he did not say much.

How Nat hated booze. How she hated his drinking because it took him away from her. Even when he was home, it was as if he wasn't there. His drinking made him quiet and sullen.

At school, Nat's temper was beginning to get the best of her. Classmates could be annoying, but the incident which caused her to snap was when one of them teased her for being an orphan. Someone had finally found out the truth about her. His name was Ian O'Neill. When the teacher stepped out of the classroom to go get a textbook, Ian's taunting made her lose control. Nat threw her math book at his head to stun him momentarily, so that she could charge him and punch him in the face until he was unconscious.

Trying hard to hide her tears, Nat sat back down at her desk. When the teacher returned, she was shocked to see Nat's hands and dress stained with blood.

"Natalie?"

Nat was unable to answer.

"Are you okay?"

Nat looked up at her with tears in her eyes. "Come with me Natalie. You're going to be okay. It's all right. Come."

Nat did as she was told, following her grade six teacher to the office, while the teacher next door, Mr. Thiessen, took Ian to the school's nurse. Sitting outside the Principal's door, it was all beginning to sink in. Why didn't she think? She lost control and got caught. As Principal Gilliam called her in, Nat hardly heard a word he was saying throughout his half hour lecture. That was until he said, "We'll have to call your father..."

Nat heard that.

"Why? I promise I won't do it ever again. You don't need to call him," Nat pleaded, scared.

"Yes we do Miss Shaw. This is very serious what you've done, and there are consequences to be paid for such behavior. Betty?"

"Yes, Mr. Gilliam," the secretary responded, walking into his office.

"Notify Mr. Shaw that he needs to come to the school immediately regarding his daughter."

"Yes Mr. Gilliam," she answered, going over to her desk phone to make the call.

"Now I have to go and check on Mr. O'Neill. You stay right here. Do not move," he warned before leaving.

It was the beginning of the end. The General was coming and when he finds out what she had done, Nat would be sent back. No matter how hard she tries to be a good girl, it didn't matter-he won't want her anymore-he doesn't even really want her now.

No one does.

Nat was trapped. The only way out, to break free, would be to go out on her own, just like Little Nat had done. Yes, she would be alone, but at least then she could be free. Not under anyone's control. No longer forced to live with people she did not want to, like her foster mom, or being stuck in a cage that was her existence at the orphanage.

The office door was open…

As the secretary busily clacked away at her noisy typewriter, Nat dropped to the floor and crawled her way past the secretary's desk, out the office's door. Free, she ran down the school's stairs and out its exterior doors into the thunderstorm. It was cold, but it didn't matter. Nat was running for her life as she sprinted across the open field.

There was no looking back.

When the General got the call that afternoon, he was perplexed. Without any detail, all he knew was that it was urgent that he get to Nat's school. Leaving work immediately, the General made his way into the office to shake Mr. Gilliam's hand. Sitting down, the General's facial expression would reveal his shock when he had learned what Nat had done. As the General reflected, why it was only just a few weeks ago that Nat had brought a stray dog home to be her new pet. Nat was very caring and tender towards the animal, never demonstrating any aggression. The person Principal Gilliam was describing was another kid altogether from the one he knew.

However, what the General was unaware of was how Nat got the dog in the first place. Walking home from school, Nat came across a crowd of boys encircled around the frightened and weak animal. A tiny cocker spaniel, the boys were throwing small pebbles, making fun of its mangy condition. Angry, Nat was disgusted with them. Taking two good size rocks, one in each hand, Nat threw the first rock as hard as she could at the ring leader. All that practice, throwing rocks at empty bottles in her back yard had paid off. It was a perfect shot, cracking the boy on the side of the head and knocking him out cold. The circle broke as Nat walked up to them, furious at what they were doing.

"Don't touch my dog," she growled. Her tone was enough to make all the boys back away from both her and the dog. Yet, there was one stupid one in the bunch who underestimated her. Laughing, he was amused by her temper. What he failed to notice was the other rock Nat held tightly in her right fist.

"Ooohh, a giiiiiiiirl," the boy mocked, turning only for a moment to get approval from the other boys. It was his mistake. "I'm so scared-"he laughed, turning back to face her but it was too late. Nat had winded back her arm and smashed the side of his face with the rock, so fast that he didn't see it coming. The boy hit the ground hard.

"Anyone else?" Nat challenged. The boys ran away, leaving their two friends on the ground to fend for themselves. Seeing that the two boys would not be getting up anytime soon, Nat turned her attentions to the dog. Bending down, she gently called him over to her. The dog came happily, eager to greet his new best friend that had rescued him. Softly petting, Nat decided to take him home right then and there. The General proved to be fine with her decision, so long as Nat looked after the dog. Nat proved to live up to her responsibility, which is why what Principal Gilliam was saying still did not make any sense.

"There's something else," Principal Gilliam continued. "She has run away."

"What?" the General demanded, rising to his feet.

"I'm sure she has not gone too far, but she ran out of the school when I left to go check on the boy."

"You lost my child?"

"She has run away sir."

"You lost her? When did she disappear?" the General demanded, wanting to know how much time he had lost.

"A little over an hour ago. She ran away after we made the call to you, otherwise we would have notified you over the phone. At the time, it was only pertaining to the boy," Principal Gilliam explained, trying to calm a man who was becoming increasingly intimidating to him. The General put back on his hat and headed for the door.

"Mr. Shaw? We need to discuss this further! Where are you going?"

"To find my daughter," he answered unapologetically, not looking back.

6

Skidding to a halt in the front drive, the General ran through his front gate, up the porch, into the house. Dark and eerily quiet, he had guessed right. Nat had come back for her dog, as the house was completely empty.

"NATALIEEEE!!!" he yelled, running out into the backyard. How he called to her with everything he had.

"NAAAAAATTTT!!"

There was no answer. Only the sound of rain as it came down hard.

"Where are you?" he whispered. Still no answer, his eyes searched the trees and fields in the distance for any visible sign.

Nothing.

Running back inside, he quickly sifted through his hunting stuff. His jackknife was gone. Nat must have taken it to use in the elements, he thought. He had after all, taught her how to look after herself in the woods over the last two years.

If anyone could find her though, it would be the General.

Six days had passed, and still no word. The General had immediately notified the police of Nat's disappearance, but to no avail. The time had come to ask for the public's help. Nat could be anywhere in New Brunswick right now. Perhaps someone else would see her and bring her back to him, that is, if she was still alive. The thought was beginning to creep in. It made him unable to sleep at night.

Waiting at the Police Station again to see if any news had come in regarding a possible sighting, the General slumped into his chair exhausted. Eyes black, unshaven, and hair disheveled, he was a mess.

No one here. He would have to wait.

Helpless, waiting was all he could do.

"General?"

A gentle voice had entered the vacant, dark room. The General looked up to see a priest standing at the door's entrance.

"Hello," the priest offered.

The General was inaudible.

"My name is Father Michael," he offered quietly, walking over to take a seat directly across from a man whom he sensed was deeply broken within. Dressed completely in black, the priest looked like death to the General, which made him unforgiving and resentful of his presence.

"I understand that your daughter is missing, having run away."

The General still refused to speak.

"I want to assure you that I am here as a friend, to offer my prayers that she return home safely."

The General still refused to look at him. What was apparent to the priest was the anger the General carried with him. It was heavy burden and Father Michael guessed that it was an anger that the General had been carrying for a long time.

So much pain and suffering.

"God wants to help you General-" Father Michael started, which prompted the General to glare in his direction.

"God?" the General scoffed with hardened eyes.

"Yes, God," Father Michael smiled, relieved to hear a response.

"You must be mistaken Father. God missed my house."

"I don't understand?"

The General did not care to explain it to him.

"He wants to help us all," Father Michael continued. "It is the reason why he sent His only Son. So that we may give up our cross, the weight of our sins to Him. There is no healing until we hand it over to God. Ransomed, we receive freedom and peace that God, through His grace, gives us all."

"You've come to save me Father? *Save* me? Well, I've got news for ya' Father. I don't need your saving. You want to save somebody, go save yourself, because I'm doing just fine."

Father Michael suspected otherwise, but he intently listened. The General needed to speak to someone. "God," he continued, shaking his head. "Where's God now? What's he doing now Father? I haven't found my little girl yet. God doesn't exist Father. If God did, He wouldn't let stuff like this happen all the time…and if He is a God who does, then He can't be any good. No, you go tell your God that I don't need Him. I haven't needed Him for many years…All that God ever did for me was take everything I cared about away. Punishing me, because we're never perfect-never good enough-"

"If bad things happen in the world, General, it is people who do it, not God. There is always a choice. Free will."

"So He'll just stand by and do nothing?"

Silence.

"It is our gift to do what we will with it."

"Well, that's just great Father. Aaaah, the world makes sense again," he mocked. "Your God abandons children, leaving them to fend for themselves, and then turns around perplexed and wonders why we don't turn to Him? What the hell did I ever do to Him? I didn't ask to be created. What have any of us done to deserve this shit world? We didn't pray hard enough? I prayed Father. I prayed so hard as a boy but nothing happened. No matter what I hoped for, no matter what I wanted, nothing changed," the General spoke bitterly.

"All of this is a part of His story and it did not end at the cross, but carried on. We all have a greater purpose, an important role to play in His story, His greater plan for your life, General," Father Michael answered.

"Well His plan," the General leaned in, "stinks-it won't bring anyone back-"

"Your daughter will come back if she knows she is loved by you," Father Michael interjected. A representative of God, truth had to be revealed, so as to confront a man greatly at odds with himself.

"She knows," the General responded defensively.

"Then why has she run away General?"

The General was silent.

"I have no doubt that your efforts as a Father are honorable and to be commended. I ask you this question, not to judge, but to help. Why would your daughter be afraid of your reaction?"

The General thought for a moment, but could not come up with an answer. He provided well for Nat. What else more did she require? *Was* she afraid of him? He would never hurt her.

One thing was apparent. Such a question hurt.

"Perhaps she needs something more from you, to reassure her that your relationship is secure."

"Perhaps she needs a mother," the General started, "someone to talk to about girl things. I haven't been very talkative to her," he said remorsefully.

"Yes," Father Michael said with a gracious smile. "Maybe she wants to talk to you more, perhaps to know you better?"

"Why?"

Father Michael shrugged.

" I'm not that interesting."

Father Michael laughed. "Maybe not to you. I think you are a lot more interesting than what you think."

As the General thought more on the priest's words, the truth became apparent. He had kept Nat at a distance emotionally as this was more comfortable for him. The General did not want Nat to alter his life too much, as he liked his life just the way it was before she entered the picture. He had tried encouraging Nat to be independent, not only for her sake but his own. It would ease the burden of his responsibility for her.

How selfish he had been.

"I have to go," the General said abruptly, standing.

"God bless you General," Father Michael offered with a smile.

"Yeah, yeah," the General muttered, gruffly walking away.

As the General continued driving his jeep down all back roads that he knew of, there still was no sign of Nat. Where could she be? After searching all day, the General retired to his empty home for supper. He had to get something to eat before heading back out to search some more. It had begun raining again, and a storm was moving in fast. He would do whatever it took to find her. Coming into the house, dripping wet, he removed his shoes and cap at the door. An unconscious ritual he had started doing since the day Nat had begun instructing him to do so.

Having soup at the dinner table, the General could not help but look over at the empty seat that Nat used to inhabit. They would hardly speak, but how he missed his little girl's company. As the sun began to set, the General grabbed every spare thing he had, including his rubber boots, a lantern and extra food in case Nat was hungry when he found her to take with him.

As he headed out the door, the thunder had begun to clap hard. The General hurried down the porch steps, looking up momentarily to catch a glimpse of his jeep in the distance.

Instead, he found Nat.

Standing in the rain, shivering from the cold, her dress drenched, his Little Nat had come home! The General stopped in his tracks.

Nat, silently searching for his reaction, began crying. Running away to the backwoods that first day with Limpy in tow, she had a secret place not too far from home that no one else knew of. An old, abandoned hunting shack that was camouflaged under many branches. Nat had actually seen the General trek past her shack that very first day she ran away. Hiding in the bushes from afar with Limpy, Nat was both scared and angry with him. Wanting to have nothing to do with the General, she would make him pay for all that he had done. Nat was pleased with herself as she watched him walk on by.

Perfectly fine surviving on her own, Nat was enjoying her newfound freedom. She was alone and able to do whatever she wanted, without depending on anyone. Yet, sitting under the star-filled sky that fourth night away from home, it was in complete solitude that she thought about her Dad. All the good times that they had together.

She was beginning to miss him some. Nat caught two fish of her own that night for her and Limpy to eat, but it wasn't the same without her Dad. Nat missed sharing the things that they both mutually enjoyed doing together.

On the fifth day she saw the General pass by again, but this time, Nat was not so angry with him anymore. Nat wanted to say something, but when he turned to look in her direction, Nat felt a lump form in her throat. The General, her Dad, looked horrible. Worse yet, the pain evident in his eyes was pain that Nat had caused.

How Nat wanted to call out to him.

On the fifth night, Nat snuggled next to Limpy and wept uncontrollably. Nat loved her Dad. She was missing him terribly. He looked so sad without her and she was sad without him.

Maybe he would take her back? Nat could tell from his face that he cared about her, but could he forgive her for all that she had done? As Nat stood in front of the house that sixth day, only a few feet away from the General, the question still lingered. Would he get rid of her?

The General slowly set down all his bags. If he opened his arms, would she even come to him after he had been such a terrible Dad? None of that mattered right now. Nat needed to get inside where it was warm.

The General reached out his arms, and Nat ran into them.

"Daddy!" Nat cried, wrapping her arms around him.

The General held her tight. He had begun crying too, but he would not show Nat his tears.

"I'm sorry," Nat said.

"I'm sorry too," he whispered gently.

"For everything. I didn't mean to-"

"Shhhh. None of that matters now. You're home, safe and sound," he said, taking her inside. Sending her upstairs to change her clothes, the General wrapped Nat in a blanket once she came back down, sitting her down for some hot soup. Inhaling her food, Nat was still hungry, so he gave her some fruit, and made her two peanut butter and jelly sandwiches. As Nat gobbled her food up, he sat down next to her smiling. They would talk tomorrow as Nat needed her rest tonight.

It was good to have his buddy back.

Safe and sound.

The next day, the General put out an ad for a domestic servant position, and many women did stop by his home those first few days. Although physically attractive, the General did acknowledge that many were much too young. Nat needed a woman who would serve as a mother figure within the home. Someone who would be there with Nat when he could not, due to work obligations. Someone who could give Nat guidance regarding womanly questions.

That is why when Eva came to the door, sitting down on his living room couch, she instantly stood out. Certainly her age, being forty-five was a factor, but her wisdom, sensibility, and calm demeanor was key. With graying hair, her complexion appeared soft despite her years of hard work raising five children who were all now fully grown. Recently widowed, the family farm had been handed over to her eldest son and his family.

"The farm house has so many memories," she explained, "that I need a change. I want to move forward, move on," she added smiling. There was something about the General she liked very much. Despite being gruff and rather burly, there was a vulnerability to him that was quite transparent, especially when he talked about his daughter. He seemed to light up then, his face becoming more animated, which contradicted very much so the way he looked. Possessing a piercing intelligence, Eva could see why he was a General. There was a charisma and strength to him that made him instantly likeable.

The General hired Eva to begin work the very next day. Unknown to Eva at the time as she shook the General's hand was how trying her position would become as time passed. How storms would be coming her way, testing who she was and her very faith, all in the name of a family that was not her own.

That her arrival would be greatly needed for what lay ahead.

Nat determined after a few days that Eva was a kind woman, whom she was happy to have help her at home, so that she could concentrate on her studies more. The General had Nat placed in another school, for a 'fresh start,' and took Nat to train with a friend of his. A military fight instructor, trained in various fighting styles and techniques, Nat's instructor was simply the best. Nat needed an outlet in a place where her anger could be disciplined and constructively managed. The General did not want a repeat of what happened before as the experience was much too hard on him. Besides, it was what he believed to be the right thing to do. Taking more responsibility, he would not be blindsided again to problems brewing. Nat's temper was a problem and it would be resolved.

Nat enjoyed the fight sessions after school. It seemed to work out any stress or fears she felt, putting her feelings at ease. At times though she would lose control on her instructor, and out of frustration and anger lash out on him. He would always then discipline her swiftly.

"Never let your emotions take over. Use your head, by keeping neutral and focused. Emotions blow focus, killing any strategy you could use to out-think and conquer your opponent. Once you are rattled, he has you. Psyche him out, make him mad, all the while tactically learning what his reaction will be, so that you will be ready to hit where he is weakest."

"How do you know what their reaction will be?"

"Observe. Always watch first before you strike. Learn all there is to know about your opponent, without him knowing that you are doing this, and never show him who you are. Observe your environment carefully so as to figure out how to best use it to your advantage. In the woods, a single tree branch could be used as a weapon if you first see it, then figure out how to best use it to advantage. It is the same with your opponent. Study him carefully. Only then will you know how to throw him off and hit his weaknesses. Someone twice your size can be defeated if you use your head first. Technique will develop precision, but it is your head that wins the fight. Got it?"

"I understand," Nat acknowledged without further resistance.

Continuing on for months, it was Eva who found her new home very 'unique.' Nat was a tomboy, no doubt about it, but her and the General were so good together. They would shoot in the backyard, go hunting, even fishing together! Eva had never seen a girl so attached to her father that she wanted to do his things *all* the time. It was really quite sweet to see.

Finding Nat to be a gracious young girl with her, Eva was curious as to why Nat kept herself always at a distance. Eva would try talking to Nat on a personal level, but Nat would only talk about her studies. Indeed the only one Nat seemed to open herself up to was the General and her dog, Limpy.

As months passed on, Eva noticed that something was awry, interfering with the father-daughter relationship.

It was the General's drinking.

Although he was home, the General would drink openly and it would greatly alter his personality. Eva could see Nat's entire demeanor change whenever the General would drink a casual shot.

Not that he was a mean drunk. Not at all. The General was just not himself, and neither Nat nor Eva liked it. They liked the General just the way he was, without the alcohol.

Eva, being older, sensed that a part of the General had something dead in him. Something that she could not quite put her finger on, but it made her wary. He could carry a coldness, a pronounced, flat demeanor, that made him unsafe to her. A man who could very well take you down with him if you stumbled too close to the dark abyss that was his heart. Eva knew his heart was good, but there was a struggle going on, a darkness at work that she did not fully understand.

Apparent was that Nat had learned at an early age to guard her heart. Was this response learned from the General? When he spoke to Eva at times, his tone could be so biting, merely because it was so colorless when he was drinking. There was just nothing there to connect with.

Hosting home gatherings for invited guests, Eva observed that the General did know how to put on a good face with others. More so, that he was a master at disguising his emotions. There was no getting close to him.

Not that the General was an evil or intentionally deceitful man. Merely someone so disconnected from himself that he did not even seem to realize his own need. Self-deceived, his lonely, isolated existence characterized his very real, quiet, unspoken desperation that he was not even aware of.

As he slept on the sofa, Eva intrinsically knew that this was not all that he was. That there was more to his story than this. More than just the broken man she saw before her. The broken man he tried hiding from her, Nat, and everyone else.

At one time, when he was younger and full of life, the General was very much alive. Eva could still see that. Beyond the harshness, his heart was still in there somewhere. Looking over at an old picture resting on the fireplace mantel, Eva saw him.

Thirteen years of age at the time, the General stood proudly next to a male friend, holding up high the biggest trout imaginable.

It was a beauty. Incapable of containing his smile, the General clutched onto his buddy with one arm, holding up the big fish with the other.

His strength was undeniable.

Eva then turned once more to the man she saw before her. What happened to him? What happened to his strength? Did it occur over time through a series of lost battles, or was he overcome in one fatal blow, where he retreated and disappeared beyond reach altogether?

Where was the adventurous, risk-taking, wild young man she saw here in this picture? How he offered his strength to his job, but not fully to Nat and not at all to himself. Did he not know how important and needed his strength was?

Falling asleep on the couch with his empty whisky bottle on the floor, Eva leaned down to put a blanket over him. Clearly the General needed to provide for his family not money, but himself-his whole self.

So it came to be one evening as Nat played outside with her dog, that Eva would say something to the General when he went to the counter to have his usual drink.

"You have a beautiful daughter sir," Eva affirmed, looking out the backyard window at Nat as she washed dishes. The General merely nodded as he poured himself a glass. "She loves you very much." The General smiled, taking a swig of his whiskey glass. "She would do anything for you. Would you do anything for her?"

The General looked over at Eva. "What kind of question is that?" he asked coldly.

"Your daughter needs you sir. She is unable to have all of you when she competes with that," Eva inferred, looking at his empty glass. It was a scary move, because she could lose her job for saying something. Still, in good conscience, Eva could not stand by and do nothing.

The General was not impressed. "You're out of line," he warned, pouring another glass.

Eva had to tell him the truth.

"Your daughter hates your drinking sir," Eva confronted, drying her hands with the dish towel. "It's clear every time she sees you do it. If you love her, you'll stop."

There. Eva had finally said it.

Now what?

Would he fire her for stating her opinion?

The General was clearly enraged. It showed on his face as his jaws tightened, but it was his silence that signaled to Eva that he had taken in what she had said. The General was a smart man. He knew the truth. The real question that remained was would he do something about it?

Eva slowly edged her way out of the kitchen, expecting to hear something. Anything. A word that she would have to leave, but there was nothing. The General let her go without uttering a single word.

The next evening, as the three of them sat down for dinner, the General brought his whiskey glass to the table following grace. That is when he saw it. Nat winced and moved her body slightly away from him.

His little girl had just moved away from him.

How he had never noticed before.

Devastated, Nat's reaction stopped him cold. Setting the glass back down on the table, the General did not take a single sip.

Eva knew. The General finally saw the negative impact his drinking was having on the family. As the General looked down at his plate, suddenly he was not so hungry anymore, his appetite gone from a sense of shame that now gripped him.

As Eva and Nat began talking about their day, the General knew that he was still purposely keeping himself on the outside.

Apart.

Distanced.

Slowly getting up, the General took his glass with him over to the sink, where he proceeded to pour it down the drain. Nat and Eva could not help but smile with relief as they watched him do it. The General hung over the sink for a bit, struggling over what he had done. If this was the right thing to do, why did it not feel good?

Why was doing the right thing so damn hard?

"Will you be eating with us sir," Eva smiled. The General could not speak. He merely shook his head.

Finally, he turned around. Walking over to Nat, he gave her a kiss on the forehead, and walked away. Nat smiled up at him. It was all he needed. It was the right thing, for both of them.

As the General went upstairs to rest in his bed, Eva took the whiskey bottle from the cabinet, pouring its remaining contents down the sink's drain. The General was exhausted. Struggling for so long had made him weary.

Fighting his inner battle, it was time to succumb. The pain was about to take over but Eva would be there to help him through it.

Going to work the next day, the General did not feel well at all. Being hung over was so much easier than this. Nauseous, the General could not stop sweating. By afternoon, his body could not stop shaking. Indeed, the General was right sick.

Finishing his work day, the General told Jeanie that he would be away tomorrow due to illness. As he came home that evening, the General weakly stumbled into the front foyer ill. Rushing to him to hold him up, Eva led the General upstairs to bed where he collapsed to sit down, slumping over his bedside. Completely incapacitated, Eva knew he needed her help. Gently removing his coat, the General let her. Next his shoes and socks. Then came the unbuttoning of his shirt, and the General weakly took hold of her hand. He wanted her to stop.

It was hard enough for him that any woman should see him in this sad state, but a stranger yet. He felt ugly all over.

Disgusting and repulsive.

For Eva to see him as he truly was, let alone take care of him was wrong. He was a General. He did not let anyone take care of him. Looking up at her, he was embarrassed. It had been quite some time since he had been so vulnerable. It was almost more humiliating to have a woman see him like this than a man.

How weak he was.

How he despised being this vulnerable.

Eva was seeing the mess he truly was, behind the uniform.

"Shhhhh," Eva soothed, "It's all right," she reassured, seeing the pain in his eyes.

For being virtually a stranger, there was something in Eva that he trusted. Somehow he knew that she would not hurt him. It made the General let go. As Eva took off his shirt, his eyes closed as she leaned him back onto his bed. Removing his trousers, Eva wrapped him up with many blankets.

Instructing Nat to keep out, that first night was the worst. The General's sheets were soaked. Dipping her cloth into the water bowl, Eva continued to soak his forehead every fifteen minutes throughout the night. In and out of consciousness he came, tossing and turning, talking in his sleep. Nightmares he would have, at times mumbling the word, "Emily," that would cause him to awake momentarily before drifting back off into sleep. Eva was always there with the light, keeping any darkness away.

The General felt like he was dying.

A part of him was.

Many times he vomited into the empty pail resting by his bedside. All the while, Eva would comfort him, holding him steady as he did so. She would then remove the pail and get a new one, once he had been lulled back to sleep.

One day off of work turned into a week. Many people phoned throughout that time, and Eva looked after his affairs discretely, telling all who enquired that he was ill with the flu.

Every night, Nat would sit at the bottom of the stairs with Limpy, waiting for permission to go up, but Eva at the top of the stairs would merely shake her head no. Nat would have to be patient and wait.

Scouring the entire house for hidden liquor, Nat and Eva threw every liquor bottle they could find into the garbage. Soon enough, the house, along with the General's health, was completely clean.

On the seventh day, the General was finally at rest. Peacefully lying in his bed, he felt for the first time in days that he was going to be all right. As Eva walked into the room, she placed a single white rose on his window sill.

"From Nat," she smiled. The General smiled wearily back. "You look good sir." Opening wide the curtains, the General squinted at how bright the sun's light was that morning. "I just filled the tub. There are fresh towels on the sill. Do you need anything else?"

The General shook his head.

"Very well. I will see you downstairs."

"Eva?"

"Yes sir?"

"Thank you."

It took her by surprise. "You're welcome sir," she answered earnestly, before leaving the room.

An hour later the General finally came downstairs. Walking into the kitchen, Eva set his breakfast plate of hot pancakes down on the table and he was actually hungry. Cleaned up and shaven, the General looked much better. Much more himself, Eva thought as she handed him a hot cup of coffee. Nat will be so pleased to see him when she comes home from school today.

Finally she will be able to talk to her Dad again.

The General would also have to break the news that they were moving. Not very far. Just across the Bay of Fundy to Hampton, New Brunswick. The General had been offered a big promotion. He would build a railway with the CNR between Saint John and Moncton, that would supply military materials and equipment for the Atlantic coast. Under the General's leadership, money was finally being put back into the Forces.

"This will be the last move," the General told Nat that night. "We'll be there awhile-at least five years."

Nat did not care. She merely hugged him, because she was so happy to have him back. *All* of him. "Sounds good Dad."

Nat was growing bored with this school anyway. At the age of sixteen, boys had begun noticing Nat, but it was annoying because none of them looked into her eyes when they spoke to her. It was her emerging physical beauty they all stared at. What Nat wanted most was to have someone to connect with... Someone who wanted her for HER. That someone wanted to pursue her soul.

Although naive, Nat was not oblivious to how most girls got their way. By flaunting their charms, the boys came running, but Nat did not want to win someone over that way. Nat was discovering that her body had a power to it, but she did not want to use it. The boys would only want her for one thing, and Nat would be letting them for only one reason. So that she may get some love, some affection, and attention that she desperately craved, even if it was only temporary.

Nat could never disrespect herself by disrespecting her body. Nat determined that she would wait for something real, a boy who would have to work hard to win her affections, because she was worth it.

Certainly the crop of boys she encountered were often either stupid, immature, or both. Nat felt superior both intellectually and athletically. There was no one special who challenged and interested her in any way. If anything, she felt defensive towards boys because they were always scoffing at her, even after she beat them in games and academics. This is why she learned to carry an air of confidence that appeared snotty. Certainly her attitude kept them away which is exactly what she wanted.

Eventually the boys would give up trying.

7

"General! Good to see you sir. How are you sir?" Sergeant Waters greeted, shaking hands. Invited by one of the locals to attend Hampton's annual Summer Fair of 1938, the General accepted, wanting to better acquaint himself with the charming shire town of Kings County. This particular weekend was the last before the commencement of the new school year, and it was a beautiful day. Not a cloud in the sky as the sun's rays glistened down on the people dispersed in the Kennebecasis Valley. As the locals played their violins next to the open gazebo, many activities such as bike races, pie-eating contests, apple bobbing, and three-legged races were all well underway.

It was interesting to Eva to notice that in a room full of men, the General was strong in presence and confident, but socially awkward in front of women and children. Perhaps it was because the General did not know how to small talk with other families. He had never had one of his own until recently, and it still took some getting used to. That's why when Sergeant Waters greeted him, the General was relieved to see a familiar face. "Where's your new house General?"

"Bonney Road. The small farmhouse up the hill."

"That's lovely, General," a diminutive woman gently smiled back at him.

"General, I would like you to meet my wife, Diana."

"Mrs. Waters," the General acknowledged, removing his hat. Patiently, the couple waited for the General to extend his own introductions.

"Hi, I'm Eva, " Eva smiled, offering her own hand. "Nice to meet you both."

"Yes, this is Eva-"

"I didn't know you got married General," the Sergeant smiled.

"That's because I didn't," the General responded uncomfortably.

"Oh, sorry…"

"Yes, I'm a friend of the family," Eva smiled. "I work at the house, helping to take care of Nat."

"The young girl you came with, is she your daughter?" Mrs. Waters asked, intrigued.

"Yes," he answered looking about. "Where is Natalie?"

"I'll go look for her. Diana, would you like to come with me?" Eva offered, knowing the General could speak with greater ease without women around.

"Certainly," Diana answered, giving her husband a kiss on the cheek before leaving with Eva. "Nice meeting you General," she smiled one last time before walking away.

Still the General wondered.

Where was Nat?

Drifting off to the backwoods, Nat wanted to inspect every inch of her new environment. How she was beginning to fall in love with the province's timeless beauty. The mountains across the Kennebecasis River were so full of mysteries that Nat yearned to learn more about.

What kind of game could be hunted in those woods?

How Nat loved the outdoors! Everything about it! Its colors, its sounds, like the branches rustling under the wind's caress. How it was like music to her ears, its smell relaxing to her. Nat would not feel at home until she explored her new, natural environment first.

A cackle of adolescent laughter spoiled her melody. A group of boys were goading each other, rather noisily, further into the brush.

"She showed her tits, *finally*," one of the boys bragged, as the others craved more details. Nat snuck in closer, undetected, until she could see the group safely from behind the shrubbery's branches.

"She was like, moaning," the tallest boy said doing his best, high-pitch, girlish impersonation, "Oh Chris, don't stop! That feels niiiiiice." The boys laughed again, wanting him to go on.

Nat was not sure if she was hearing what she *thought* she was hearing.

"No way!"

"So what happened next?"

"Yeah, tell us, tell us!"

"Tell us!"

"Okay, okay. So, things are going good, and so I slide my hand down-"

"Yeah?"

"-and she lets me!"

"Whoaah," the guys all nodded in unison.

"Don't believe what you hear about Catholic girls," Chris gloated. "Get past all that good girl stuff, and they are wild underneath. I couldn't stop her screaming," he laughed, as the guys patted him on the back.

"Did you-?"

"Of course I did," Chris scoffed. A small lie, but he was in front of the guys. Certainly none of the other small town boys were lucky enough to get close to touching a girl's tits, but then again, he was Chris Woods.

"The Master."

The guy was a magnet for the local girls, and the guys hung onto his every word because he could possibly get girls to talk to them by mere association.

Chris had everything going for him. At fifteen years of age, his lean physique and six foot two frame gave him the appearance of being older than he actually was. While the boys still looked like boys, zits and all, Chris' athleticism and incredible good looks made all the girls notice him.

Needless to say, Nat was disgusted by that Chris something, and that kind of talk! That boy is a disrespectful pervert, she thought to herself. Heading back to the party, she was not going to listen to another word from boys who were *so* immature.

Walking up to a flower bed to pick some flowers for Eva, Nat could not help but shake her head. The boys in this town, she would have to watch out for. Especially that guy who did all the talking.

What was his name again?

As the boys headed out of the bush to join the County Fair, it was Chris who could not help but do a double take on a new girl he saw in the distance.

"Who is that?" Chris asked, seeing Nat bent down amongst the flowers. Dressed in a beautiful, one-piece cotton dress with spaghetti straps, her long, shiny, black mane of Irish hair blew carelessly in the wind. "Anyone know her?" he asked, a bit mesmerized by the visual. That face, so pale, with her ruby colored lips seemed almost exotic. No other girl he had ever met had such a look, making her very interesting to him. Someone worth getting to know right away-before anyone else did.

"Yeah, she just moved up the road from us, the old farm," Steven piped up.

"What's her name?"

"Natalie."

"Excuse me boys," Chris said, as the guys stayed back to watch the master go to work.

Nat saw the pervert boy in the distance coming towards her, and it made her rise quickly to her feet.

'Ha, she must see me coming,' Chris thought to himself. Maybe she's shy? He could change all that.

Turning her back, Nat hurried out of the flower bed to get away from him!

'Oh, playing hard to get?' Chris smiled to himself.

"Hi!" Nat heard a voice from behind call to her. That was the same voice she had heard before. Turning around to see for sure, Nat cringed when she saw that it was indeed the same boy.

The pervert boy.

"Chris Woods," he smiled a cocky grin, extending his hand. This girl was even better looking close up. Fully developed, her boobs were big!

"Hi," Nat said, refusing to shake hands with him. "What do you want?"

Taken a little off guard, Chris worked his charm. "Well, I was wondering if you needed help learning your way around here. I could introduce you to everyone-"

"I think I can handle it," Nat answered flatly, slightly annoyed. How stupid this boy was. He obviously didn't know who he was talking to. Far too arrogant to her liking. "What's your name again?"

"Chris. Chris Woods," he uttered slowly, his confidence dwindling.

"Well Mr. Woods, you are hindering my way, so if you don't mind," Nat said turning her back on him, "my father is calling me."

Speechless, Chris felt himself unable to say a word as Nat walked away haughtily, wanting nothing more to do with him.

"I see you met someone," Eva smiled enquiringly as Nat approached.

"No," Nat said, firmly shaking her head, "I did not."

"He's such a nice boy Natalie, being the Pastor's son and all," Diana added, hinting at a possible future union.

Nat was shocked. "He's a preacher's kid!?"

"Yes. A very handsome one at that, wouldn't you agree? His father is our minister at the Hampton Village Baptist Church."

"I wouldn't know," Nat said defiantly.

As the three women walked over towards the General, Nat could not help but look back at him, only he was gone now. Putting on his best face before turning around, Chris puffed himself back up and headed back towards the guys.

"So?"

"What happened?"

"What did she say?"

"She has a boyfriend back where she's from, so she's not ready to date yet," Chris lied again.

"That will soon change though, eh?" one of the guys said.

"Most definitely. In due time," Chris assured, watching Nat walk up the gazebo's stairs to have a waltz with her father. As the guys began to talk about the new school year approaching, they were unaware of Chris' feeble smile. Never rejected before, Chris felt a little embarrassed actually. Still, something pulled at him, as he felt drawn to watch her. Possessing a beauty that was undeniable, Chris was drawn to her and her laugh as she danced with her father.

School was just around the corner.

Natalie had not seen the last of him yet.

Nat's first day at Hampton Consolidation School was daunting, but Anna, made it much easier. She was a sweet girl who knew and liked everyone, loyal to no one particular group of kids. A little chubby, Anna's inquisitive, blue eyes, behind a veil of strawberry-blonde hair were playful and fun. Going to math class that afternoon, Anna could not stop talking. That is until the group of guys came in, taking their seats from across class.

That is when Nat saw him again. It was Chris Woods from the annual summer fair.

"Nat?"

"Yes?"

"Isn't Chris dreamy?"

As Nat looked over, Chris let out a loud belch, followed by more laughing amongst the boys. Competing, they were trying to see who could belch the loudest. Chris looked over at Nat to see if she was impressed.

"I wouldn't say dreamy." Nat could not be bothered with him. There was not much substance there.

"He is so cute," Anna gushed.

"Welcome back everyone. Mr. Woods, sit up," Mr. Hayes, Nat's new English teacher sternly said entering the classroom.

"Yes sir," Chris replied dutifully.

"Before we begin, I would like you all to help me welcome a new student to our school," he motioned Nat to stand, which she did. "Miss Natalie Shaw is from Kentville, Nova Scotia-"

The boys broke out into unanimous clapping and cheering, as Chris whistled and hollered the loudest. Nat gave them the entire group the strangest, most annoyed look. Boy, were they immature!

"Settle down now!" Mr. Hayes yelled annoyed. "What's the matter with you boys? Where are your manners? Be respectful."

The boys quieted down. They sure were a rowdy, rambunctious group their first day back. "Miss Shaw," Mr. Hayes apologized, "behavior in class is more civil than demonstrated today. Behavior that will not be repeated in my class," he said, sternly looking at the boys who were trying to muffle their chuckling. "You may sit Miss Shaw. Welcome," he finished, as the girls politely clapped, greeting Nat. Nat could see from the corner of her eye that Chris was looking, but she pretended not to notice him. Maybe if she ignored him long enough, he would just eventually go away.

"Hey Anna," Chris strolled by, walking past Anna and Nat in the hallway later that afternoon. "Are you coming?" he asked.

"Sure Chris," Anna answered without hesitation. "Where is it at?"

"Smithtown, the Covered Bridge…" Chris said, eyeing Nat who was reading her French Language textbook. "That book is fascinating," he smiled, adding, "you know, French is the language of lovers."

That should bug her and get her goat!

"You understand French?" Nat challenged skeptically.

"Mais oui mademoiselle, je sais un peu," Chris responded, catching her off guard.

"Combien?"

"Come to my house and find out," he teased.

Nat did not know what to say to someone who was so bold. "You get your manners from a barn?" Nat asked, annoyed.

"At least I don't read French books upside down." Nat looked down, seeing that the book's cover revealed that she was indeed reading its text upside down. Trying so hard to quickly ignore him, she was busted. "Bring some booze, if you can sneak it," Chris invited, his gaze returning back to Anna, "and be sure to bring your new friend," he winked. Nat looked firstly at Anna, then back at Chris who was loving the attention Anna was giving him. An insincere charmer, Chris was merely having fun at the fact that Anna was drooling over him. Could she not see what a phony he was?

"Someone sure likes you," Anna teased, a little envious, once Chris left.

"He likes everyone, including himself," Nat said shrugging it off.

"There's nothing wrong with a little confidence," Anna defended, relieved that Nat was not interested in him.

"There's a difference between confidence and arrogance. Confidence is something real, coming from experience. Arrogance is thinking you're something you're not when you have no experience to back it up. He's too full of himself," Nat explained candidly, watching him swoon his way down the hall. "Not my type."

"What is your type Nat?" Anna asked incredulously, as she found Chris impossible to resist. Charming and seductive, he said all the right things.

"A real man, like my Dad, and not a boy," she answered firmly. "I'll see you tonight."

That evening the bonfire reflected off the calm waters, lighting the entire river bend where all the kids were. Nat was surprised at how many kids were there. Perhaps they had all told their parents the same thing as Nat had. That they were all studying at a friend's house that Saturday night.

Nat did go over to study, just not the whole night. A partial lie.

Anna had helped Nat dress, doing her hair, but Nat refused most makeup with the exception of lipstick and blush. If Anna's parents knew that Anna had makeup on, she would be grounded for a year. Okay, maybe not that harsh, but makeup was perceived as being worn by loose women, not good girls.

"You ever see Jean Harlow, Nat?"

Nat shook her head.

"You have her complexion. One day, when my pimples go away, I'll have it too. That's how I want to look," Anna spoke wistfully. "I want to be beautiful like Harlow, so that when I walk in a room, everyone will just stop and stare. All men will want me."

Nat broke out laughing.

"What? I want to have suitors clamoring over me so that I can pick the best man. A man who will adore me and take care of me. A man who is strong, daring, and romantic! A man who will bring me home flowers and tell me how beautiful I am. You probably think I am vain," Anna confessed, concerned about Nat's opinion.

"No," Nat reassured. At least she was not the only one who felt awkward about who she was, or insecure at times. "I think that you are pretty right now, as a person, and that's more important than looks."

"Easy for you to say. You have your looks Nat and the guys look at you. I've noticed," Anna said, a tinge of envy in her voice.

"That's only because I'm the new girl. After a month, I'll be just like everyone else. I know because I have moved around a lot. You'll see. You are a swan...and a sister," Nat smiled.

"A sister huh? I have an older sister, but she is not nearly as nice as you are Nat. Sisters we are," Anna said giving Nat a hug. "Is my makeup pretty?" Nat felt it was a lot, but Anna liked it, so she nodded. "I don't care if my mom finds out," Anna said defiantly. "I'm going to have fun tonight."

So the two of them headed for the Covered Bridge, biking down the Damascus dirt road. Chris was with his buddies and had been watching for Nat to come, but to no avail. Finally, he saw Anna walk out from behind the hill, but her friend wasn't with her. As Anna neared closer to the fire, he then saw Nat was actually behind, following her lead. Feeling a tinge of excitement, Chris looked back to his friends and started telling a joke. The group broke out into laughter, and it caught Nat's attention to his delight. Chris pretended not to notice her arrival, and carried on as if he was the ring master in full swing. That would impress her.

Nat could not help but notice him. Everyone always seemed to be around him, wanting to hang out with the guy.

As Anna greeted Suzy and Shirley by the bonfire, introducing Nat, others joined them. That meant the boys too, as she was one of the prettiest girls in the school. Chris took notice.

He had better make his move, but in a minute. He wanted to just watch her first. Wearing a simple, two-piece, pink cotton dress, that revealed Nat's bare shoulders and exposed neck, her skin looked so soft. The hemline rested just below her knees, revealing calves that were so smooth, round and supple that he could imagine going up that dress with a body like hers!

As Nat looked up, she caught Chris looking at her again. He had to approach.

"Bonjour mademoiselle," Chris smiled down at her. She looked to each side of her, but unfortunately he was indeed talking to her. Nat eyed him carefully.

"What do you want?" she replied suspiciously. Chris sat down next to her.

Close.

Too close.

Did he not have a sense of personal space? Nat moved over, but Chris moved in close again.

"I don't bite," Chris laughed. He had been drinking. Nat could smell it on his breath. "Mmmmm, Natalie," he murmured. "That is a beautiful name for a beautiful girl," Chris said sweetly. Nat looked away.

'What a lying louse,' she thought to herself.

"Ga-gonk, ga-gonk," Chris began repeating, trying to get Natalie to look at him. "You hear something?" he asked. "Ga-gonk, ga-gonk." Nat looked at him strangely. "That's the beating of my heart for you, Natalieeee," he laughed, knowing full well that he was being cheesy. Nat tried hard not to laugh, but could not help it.

"That is terrible," she scolded him gently, breaking out into a grin. "Terrible."

"I know," Chris shrugged, taking another swig.

"Does that really work?" she smiled.

"You're the first one I've tried it on. You tell me." Nat did not answer. "Oh, I just wanted to see your beautiful smile," he charmingly flirted again.

"You are so full of it!" she smiled, incredulously.

"What? I mean that one! Like no guy has ever told you what a beautiful smile you have?"

Nat felt herself being caught up in him, and she had to pull back. Don't forget what you heard, she told herself. That's what he's about. "That still does not change the fact that you are full of crap, Chris Woods."

Chris was a bit stunned. No girl had ever told him that before. Not that she was wrong. Chris knew he was being pretentious with her. It was strange because no girl had ever seen through him like that before. Nat could not be conned.

"Did you want to go for a walk?" Chris asked, intrigued.

"Why?" Nat asked again, her eyes suspiciously narrowing. Was he going to try something on her if she went alone with him somewhere?

"Just to talk, honest," Chris answered with his hands in the air. "No hands. I just could probably use some sobering up, if I'm going to try to hold a conversation with ya'."

"And risk losing all your drunken charm?"

Ouch. Another blow.

"You may not believe this, but I wouldn't mind getting to know ya better, Natalie Shaawwww," he slurred. What did he just hear himself say? He never wanted to get to know girls better! Certainly not as people, as that was too much attachment. Yet, the real question was, why was he being so real?

Nat took a moment to consider him carefully, before deciding that he was harmless. Besides, she could easily defend herself against him if he did get fresh. "Where shall we walk?" she asked, rising to her feet.

"Down the dirt road," Chris said, staggering to his feet. Only a little tipsy. "It has some great views." Anna came back.

"Anna, we're going for a short walk-to help him sober up," Nat reassured, adding, "I'll be back shortly." Anna was not worried, trusting Nat on her word that she would not make a move on a guy she liked. As the two walked along the river side, once out of view, Chris swung his arm around Nat's neck, and began to sing:

"Show me the way to go home,
I'm tired and I want to go to bed,
I had a little drink about an hour ago,
And it went straight to my head."

"Get off me!" Nat said throwing his arm off of her. Nat would walk alongside of him, but at a distance that respected her personal space.

"Oooohhhhhh, wherever I may roam,
By land or sea or home,
You can always hear me singing this song,
Show me the way to go home."

As he began to sing again, Nat shushed him. "All right, ENOUGH! You are being too loud!" she said annoyed. Chris started laughing. "What's so funny?"

"You."

Stopping, Nat confronted him irritably. "What about me is so damn funny?"

"Are you French?"

"Why?"

"I thought so," Chris said, resuming his staggered walk.

"What does that mean!?"

"Nothing."

"Yes it does. What?"

Chris stopped and looked deep into her eyes. It made her feel she needed to be on guard. "Passionate," he said, proceeding to look her up and down. "Very passionate," he said, leaning in. Nat stopped his kiss with her index finger.

"You've got the wrong girl. I'm mostly Irish," Nat said, heading back to the beach.

"French-Irish-now that's even better!" Chris called out. Nat continued to walk away. "Come on, I was kidding! Come back girl," he yelled, beginning to call her as if his dog. "Come on girl. Be a good girl. Come here. Cooooome here!" he began barking like a dog. As Nat turned around to look back at him, she couldn't help but give him a dirty look as she watched Chris laugh at his own comic genius hysterically.

What an idiot.

Following the weekend, Chris would be more than that. Chris would be a dead man.

The things with boys is they have a way of elaborating and embellishing the truth. On Monday morning, news had spread fast throughout the school about Chris and the new girl. When pressured by the guys to know what happened between him and Nat, Chris had succumbed to lying. It slipped out that she was 'easy,' but that this had to remain in the strictest confidence within the group.

By noon hour, the word had spread and everyone in the school was talking. Nat was frustrated at having so many boys ask her out that morning, particularly the one who stood by her locker.

"I don't even know who you are, so why would I go out with you!?"

That is when Anna told her. When Nat was eating her lunch quietly outside on the school's steps, Anna, knowing intrinsically that Nat would not do something like that, told her the rumor. That Chris said they had 'done' it when they left the party briefly.

"WHAT!?" Nat screamed horrified, rising to her feet. "Where is HEEEE!?"

"By the gym lockers, with the guys," Anna answered, scared.

"Where is that?" Nat steamed.

"What are you going to do?"

"Show me where Anna."

"Okay, follow me," she said timidly, as Nat followed behind. When they reached the end of the hallway corridor, Anna stepped aside as Nat finally caught sight of Chris. Seeing the little, little man, her footsteps carried an impending fury.

"Hey look, there she is," Johnny pointed in the direction where Chris' back was turned, as Nat made her way towards the group. Chris gulped hard being afraid, but put on his best face when he turned to greet her, "Nat, hi-"

Swiftly moving in, Nat throttled Chris with her best punch. It sent him flying back into his locker.

"Don't you hi me!" Nat yelled. Bouncing back up to face her, Chris was pissed.

"What the hell's your PROBLEM!!!?"

The question enraged Nat even more. Nat slapped him fast and hard against his left cheek. As all the guys backed away, they winced at the slap. It was loud on contact. That one had to hurt.

"Don't pretend you don't know what my problem is!? How dare you say lies about me!!!?" Nat yelled, reaming him out. "Who the hell do you think you are, saying we *did* it! I wouldn't do you, if you were the last man on earth and the whole human race depended on it!!!"

A crowd had gathered around the two of them.

"Hey baby-" Chris nervously laughed, trying to save face.

"Don't you baby me you jerk! I'm NOT your baby! The only way I could be your baby is in your dreams buddy because you wish! For the record everyone," Nat said addressing the crowd, "Chris and I did **NOT** do it. Chris Woods is a ball-faced LIAR!" Nat yelled. "You just keep away from me," she scowled, finally storming off.

As the crowd dissipated, the guys started to walk away from Chris, without saying a word. What could Chris say? Busted in his own lie, Chris knew he may have deserved something, but not that! This girl had just humiliated him in front of everyone! After he had said it, Chris knew it was a mistake. That's why he told the guys not to tell, but they couldn't keep their big traps shut.

How in the hell could she punch him like that!!?

Fine.

Chris did not want anything to do with her anyway. That new girl was crazy. From this point on, they would be enemies. No more Mr. Nice Guy.

As Chris and the boys took to the field to play football, all Nat knew was that she was just itching to play the sport again. After all, she had played lots back in Nova Scotia, and knew how to play the game well.

Heading to the bathroom, she took out a pair of men's pants her Dad had bought her the previous year. At the time, the Principal had called the General in to discuss the 'situation.' Distraught, the Principal was very concerned N that had been caught wearing boys pants, and this was not only against the school dress code, but was rebellious and unnatural behavior in a girl that the school did not support. The General simply shrugged. "Winters are cold. My daughter is supposed to wear a dress through snow, exposing her to frostbite, because pants on a girl makes you feel uncomfortable?"

"You are missing the point Mr. Shaw. Natalie is not exhibiting the kind of female behavior our school community values as important. If we let children get away with anything, we have to wonder where it all will lead. What will happen next, down the road, as a result of this?"

"Nat wears pants when we go hunting. In my family, it is not an issue, so if I have to take Natalie to a different school, because my values don't agree with yours, so be it."

"Nat?" Anna called from the school's front doors, as Nat walked past her. "The girls are here. Where are you going?"

Nat turned with a mischievous grin, heading straight for the field. "I'm going to play football."

"Nat!" Anna's voice rose in urgency, as she ran after her.

That's when Chris saw her coming. All the guys did and they stopped what they were doing to get a closer look at the strange apparition that was moving in.

What the hell was she doing?

Why is she wearing pants?

Bizarre.

"Hey fellas," Nat waved walking up to them, stepping confidently onto the field. No one responded verbally, their glances condescending. "Hey," Nat smiled, "I was wondering if I might join you in a game of football? I assure you, I am very good, and will not hold my team back," Nat proposed.

The team leader, all Chris knew was that it was payback time. "I'm sure that you're good at many things, like fixing your hair, painting your nails pretty, having a tea party with the other girls, but this is a man's game little girl. I think it best if you go giggle your way back to the other girls over there, before you get hurt playing with the big boys."

Nat was not impressed.

Good. He had embarrassed her. "Run along now," he dismissively said. Satisfied, Chris turned his back to walk away, knowing that he had put her uppity manner in its place. No longer interested in a mouthy girl, Chris could feel her glare penetrate his back, but he did not care. The guys huddled up again to renew their game.

No one can talk to her that way! Especially not some jerk who thought he was so mighty. God's gift to women everywhere, my foot! Nothing made her want to vomit more. No, the way he just talked to her only made Nat want to beat him even more. "Would you want to bet on that Big Football Boy?" Nat mockingly yelled out to him.

"You're hysterical. Absolutely deluded you know that? Look at you," he mocked. " You're wearing pants for crying out loud. You're completely mental."

"I've got money to bet." All the guys turned back around. "Bring your best guy to hit me down. I dare ya," Nat challenged. "Hit me down and this ten dollars is yours to split amongst yourselves."

"I will," Charlie volunteered, anxiously stepping forward.

"Hold it," Chris said, stopping him. What the hell was she doing? Why couldn't she just shut her trap and go away quietly? If she wanted to make a point, this was not the way to go about doing it. If anyone else had punched him, Chris would have pulverized them. The only reason he did not hit Nat back that day was because she was a girl. Now she was just acting plain stupid. "I'll be right back."

Leaving the group, Chris walked over towards Nat. A crowd had begun gathering at the sidelines to see what was going on as an uncomfortable tension filled the air.

Chris went up to her to speak face to face. Towering, Nat was so small in comparison. Five foot six, maybe a hundred and twenty pounds on her. What was she thinking?

"What are you doing?" Chris quietly demanded, so that no one would hear him but Nat. "If you're mad at me for what I said, it's over and done with."

"Oh no, I'm mad at you for what you just said now!" Nat hissed back. "This is all new!"

"Quit acting like a stupid school girl and get over it."

"I am not a stupid school girl! How dare you talk to me like that! Who do you think you are?"

"Go away," Chris said firmly turning his back on her.

"You want me to go away!?" Nat attacked, following him.

"YES!" Chris yelled back, not liking her tone of voice, as he continued on walking.

"You are by far the stupidest boy I've ever met!" Nat screamed at him. Chris whipped back around.

"If you don't go away, I'll take you off the damn field myself!" he firmly warned.

"Oh really?"

"Yes, really!"

"Is that so?"

"Yes, that's so!"

"Can't threaten me with a good time!" Nat mockingly yelled back, knowing this would antagonize him. If he wanted a verbal battle, he was way out of his league.

Chris opened his mouth to respond, but he had no comeback.

"Ooohhh, the great Chris is caught speechless! Oh hi," Nat imitated his demeanor, "I'm Chris and I'm an idiot-"

For Chris, this girl had irritated him long enough. Furious, he would show her who was boss and put her in her place. Aggressively picking her up, Chris slung Nat over his back and began walking off the field.

"Hey!" Nat screamed. "Put me down you big lump of coal!! You human version of an ape! Put me down I said!"

The guys began laughing and clapping as Chris physically removed her from the field.

"PUT ME DOWN!" Nat yelled, kicking her legs and beating her fists on his back.

"You want down?"

"Yes!"

"You're sure about that?"

"YES!" Nat answered enraged.

"Fine," Chris said, throwing her off his back into the watery mud pond. "As you wish your highness," Chris bowed before walking away.

"How dare you!?" she screamed at him. Chris smiled as Nat was a muddy mess. 'That would show her,' he thought walking away.

Nat rose up and grabbed with both hands the biggest chunk of mud sludge she could find. "Chris!" she called, crawling out. "Hey Chris!" she called but he continued to ignore her, opting to return to the field.

Making his way back, Chris called out to the guys, "Okay, let's go-"

Chasing after him, "I'm playing whether you like it or NOT!" Nat screamed, throwing a large chunk of mud sludge that exploded on Chris' backside. Hitting hard, Chris flew forward with its impact. Veering around to yell at her, he found himself encountering a second throw of mud, this time exploding in his face! Nat furiously stomped towards him as Chris struggled to gain his sight back, clearing the mud from his eyes.

"What the hell's the matter with you!? What the hell? Dammit woman! Are you CRAZY?!" Chris yelled to her face.

"With the hell's wrong with MEEE!" Nat yelled back, fists raised. "There's nothing wrong with me! What's the hell's wrong with you!? Tossing me off the field, Mr. Big Shot! I didn't know that you owned the entire field!!!"

"They're just like my parents," Charlie commented to Pete, who nodded in agreement.

"Yeah, it's like they're married or something," Johnny commented, as the other guys stood by watching the spectacle unfold.

"I'm trying to help you, GOD!"

"Oh really? How? By throwing me into the mud?" Nat charged.

"You fell. I didn't throw you in," Chris corrected Nat.

"You threw me in the GODDAM mud!!"

"Well, you deserved it, carrying on with a tantrum when you don't get your way!" Chris yelled back, oblivious now to the crowd watching him.

"Why can't I play? Tell me why?" Nat demanded. "Give me one good reason and I won't bother you!"

"Why?"

"Yes, WHY?" Nat screamed.

"You're a GIRL! You'll get hurt. I am only stating the obvious. I'm just trying to get you to act smart. For someone who is supposedly a smart girl-"

"Person," Nat corrected him.

"Whatever-you're not acting very bright. Charlie, our biggest guy is twice your size," Chris said. "He'll break you in two if he wants," Chris said.

Nat bypassed Chris altogether, yelling out her offer for the guys to hear. "If I hit Charlie, and he goes down, then I get to not only keep my money, but I get to play football today and any other day I damn well feel like."

"Come on Chris," Charlie urged wanting the money.

"You're not helping things Charlie," Chris yelled back. Why wasn't she listening to him, the voice of reason?

"I'll take it easy on her. Bring that money over sweetheart," Charlie called.

Chris could not do anything about it now, but he knew he wouldn't be the one to hit her.

"If you get hurt-" he warned.

"Then I'll tell the school I fell off a bank while walking home last night," Nat strategically countered. Nat stared hard at Chris, forcing his hand open, to forcefully place the money in his palm. Determined to prove him wrong, and wanting to play football again, Nat defiantly pushed her way past him. It was then that the girls started cheering Nat on, as Charlie, the biggest guy on the team stood ready to go.

"This will be easiest money I've ever made," Charlie muttered under his breath. "I'll give her a little push, and she'll go home crying to her mommy," he laughed, as did the others. Nat walked up, assessing Charlie for weaknesses. He was big-slow and uncoordinated she determined.

"Whoever goes down first right?"

"Right," Charlie confirmed. Nat got into position and the guys could not contain their laughter.

"Hey, I want to be quarterback," one of them said, standing behind Nat in her squat position. Charlie was beside himself. "You look cute sweetheart. You'll look even cuter when I lay you down," he said, taking position. "I promise I'll be gentle," blowing her a kiss.

Yet, Nat no longer heard Charlie, the group's laughter, nor the crowd. She had honed in on her target. He would not know what hit him. Chris begrudgingly walked back to the group.

"On two?" Chris said. Charlie nodded as Nat looked up at him. "On two," he repeated to ensure that she was ready. Nat in position looked back at Charlie. A part of him wanted Charlie to smash her down so that she would pay for what she did to him and finally go away. The other part of him though, did not want to see her get hurt. Although she was tough and maybe needing someone bigger to stand up to her, she was still just a girl.

"Ready," Nat said, completely focused.

"Three fifty one, three fifty one, hut, hut!" Chris yelled. Nat sprang up with such force, she looked like a cheetah breaking out from its cover. Charlie stumbled up, opening his arms to take her down, but Nat ducked and twirled around underneath his grasp, to give him a push from behind. Falling forward onto his knees, Nat smiled in triumph as the girls cheered. Chris was relieved and a bit surprised.

Charlie was enraged as he rose awkwardly to his feet to protest her methods as unfair.

"I beat you fair and square you big lug," Nat snapped back.

"She pushed you down 'fair and square'," Chris quoted, shrugging. "What do you want me to do about it?"

"I want two out of three," Charlie argued.

Nat was annoyed. "You want another chance, eh?" she challenged, walking towards him.

"Yes."

That's when Nat kicked him in the groin with all her might. Startling everyone, including Charlie, no one saw it coming. Charlie's eyes went cross-eyed as he dropped to his knees like a pile of bricks.

"There. There's your chance!" Nat yelled.

Charlie was unable to breathe let alone speak. The field went quiet, the only audible sound being the moaning of Charlie's voice. The guys were surprised, but impressed.

"Anyone else need me to give them a second chance?"

All the guys immediately shook their heads, consciously covering their hands over their groin area.

Unreal. Charlie just got beat by a girl!

Nat looked back to Chris.

"That's two out of three. Now can I play football?"

Chris could not help but smile. She bagged him pretty good. No guy he had seen came close to that hoof. Charlie was still rolling over in pain. How easy it was to underestimate her, perhaps because she was so good looking. Probably more so because she was a girl. Nat sure did not act like a girl is supposed to. It was a quality he very much liked, but would keep a secret for himself.

"Yeah," Chris nodded, "but, we're not going to play soft because of you. You've got to hold your own. You know how to play?"

"Chris, you can't let her play," one of the guys objected.

"A deal's a deal. You can't refuse the deal because you didn't like the result," Chris argued.

"I know how," Nat answered, impatient.

"All right, you can play on my side. Charlie," Chris yelled, as Charlie struggled onto his knees. "Come on, get up. We need ya. We're going to start a new game."

"Heads or tails?" Pete asked.

"Heads," Chris answered, as the coin was flipped and Chris won the draw.

"Let's huddle up guys," Chris called. The guys did so, keeping Nat out of their huddle. Nat pushed her way in. The guys all looked at her, but Chris was unfazed. "The line will stay the same. Play wide for the rest of ya'. I'll call it on one. Whoever is open, the ball is coming. All right? Break." As they took to the line, Nat went wide once the ball was snapped. Although she was open, Chris did not throw her the ball, and no one bothered to cover her.

So it went, play after play. It was as if she wasn't there. They were letting Nat play, but not *really*. That's when Nat decided to take it for herself.

Reading the play, Chris sent the ball flying to Pete, but Nat intercepted and ran. Ran like the wind, so fast, that no one could catch her.

The game ended with her touchdown, as Anna, and the rest of the girls ran up to her.

"Nat, that was great, but you've got dirt on your clothes," Anna said, dusting her pants off.

"I'm fine Anna. Next time they will pass to me," Nat said, still angry.

"What do you mean next time?"

"Tomorrow. And the day after. And the day after that. Eventually they will get sick of me, and finally pass me the ball so that I go away. Only I won't Anna," Nat vowed.

"Well, well, well Christopher," Betty smiled, flirting. "You certainly had an interesting game." As Chris walked over to her, Betty's girlfriends left the two of them to give them some privacy. "So, who is that new girl, or is she really a boy in secret?"

"I don't know. Maybe. She knows how to play though," Chris said, trying to incite a tinge of jealousy. Chris had always liked Betty, but she had been going steady with Frankie for two years now. If Betty was to become threatened by Nat, she might finally turn his way once and for all.

"Who is that?" Nat asked, seeing the two of them across the field.

"Oh, that's Betty O'Reilly. She teases Chris terrible even though she is with someone else," Anna replied candidly.

"Does he like her?" Nat asked.

"Why do you ask?"

"No reason. Just conversation," Nat shrugged noncommittal.

"Chris has liked her since elementary school, but they have never gone steady. Betty is full of herself because she is so pretty, and she has said she will only date 'marriage' potential." Nat was confused.

"Money," Anna explained. "She comes from one of the wealthiest families in Kings County."

"What does it matter?"

"For you, me, yeah, but Chris is a preacher's kid. Chris is not the doctor type, like her daddy, so he will never be good enough for her taste. That doesn't mean that she doesn't tease him though." Nat took a closer look at Chris. He was charming no doubt, but it seems hard to imagine any girl resisting him, aside from herself of course. Certainly not over money or supposed potential. If anything, Nat thought that she had been the only girl to reject him. The way he carried himself was the main reason why she was so harsh towards him. He had only one thing on his mind, and he seemed to believe he was entitled to get it.

Nat did not want to be just any girl. She wanted a man who would make her his *only* girl. Jesus had said to treat your body as a temple, and Nat did. It would only be for someone special, and that would be in marriage. Yet, Nat intended to never marry. At least not until she met someone who was her equal.

Then the thought of Chris deserving more passed through her mind. What? What was she thinking? Well, he should not cow down to a girl who believed him to be inferior. Shake it off, she told herself. He deserves whatever he dishes out, and that is a lot!

"She sounds charming. Can we be friends with her?" Nat asked.

Anna laughed.

What was an ideal man though? Interesting question. For Nat it was a man whom embodied the qualities of goodness. He had to have a gentle spirit, be loving, resourceful, self-sufficient, and above all, intelligent. Someone who could hold a good conversation.

"Studying tonight?" Anna asked.

"Yeah," Nat said.

"Okay, see ya tomorrow Nat," Anna said leaving. Nat turned back to Chris who was now leaving the field alongside Betty. It was at that moment that Chris discretely looked up to see Nat watching him go. As Betty rambled on with her incessant chatter, Chris could not help but look around him. Was she really looking at him? Could it be that she liked him?

Something was becoming clearer to him.

He kind of liked the new girl.

8

Those first few months of school were exhausting for Nat. The guys begrudgingly let her play football that fall, after awhile throwing her the occasional ball. Nat had made a best friend who felt more like a little sister to her.

Just like Mary had been when she was younger.

Classes were challenging, but every night, after her fight regimen, Nat would attend to her studies. The General was away most of the time, leaving Nat bored, so she had extra time to ensure that she excelled. Besides, she wanted to ensure that Chris Woods who continued to ignore her every day at school and on the field, could see that she was something special. That Nat was really smart, and that a boy like him could never be good enough for a girl like her. Nat was going places, beyond this small town, beyond the Maritimes, and that nothing was going to get in her way!

That Christmas, the family spent time together, but it would be short-lived. Things were happening that consumed her father's time. Eavesdropping from the staircase above, Nat listened to her Dad share with Eva how "Canada was living in a dream world, refusing to see the truth. That a mass hypnosis of peace had gripped the country" that no one wanted to come out of. "Isolationist attitude," the General stated. "What happens overseas won't affect us, but just wait. When war does break out, Canada will need to defend her own, but won't be able to."

The last twenty years had experienced such devastating cuts to defense spending, that the government money coming in now would not be enough to repair the damage done.

Truth be told, the Canadian military possessed not a single tank, modern anti-aircraft gun or artillery, nor aerial bombs of any kind. Moth-eaten uniforms, ancient Lewis guns, ninety minutes of total ammunition, and two-hundred and seventy obsolete aircrafts were what remained for use, remnants of the Great War fought well over twenty years ago. 3,100 men represented the entire Canadian Air Force, and out of that, only nineteen men were competent enough to fight in combat with the Hurricane fighters.

The Navy was even smaller with a tiny force of only 2,200 men, while the Army being the largest force, carried only a total arsenal of 29 modern Bren guns for 4,500 of its men serving. There was so little to build on, that it would take years to catch up, and war, seemed just around the corner. That a man named Hitler posed a serious threat that world leaders, including our own Prime Minister, seemed to be ignoring.

It all sounded very serious, making Nat determine that she would not be too demanding of her Dad's time. His presence and intellect was needed by the Canadian government and our country at this time, so she would wait for him.

As Nat buried her dog Limpy with Eva's help that spring, the General still phoned home to make sure she was okay. The dog was old and haggard looking from the first day Nat brought him home, but still. Limpy was Nat's dog, and he meant a lot to her. A difficult time, Nat made it through.

An early melt, Nat could not help but head out into the woods to explore all that the landscape offered. Drinking in its smells and sights, the Hammond River never looked prettier as its waters cast a reflection of the woods surrounding it. The early mist had nearly finished its ascension, as the sun filtered through its mystery, warming Nat to the bone.

It would prove to be too tempting.

Slyly scanning to see that the coast was clear, Nat lifted up her arms to remove her shirt, followed by her skirt and shoes. What the hell? Who needs undies anyway? Tiptoeing into the water, Nat eventually dived in once the water was deep enough.

Up and out of the water she came, swimming about on her back, enjoying her newfound freedom. Where Nat could do anything she wanted because this spot of heaven was hers.

Initially cold, Nat did not mind. How refreshing it was. Plunging deep into the water again, Nat glided along the bottom floor before rising up eventually to catch her breath. How Nat loved the water, a consequence of being around the ocean all her life. A strong swimmer, a real Maritimer is secretly a fish on land!

It was only as she cleared the water from her blurry eyes, did she scream at the apparition before her. Pushing herself violently back into the river's deepest part, so as to veil her body, Nat screamed again. "What the hell are you doing here!?"

"What am I doing here? What are you doing here? Taking your morning shower?"

That Chris was such a smart mouth! Standing by the shoreline, he was being a pervert!

"Ha, ha, very funny. That was so funny I almost forgot to laugh. Oh wait, I didn't laugh," Nat replied sarcastically with her arms crossed, so as to cover her breasts. "Did you follow me!?"

"Oh it's all about you, isn't it? You wish," he answered smugly, beginning to enjoy this new situation he had by chance stumbled onto. "I was on my way to play a game with the guys, and happened to take a shortcut-"

"Well, how long have you been standing there?" Nat interrupted him, concerned.

"Oh," Chris pretended to ponder, "long enough."

"Long enough for what!?" Nat demanded.

"Long enough," Chris said, picking her clothes up off the ground, "to see that you have no clothes on."

"Don't you touch my clothes," Nat warned. Chris smiled teasingly, knowing he had Nat just where he wanted her. "Those are my personal things and you have no business touching them!"

"What do you mean?" Chris asked coyly, playing dumb, continuously poking her clothes with his index finger. "Touch...touch..."

"You know damn well what I mean! If you don't set them down-"

"You'll what?" he asked, inspecting her panties.

"I'll, I'll-"

"What?"

"Do you know who my Dad is? He's a GENERAL, and when he finds out about you, he'll kick your ass!"

"Do you know who my Dad is?" Chris mimicked Nat in a high falsetto, "He's a General, blah, blah, blah." Chris made himself comfortable by sitting on a nearby rock.

"What are you doing!?" Nat sheepishly asked, feeling a little helpless.

"What?"

"Well, you said you had a game. Aren't you going?"

"I like the scenery better here," he smirked." Besides, you don't *own* the river."

Nat was furious. "Go away!!!"

"You want me to go away?"

"**YES**!"

"Okay," he shrugged, slinging her clothes over his back to take with him.

"Wait!" Nat cried out. "What are you doing? Leave me my clothes!"

"Ah, so now you want me to stay," Chris smiled, coming back, having fun with torturing her so. "I always knew you secretly wanted me to see you naked."

"Look, I want you to go and leave my clothes."

"But they are attached to me, see?" Chris said, pretending that her items were sticking to him, like glue as he tried to pull them away. Dramatic, he exaggerated his battle with her clothes. "They are attached to me like someone else I know..." he winked.

"You are so full of yourself, Christopher Woods."

"*I'm* full of myself. Yes, Miss Queen-"

"If I was your mother, I'd be ashamed of you, acting this way with a young woman. Not very gentlemen-like-"

"Who said I was a gentleman? According to you, I'm an idiot. Well the village idiot says that if you want your clothes back, then you've got to come and get them," Chris challenged, putting her panties on a stick to dangle out enticingly in front of Nat.

Taking a deep breath, Nat disappeared into the water without a trace. Chris stood up, fully taken back. Was she swimming towards him? Not that he would mind! The thought made him smile. Still…after a few uneasy seconds of waiting, Nat's head finally popped out of the water. Smiling too soon, Nat threw a big stone at him, barely missing his face. Throwing three more in quick succession, Chris darted and ducked, the last stone hitting him on the arm.

That one hurt.

The two of them stood their ground, staring angrily at one another, both refusing to budge. Their standoff was at a standstill. A part of Chris was satisfied being kind of mean to her because Nat was so mean to him. He had the upper hand and he wasn't going to back down. Looking her directly in the eyes, that's when he saw her. The moment when he really *first* saw her. Nat glared back trying to hide her embarrassment behind a defiant stare, but the fear was evident in her eyes. There was a vulnerability there he had never felt from her presence before.

The girl was human after all.

He was clearly the victor, but he would not rub her nose in it. "Here," Chris offered, setting her clothes back down on the rock. "I'm going to stand over there with my back turned, all right?" Even though he wanted to hate her for all the humiliation and constant rejection she committed against him, Chris offered her grace.

"Why don't you go? I'm fine staying," Nat argued.

"You won't want to stay when Charlie comes through here. You should know I'm not the only one who takes a shortcut to the field."

Nat began to look around the river bank nervously. No one was here.

Yet.

"You promise to turn your back?"

"Yes. I'll be over here," Chris pointed, walking over to the tree line with his back turned to Nat.

"You won't look?"

Chris turned to look back at her tiny figure in the water. Nat's vulnerable demeanor affected his response. "I promise," he said gently, smiling. Something in his voice made him trustworthy. Self-consciously walking out of the water, Nat tried to keep her eyes on Chris the whole time to ensure he didn't look, but as she began putting on her clothes, Chris couldn't help but sneak a peek here or there.

"Done?"

"Yep," she answered sheepishly.

"Here," Chris said walking over, handing Nat her shoes.

"Thank you," Nat spoke quietly, too embarrassed to look at him.

"Your hair," Chris said reaching but Nat intervened.

"I'm fine," she said pulling away to remove the leaf from her hair. "I can do it."

Chris knew it then that Nat's pride had been wounded. "You swear you didn't see anything?" she asked, looking up at him, searching his eyes.

Chris stopped for a moment.

"I swear."

It would be his best lie yet, as Nat believed him.

"You won't tell anyone will you?"

"No. It's not a big deal," he smiled. With his reassurance, Nat turned to go.

"See ya," Nat said, disappearing into the brush.

"See ya."

As Chris watched her go, he would have a hard time falling asleep that night, unable to stop thinking about her. Having the best dreams of his life, he dreamt that night of only one thing.

Natalie Shaw.

When Monday came around, Nat showed up on the field looking rather meek as she huddled up with the guys. Looking to Chris who was making the call for the next play, he acted no different towards her. It was like it never happened.

No big deal.

If anything, Chris passed the ball to Nat a little more than usual, the last throw resulting in a touchdown. With a wink, Chris had demonstrated to Nat that they were friends, and friends could trust one another to keep a secret.

As their friendship grew, Nat was invited to hang around with the guys all the time. Sitting in their circle, whether in class, the cafeteria, out on the field, or at everyone's favorite hangout, the Fish and Chips Shop, Nat was having a blast! Boys were so much more fun than girls. They would go out at night cruising along Lakeside Drive, hitting mailboxes with a bat, or setting off firecrackers in a remote, isolated place out in Kingston. When Natalie went to the Hampton Courthouse to check out some of the county's law cases being tried, Chris and Charlie took her by the old jailhouse residing next to its building. A familiar scene, the prisoners would often heckle the local kids from their barred windows. Chris started heckling and taunting back.

"Hey Dad?" Charlie called.

"Yeah?" a voice yelled back.

"When you getting out?"

"Tomorrow. Tell your mother I'll be home for dinner."

"Sure thing Pop," Charlie said.

"Hey Mr. Walker.-sorry about that," Chris apologized. "I didn't know that was you sir. I was just having fun."

Charlie's Dad gave a wave before retreating away from his tiny barred window.

It wasn't a big deal. Charlie's Dad had started a fight at the Hampton Bar the night before. A little too much to drink, he would have to serve two days in the slammer for it.

As for Chris, he had a new girlfriend practically every month. That is if they even lasted that long. Nat paid no heed to it at all. Chris did not let any girl affect his friendship to her or the guys, so Nat did not really care. A lot of the girls were becoming increasingly jealous over Nat's inclusion, particularly Betty, who saw that Nat had all the guys. As summer fast approached, the group wanted to get together again to party before school was out, but where? The old Irish pub in Sussex seemed the perfect remedy for such an ache, as the kids headed out that last Saturday night in June. Nat had actually declined at first, not interested in drinking, but it was Anna who would convince her to go. Nat knew all the boys, so Anna would have the chance to get closer to Robbie, a boy she liked if Nat went.

Still, the matter pressed. How could she get out of the house so late? Even with her Dad gone away on business, Nat's curfew was strictly set at nine p.m. Waiting until Eva went to bed, Nat would finally get her chance at eleven that evening. Climbing out her window onto the porch roof, Nat used the tree to crawl her way down to the ground. Racing to her bike with her best dress on, Nat sped off down the road to meet Anna by the old tree. Anna had promised that she would not leave until Nat showed up, and true to her word, she was standing there waiting for Nat. From there the two of them biked towards the Hampton Gas Station where Charlie was waiting to pick them up. Arriving in Sussex twenty minutes later, both girls ran inside the pub doors.

Everyone was there, including Chris, who had noticed Nat immediately. Stunning as always, her beauty made him go to her.

"So you finally decided to show up!" he yelled above the music. Nat smiled. "Come on. The guys are over here," he urged, showing her the way. That's when Betty came between them.

"Hello Chris," she cooed. "You haven't forgotten me, have you?"

"What boy could forget you Betty," he charmed. The whole exchange made Nat want to vomit. "I've got to get another drink first." Betty haughtily looked Nat up and down, but Nat refused to be intimidated. The girl was stupid and had nothing over her. Nat knew she was better. "Promise," Chris said, walking away. Sitting down, he bought Nat and Anna a drink.

"I don't drink," Nat said flatly.

"What the hell? You're a Maritimer, are you not?"

"Yes."

"And Irish?" Chris had remembered from that night of the bonfire what Nat had said.

"Yes, but still, I-"

"But still, my ass! Have this pint. Come on! You don't want to offend me by not accepting my offering?"

"Just one?"

"Just one drink," Chris urged. Nat took it carefully, smelling its contents before taking a sip. "Eh? Now that's good Maritime brew."

"You know, you sure don't act like a preacher's son!"

"Thank you," Chris smiled again, taking it as a compliment. "Cheers!" The two of them clinked their glasses and took another swig.

As Chris got up to go dance, he turned to Nat, offering his hand. Nat shook her head. "I can't dance."

"I'll teach ya'."

"You teach me? I wouldn't trust you to teach me for a second."

Chris grabbed hold of his heart. "Oh, that hurts," he said mockingly before leaning in, "I wouldn't trust me either." Did he just flirt with her? Of course he did. Chris flirted with everyone, even friends. Taking off to the dance floor, Betty swooned her way over, trying to impress him with her fine Irish dancing.

How pathetic, Nat thought to herself, watching from the sidelines. Drinking down another pint, the way Chris was looking at Betty was different. Chris had never looked at a girl like that before, even his girlfriends. More like a puppy dog.

It made Nat cringe.

Only a little.

A small speck of jealousy crept into her heart.

That's when Nat rose to her feet and began walking over to Chris, who could see her move towards him from behind Betty. Chris couldn't help but stop what he was doing to look at Nat. Betty turned to glare at Nat, taking a stance beside Chris. It was then that Nat looked to him, and Chris knowing that she had something to say, waited. That's when Nat raised her skirt above her knees, and started to mockingly imitate Betty's Irish dancing, never taking her eyes off of Chris. Kicking her legs stupidly up, Nat had succeeded in winning his attention and affection, as Chris laughed hard before moving in towards her. Pulling Nat close, the two were attracted to only one another, out of all the people in the room. It made everyone look. Something was up, as even Betty sensed it.

"So you think you can dance,eh?" Chris asked, laughing at her keen sense of humor.

"Oh yeah," Nat said playfully.

"Let's go." Chris sped away with her, swinging her about, before dipping her down at the end of the song. As Nat slowly rose up, her cascading hair following, the two of them looked into one another's eyes.

The chemistry between them was undeniable and obvious to all.

"Eva!!!" the General yelled from upstairs, before tearing his way down the staircase towards the kitchen. Dressed in her housecoat, Eva disoriented and alarmed, entered the kitchen half asleep.

"What is it, sir?"

"Perhaps you might explain to me why when I come home earlier than expected to see my daughter, that she is **not** in her bedroom!" It was one o'clock in the morning and the General was furious. "Where the hell is she?"

Eva was shocked. "I don't know. She went to bed before I did. I fell asleep sometime after ten. She's not upstairs?"

"I leave you in charge, and this is how you look after my house when I'm away." The General obviously needed someone other than Nat to blame, but Eva refused to take it.

"I have done my job," she stated firmly. "If Natalie chooses to sneak out of the house past her curfew, without my knowing, there is not much I can do-"

"I will not let this happen again," he vowed, storming past her into the living room. Pacing, he needed room to think and breathe.

"What happen again?" Eva said, following cautiously behind him, keeping her distance.

"She will not end up like her-"

"Who?"

The General paused long before speaking. "Emily."

"Who is Emily?"

No one had ever asked him that question before. Then again, he had never really spoken of her. After all this time.

Sitting into his chair, the General could not make sense of what he was feeling. Eva waited patiently.

"Emmy," he said finally, "was my little sister. It was only me and Emmy. We lived on a farm in Oromoncto," he recounted quietly. "I never really knew my mother, because she died giving birth to Emmy."

Eva moved in slowly, unaware that the General had even had a sibling. In the years that she had been working, Eva had never seen a photograph, nor anyone visit from his family. "One day," he finally spoke, "I was supposed to watch her, but I got distracted. The neighbor's kid came over and I wanted to go play with him in our field…My father had started drinking when my mother died…"

"Yes," Eva gently encouraged.

"I was coming in," he finally continued, "when I saw Emmy."

How painful the memory was.

"Sitting, playing with her doll…She saw me coming, smiling and waving at me as I approached…That's when my Dad, threw the tractor in reverse…"

Eva held her breath.

"Emmy got up fast, trying to get away, but the wheel caught her foot…"

"Oh my, I'm so terribly sorry," Eva said regretfully. "How old were you?"

The General was silent for some time before finally answering. "Twelve…My father was so drunk, he ran over his own daughter without even knowing she was there."

Eva felt the tears start to well up in her eyes. "How old was she?"

"Ten…She was so strong. She was," he affirmed, reliving the memory as he recalled it. "She screamed," the General said shaking his head at the visual of it all. "I ran to her, yelling at my father to get the tractor off... There was blood everywhere. I held her, telling her that she was going to be okay...She just kept whispering, 'it hurts Robbie,' and there was nothing I could do. I just held her hand. She struggled to breathe...I told her that I was sorry, that I should have been here...I was supposed to watch her," he spoke painfully, expressing the weight of his guilt all these years. "Then she looked at me," he whispered, looking down as the memory was too much. "I'll never forget that look...I love you Robbie...I love my big brother...and I saw her life leave her eyes. She let go..."

Eva went to him, wrapping her arms around him. "I'm so sorry."

"Love me? How could she love a brother who didn't take care of her? I let her down," the General spoke with an overwhelming guilt and shame.

"It wasn't your fault. You didn't do anything wrong," Eva consoled. "You took care of her. It was your father who hurt her."

"Nat is Emmy. I have to look after her. Nat has to be watched. I don't want something like that to ever happen again-"

"I understand," Eva murmured soothingly, caressing his hair.

The General absorbed the nurturance Eva offered, resting his hand in hers. He had never ever told anyone about Emily before, but as he looked into Eva's eyes, he knew. Something he had known from the day he first met her. Eva was a kind, compassionate, safe woman to confide in. Eva would never betray his vulnerability. It made him want to reach out. Touching her cheek with his finger, the General took her hand once more and gently kissed it, before rising to go to the kitchen. Eva smiled tenderly back at him, supportive of his intimacy. Following him into the kitchen, Eva prepared the General some coffee, both of them knowing that it would be a long night.

Drunk, Nat fell over on her bike a total of three times trying to steer her way home. Both Chris and Charlie had offered to give her a lift, but Nat insisted that she was fine and able. "Nothing wrong with me," she slurred. Getting back up on her bike, Nat giggled as she reached the hill.

Why not walk through the front door? If she was quiet, Eva would never hear her. What Nat failed to notice in her drunken stupor was her Dad's jeep parked up alongside the barn at the end of the driveway. Coming in, she took her shoes off, and proceeded to tiptoe in.

The lights came on. It was her Dad standing in the hallway with Eva behind him, and he looked furious. Looking down, Nat was caught.

"Where have you been?" he demanded, "It's four o'clock in the morning."

Nat tried to act like nothing was wrong, but her slurred speech gave her away. "I was out, for a walk-"

"Don't lie to me Natalie! You don't lie to me ever, you understand!?"

"Yes, sir," Nat said, knowing it was going to be an even longer night than it already was. Reaching for a nearby chair so as to take a seat, Nat missed and fell to the floor face first, knocking herself out cold. As Eva stood by, the General bent down, turning her over, trying to revive her.

How it all reminded him of Emily, and his own failure to look after either of them.

Nat's eyes were closed. Intoxicated his daughter was, and it frustrated him so.

"Eva, if you could get her bed ready, have a pot by her bed and a jug of water."

"Yes sir," Eva said, rushing upstairs.

Just then, Nat opened her eyes. Nat was drunk but she could still see the disappointment and pain in his eyes.

She blew it.

Again.

No matter how hard she tried, she always ended up blowing it.

"Dad?"

"Yes Natalie?"

"I'm sorry," she whispered, before passing out again.

"I know," he said lifting Nat up in his arms and taking her upstairs to bed. "It's okay." Nat would be sick throughout the morning as she fell in and out of sleep, and Eva would care for her while the General waited. Once Nat was feeling better, the General announced that she would be packing her bags and coming with him to Kentville over the summer. Whatever bad influences she was falling into, the General would ensure these influences would never let her falter again.

As the General lectured Nat, she agreed with him that she had to keep on target. If she wanted to go to university, she would need to keep up her grades to win a scholarship. Nat planned to eventually go to law school at The University of Toronto. This was the same university where the General himself had achieved his respective B.A. Honors and Masters degrees in Engineering and

History. If she wanted to be a lawyer, she would need to focus on what's important, because education was not cheap. The General had money saved, but Nat would need to do her part to ensure she could afford room and board.

It became understood that boys and parties could come later. Nat's senior year would prove to be the most pivotal for her future, and the General did not want her to blow it.

Breaking off all correspondence with everyone in town over the summer break, Nat stayed with her Dad in Camp Alders hot. Returning to school that sequential fall, Nat was focused and ready to achieve the challenges that lay before her.

Then the news across Canada hit. Britain had declared war on Germany, September 3rd, 1939, in reaction to Hitler's invasion of Poland. Within a week, Canada did the same and the General was sent immediately that Fall to train the 1st Canadian Division that would be sent over to Britain.

Nat felt her world turn upside down.

Although predicted by her father, Nat was still surprised when the war did break out. Her father had been pushing for greater defense spending and training over the last two years in anticipation of what he called Hitler's "true intentions." A part of Nat secretly hoped that a small skirmish would break out so that she could see the men train and possibly fight. To have them return home and tell their stories to her, as her father had done countless evenings.

Stories that spoke of courage, character, camaraderie, and integrity.

Every day Nat went to school, her eyes remain fixed on the bigger picture that lay beyond her world as she knew it. Nat fit in and was accepted, but ultimately, she was tired of the same old picture. Nat loved Hampton, but knew it was all only a matter of time.

Patience.

Nat would not be here for very long. Other people to meet and new places to explore awaited her. How so many days in the orphanage she dreamed of breaking the gates open, to see the world that she was missing. If Nat had the brains and opportunities to do something important with her life, she ought to make use of her gifts and blessings. Follow God's plan for her, and make her mom and dad proud.

Nothing would get in the way of that.

When the war broke out, Nat made sure that she was one of the first people in Halifax to watch Canada's first trained, infantry regiment leave its port in December. Nat's intentions before she went were to stay on track with her dream of becoming a lawyer, but as she waved goodbye to the men, something lingered. Nat remembered the time her Dad had taken her to her first Remembrance Day ceremonies. She was eleven and saw the men, young and old, enlisted and veteran, marching in unison towards Memorial Hill to pay their respects. Nat struggled her way through the crowd lined alongside the streets to clap them on in respect. These men were heroes for defending our young nation, our land so proudly. Some were disabled, but most were modest. Nat found herself in awe, impressed by their stature which seemed so grand in her eyes at the time.

Only thing was this same awe had not changed. Six years later she was still taken with their hopeful eyes that she felt it all over again. Something forgotten she had said to herself that first time, but dismissed all too readily.

"I wish I could do that..."

A touch of envy.

These men were off to see the real world beyond their maritime border. They were off to see other cultures, lands, and experience adventure first hand. It was a world Nat was only familiar with through books she had read. Nat was stuck for the time being, trying to finish school and move on. How she wanted to do something and be somewhere beyond here. To make her 'mark' on the world.

Seeing the men leave, only reminded Nat of how repressed she felt by her own ordinary, mundane, simple existence.

Always waiting.

Why couldn't she just get to what she wanted? God, why must life be so tedious?

Absent since the war broke out, Nat returned home with Eva rather than her Dad. Restless, Nat knew she should be happy, as she had everything any daughter could hope for. Dad and Eva cared for her, a good friend, Anna, and a school record that had her at the top of her class.

Something was missing.

Why a burning desire to never sit still?

What is it that I need to know God?

What am I still missing?

It was not in her faith, because she read the Bible daily and largely understood its teachings. She was inspired in her relationship to Christ, trying her best to live a life of integrity that pleased God. He had big plans for her as he did for everyone, so what was eating away at her? Nat felt that if she sat still for too long, became too content, something was always at work, eating away at her inside. That she was trapped in some way between two worlds. The world that was her daily existence, and the other world that she knew existed beyond her. Where did she belong because this one left her so restless, yearning to live in a more 'grand' way?

Silent on the ride home, Nat sat down on her bed. Looking up at the picture of Christ's kind face smiling down at her, Nat was confused. No matter how much she tried as best she could to please those that she cared about, achievement gave her a high feeling that never resonated any permanence.

Fleeting.

Existing only for a short while before passing, and she remained as unhappy as she had been before.

WHAT did she want?

To be a good daughter and to be a good person, whatever that was.

Nat knew she wanted to break loose from the very chains she had created for herself. It was a prism of perfection she was always trying to reflect back to others that was not fully authentic. Why couldn't she just accept what everyone wanted and expected from her?

She was physically a beautiful girl, many features inherited from her dear mother. A handful of boys would court her if she didn't scare them away. Partly intentional, Nat did not want them slowing her down, and that included Chris. Although always present in her life, Nat kept him at a distance. The thought of marriage and children, a dream so many other girls her age talked incessantly about, terrified Nat.

Of course she yearned to be loved at times, yet boys her age were frustratingly disappointing. Inferior intellectually and personally, lacking any sort of character or maturity, how could she ever talk and be with someone whom she could not relate to, nor have a conversation with?

If she could meet a man who was not only incredibly intelligent but would let her be herself, doing all the things she wanted to do, Nat would find love a possibility.

Yet, there would be no such man. Perhaps when she was older, at college, she could meet someone who would accept her as an equal, looking beyond only the physical as a prerequisite.

If Nat didn't belong with her mother, an orphanage, a foster home, or a small maritime town, then where was she meant to be? What was a normal life anyway? Who was she!? The Nat that everyone had come to know, or was she really something more? Someone else who had yet to come out?

Nat knew instinctively that she was a fighter. Just like her mom was, and her Dad is. Repressing this impulse consumed a great deal of her energy. To the point she felt starved for a fight.

No…There was no woman that had ever been accepted into the Canadian army, let alone any military before that she had heard of. Doubts were pervasive, but she had to stay on course. This was her reality, and her pragmatism dictated having greater patience. Soon enough she would be out of here, this place, and be who she felt she was meant to be.

Sitting in history class before the Christmas break, Nat couldn't help but let her thoughts wander elsewhere.

"Now Joan of Arc was a young, fifteen year old peasant girl when supposedly she claims she heard the voices of God instructing her to lead the French army into victory," Mr. Saunders lectured. Saint Joan had caught her attention. Nat raised her hand.

"Yes Natalie."

"Do you suppose that what she heard was her own voice Mr. Saunders?"

"What do you mean?"

"Well that maybe it wasn't voices from another person, but a voice within her? Her soul spoke to her of her innermost desire? I mean your soul is a part of God, and the holy spirit is within us, but maybe it wasn't God talking to her directly. It was indirect but either way, she appears crazy. Maybe he was talking within her because she was far from crazy. Maybe Joan was just an ordinary girl who heard her own voice truly for the first time of how she had been created to be. He was calling out who she really was and destined to be," Nat reasoned. "Her courage and strength all from him."

"I've never thought about it that way. History reports, but it can never attain the whole story. You may very well be right Miss Shaw as she was an unusual woman, especially in such a time," Mr. Saunders smiled.

Nat now understood what Joan of Arc was really doing. She seemed crazy because her inner voice was telling her to go against what her female self was expected to do. According to this world's rules.

Not Nat.

If Joan could do it, if she could find a way, then certainly Nat could too.

Nat would need to train, but who could she get to help her? Someone she could trust to keep it all a secret?

The answer would be closer to her heart than expected.

9

For Christmas Eve, Nat and Eva had accepted an invitation by Chris to have dinner with his family at their house. Without the General around, heading over to the Woods residence seemed a welcome remedy from the loneliness both women were feeling. As the snowstorm picked up outside, the two of them dressed in several layers of clothing to keep warm on their horse buggy ride over. Stepping outside, the cold wind gusted upon their faces, but beyond its snowy haze, Nat saw a figure emerging, stomping his way through the deep snow.

It was the lone figure of the General slowly approaching.

Sliding his jeep off the Trans Canada Highway into a ditch, the General hiked his way down the road, knowing he was maybe a mile away from the farmhouse. Nat and Eva both ran to him with full hugs, ecstatic that he had come home in time for Christmas.

Dad had come home!

Sensing his fatigue, they both helped the General back inside to warm up first, before heading out.

"I can't believe you're here Dad!" Nat delightfully hugged her father once more.

"Of course I'm here. I had to see my girls," he said with a wink to Eva.

Nat knew that a mutual respect and fondness between the two had developed over the last two years. Good friends, Nat knew she would approve if they decided to become something more. Eva was a part of the family and Nat felt no jealousy towards her possibly replacing her father's affection. Nat knew that her Dad would always love her, with or without a wife. Nat desired though, more than anything, for the General to have someone to look after him after she was gone. Possibly away at university next year, the General deserved someone in his life always.

Dad should never be alone again.

As the three of them arrived at the Woods residence, it was at the dinner table that Eva saw for the first time Chris and Nat interact with one another. Talking with Mrs. Woods, Eva could not help but keep glancing over at the two of them. Sitting next to each other, Nat was talking to Chris with such ease, she was completely relaxed. Giggling at Chris' jokes, it was when they looked at one another, locking eyes, that Eva knew this boy was something special. He had done something that no other boy had previously.

Chris had got through Nat's defenses to uncover the young woman underneath waiting to be discovered. Talking to Mr. Woods about their fishing experiences, the General was oblivious, but Eva knew.

Still, there would be no prying. When Nat was ready to discuss it, she would, and Eva would not press the matter further. As January came, Nat knew only one person she could trust.

"Chris, have you ever trained anyone before?" Nat demanded at his locker as he reached for his textbook.

"Good morning Nat. Happy New Year to you too." Gosh, how she could be so abrupt, he thought to himself.

"Sorry, good morning," Nat smiled.

"Good morning," he said, quite grouchy to be back to school so soon. Besides, he hated it when Nat only seemed to talk to him about things that were not about him. It simply annoyed him that she never enquired about him.

"I was wondering if you have ever trained anyone before?"

"You mean physically train, like a coach?"

"Yes."

"No," he said, taking a sip from his coffee. Chris still needed coffee to help his hangover from two nights before.

"Well, I want you to train me for the army!" Nat blurted out excitedly.

Chris choked on his coffee, coughing some of it out.

"Keep your voice down," he scolded, closing his locker door. "What? You're not serious, are you?"

"Yeah."

"What are you talking about? I thought you were planning to go to law school?"

"That can wait. The war may be over then. I want to be a part of it now!"

Chris walked away from her. What was she thinking? For someone being so smart, she was certainly dumb at times in her thinking.

Yet, he would not see the last of Nat, because she would continue to persist whenever she saw him. This time it was at his table in the school cafeteria.

"Why not?"

"Because you're a woman!" Chris stressed. "They're not going to let you in, even if you did apply, which you have to do, before you can get in!"

"That's where you come in. You show up with my application, and complete the physical for me. By the time they figure out what happened, it will be too late. I'll already be in," Nat explained. "Then they can't get rid of me. That is unless, I don't make the cut in basic training."

"So let me get this straight. Not only am I supposed to train you, I'm supposed to lie for you?"

Nat nodded.

"Yes."

"Why would I do that?"

"I'm your friend. I need your help," Nat pleaded. What Nat did not know was that Chris would do it for her, but something in him resisted. Chris had helped out his friends before, lying or not, but this was different. Chris was reluctant, not because he doubted Nat's ability to go ahead with something like this for a second, but because he could not stand to see her get hurt.

For his own self, he did not want Nat to go.

"No," he answered firmly, walking away from her again.

"Then I'll do it without you!" Nat yelled.

"Fine, do it without me!" Chris yelled, not looking back.

That winter Nat began her own training, while still pestering Chris all the while. Eventually, he just tuned her out whenever she started talking about it again. Running through trails packed with snow, she would build up her muscles first, as Nat needed more physical strength. As March came, so too with it did the melt, and Chris realized that no amount of ignoring her, would make her give up this idea of joining.

With the snow all gone, Nat found herself standing alone by the water once more. It was her favorite place to be. Gazing out over the blue horizon before her, Nat knew that it would not be long before she crossed over. Soon she would fly over to the other side of the world and see all the beauty it had to offer.

How far away the rest of the world looked.

Catching the train that morning to St. Martin, Nat started her early morning jog through the dew along the Bay of Fundy trail. With her feet pounding the earth, her legs in full stride, Nat knew she needed more endurance. With sweat rolling down her forehead, she kept running alongside the ocean, feeling the warmth of the sun through the chill of the spring air. Panting hard, Nat continued on, but her stride was slowing, and she was getting frustrated by it all. At this pace, she would never be ready in time.

That is when Nat heard the sound of feet pounding behind her. Glancing behind, Chris ran up alongside her.

"What are you doing here!?" she asked shocked, but continued her jog alongside him.

"Never mind that, Private. You get your ass going now, and I mean it!" Chris teased, slapping her bum.

Chris took off in full sprint, knowing full well he was in for it.

"Why you-I'm going to get you!" Nat yelled laughing, chasing after him along the beach's shoreline. Both laughing, they raced towards the cliff's end as Chris constantly looked behind him to see if Nat would catch up. Eventually he slowed so that she could. Standing at the forty foot cliff that stood high above the day's tide coming in, Nat gave Chris a light slap on the arm while trying to catch her breath. "I thought you weren't going to help me," Nat said coolly, trying hard to disguise her surprise and genuine gratitude.

Happy to see Nat so happy, Chris stood up straight. "What? And miss my golden opportunity to coach my first athlete? I do admit, looking over ya', it isn't going to be easy, but I can make a soldier out of you yet."

"I'll be the best person you'll ever train," Nat stood confidently. "Just tell me what to do."

"That's a first," Chris said with a sly smile, but Nat wasn't fooling around. Truth be told, neither was Chris. "Well, I'm not going to feed you to the lions," he said intensely. "Those guys will tear you apart as it is, and if you can't keep up-"

"But I will," Nat said, cutting him off. "I know I can do it. I just need to get in shape," Nat asserted.

If only she was listening would she be able to hear in his words how Chris was really saying, 'I say this not because I don't believe in you, but because I *care* about you.'

"You'll need more than that. Do you have any idea what you're getting yourself into?"

"Are you trying to talk me out of it?"

"No, I'm just-"

"Good, because I am still going to do it, whether you help me or not."

Chris nodded in agreement. "I know."

That was Nat. Once she set her mind to something, there would be no use trying to convince her otherwise. "I'm here, aren't I? I will help you, that is…"

"What?"

"If you still want my help?"

"Yes, I do," Nat answered firmly, trying to stifle her smile. Secretly she was overwhelmed to have Chris train her. Under his tutelage, Nat would be in amazing shape for basic training. "I suppose you'll do," she said, playfully pretending to be haughty.

"You know what I think?"

Nat hadn't a clue. "What?"

"I think you're going to enjoy this just a little," Chris smiled.

The two stood and looked at one another for a moment. The answer was clearly yes. Nat recomposed herself. "So, where do we begin coach?"

It was back to business.

Chris pulled out a piece of crumpled paper from his pocket, and opened it up. "I've got a schedule here. We'll get you running at one kilometer a day for the first week, and work it up to two the next week, and that is not slack either. You sprint and run fast. No taking it easy and coasting through," he instructed.

"Sounds fair," Nat nodded.

"I've got a weights program worked out for you too. You've got some tone, but your muscle strength could be so much more. You need to be able to fling a man over your back, and you can't do that at a hundred and twenty pounds. How tall are you?"

"Five seven."

"Okay. We'll get your weight up to 150 with the muscle building. How does that sound to you?"

"Looks like a good plan Chris. Seems like you went to a lot of work on this, didn't ya'?"

"No," Chris insisted. He wasn't about to let Nat know that he had put effort into her. "I like doing this sort of thing, that's all. Let's get started."

"Okay," Nat agreed.

"Let's do it. Come on, let's go," Chris ordered and Nat obeyed. Off running they went as this would be their routine for the next few weeks. Chris would run alongside her, pushing her hard to accelerate, the thing most surprising Nat was how tough Chris was on her. When she did do push-ups, weightlifting, Chris wouldn't tolerate any whining or complaining. Not that Nat did much, but every now and then she would feel slack, and he would be right there to push her along, without mercy. Chris as it was turning out, was the perfect coach in both guidance and discipline.

Yet, what began to surprise Nat the most was how his sense of humor and sly wit made him so much fun to be around, even while training. Nat knew that Chris was much fun, having been his friend for awhile now, but how his sense of humor seemed less offensive to Nat. That there was a depth to him that she was intrigued to learn more about.

Chris was seeming more like a person to her now, rather than just a kid. Someone who was very real, not the fake Nat had initially assessed him as. Naturally opening up to Nat more and more with each passing day, Chris was beginning to enjoy seeing Nat's softer, more vulnerable side. How the two of them saw and understood each other in a way, that no one else had discovered before. All Chris knew was that he had to pursue Nat further, which is why he decided to take her to his 'secret' place. It was a place where no one else had ever been invited to come before.

"You're not going to club me and drag me off to your cave now, are you?" Not that Nat would mind. Lately, all she had done was dream about Chris at night. Wonderful, dirty dreams that only she knew of and could delight in. Everything about Chris she liked, desiring him to pursue her further.

To come closer to her.

Chris picked up a good, sturdy stick and looked over at Nat mischievously. "Not a club, no...Follow me," he smiled, leading the way. As Nat followed him in, she was surprised to find a place that was more like a home away from home. Chris had blankets, a fire area, card games, two wooden chairs. It was his own little haven away from everything.

"No one else knows about this place but you," he said, "and I expect you to keep it that way."

"Of course," Nat nodded. How he kept her secrets for so long. Making a fire, the two of them relaxed in the cave, drinking that afternoon and talking. "Why do you have this place?"

"It's quiet. There are no expectations when I'm here. I can just cut loose and be myself."

"What expectations?"

"Don't you know? I'm the pastor's kid. I'm going to be a preacher like my Dad when I grow up." Nat started to laugh uncontrollably. "That or medical school…What? What's so funny?"

"You…being a pastor." Chris did not know whether he should take her statement as a compliment or insult. "I mean you're a good guy," Nat explained, as Chris leaned in towards her, wanting to know what she thought of him, "but I just don't see it. I see you being a teacher sooner, doing sports, coaching." Chris had never thought about it before, but it was an idea to consider. It sure would be fun, doing sports as a part of his work every day.

"So you think I'm a good guy?"

"I *know* you're a good guy."

"Good enough for you to go to the prom with?" Nat set her drink down.

"Yes," she said, hoping he meant it.

The time had come. Chris leaned towards her and Nat leaned in towards him.

Chris came in and touched Nat's lips. How his kiss tasted so warm that it made her tingle all over. Looking into each other's eyes to see the other's reaction, Chris knew it was okay to pull Nat closer. Kissing her again, Nat wrapped her arms around him, the two of them unable to stop kissing! It was as if being held in for so long, their passion for one another had finally ignited. It was Nat who told herself to stop.

"I have to get home. My Dad will be worried about me."

"Really? Can I walk you?" Nat nodded, as the two of them headed back, through the rain. As they came close to the house, Nat turned and gave Chris one last passionate kiss. "See you tomorrow," she waved.

"See you tomorrow," he smiled back.

Only tomorrow would have to wait.

Sick in bed with a bad cold from having walked home through the rain that day, Nat would not be at school for the remainder of the week. Word had spread fast that Chris had asked Nat to the prom, as the planned bonfire for the coming weekend approached, and it was Betty who was furious. No longer dating anyone, Betty had purposely refused other boys because she was waiting for Chris to ask her and now he had asked Nat!

Insulted, Betty knew who the real winner was and she would prove it to herself and Nat this weekend. Flirting with Chris all that Saturday night, Betty asked Chris if he could walk her to her car that was parked down the road.

"I'll be right back guys," Chris said before leaving with her, intending to be gone only briefly. However, it would be awhile before Chris would return, making his way back.

A bit shaky, Chris sat down quietly next to the guys. Something had just begun to surface within him from deep within his heart, only he did not fully understand it.

What he couldn't figure out was that he had betrayed his own heart that night.

Chris had made a big mistake.

Nat slammed the house door and ran past Eva, up the stairs. Hiding in her room, she slammed the door behind her, choosing to crawl up into a ball on her bed and cry. Nat cried like she had never cried before, gasping for breath. Eva knocked gently on her bedroom door.

"Natalie? Are you okay?"

"I'm fine. I just need to be alone right now," Nat whimpered.

"You have school today?"

"I'm sick." It was only noon, and Nat refused to open the door. Calling the General first, Eva went back upstairs to try again.

It was Anna who told Nat the news. News that she did not want to tell, but had to as Nat was her friend. She should know what Chris is like.

Nat did not hate Anna. She was only being a good friend.

"Yes. I'm not feeling well Eva. I can't go back to school," Nat said choking back her tears. The door was locked, and as Eva waited, it would be some time before she would hear its lock open. Seeing Nat on the bed, Eva knew that something was terribly wrong. Eva walked slowly over to the bed, wanting to help, but at the same time, give Nat her space.

"Oh Nat…What's wrong?"

"Oooh Eva," Nat said crying again, reaching out her arms. Eva took them and held her, cradling Nat in her arms. She had never seen her so upset before. "It hurts so much."

"What does Nat? What happened?"

"He fooled me Eva. He tricked me. "

"Who Nat?"

"Chris," she sputtered out, weeping. "I actually thought he cared about me, but he didn't. The whole time he didn't. The only person he cares about is himself," Nat cried. "I just feel so stupid for believing in him Eva. I just want the pain to go away." Nat's body trembled because she was crying so hard.

"You were quite fond of him before Nat...What did he do?"

"He went and slept with another girl!" Nat cried. "What's worse is it's a girl I despise. Why did he do that? Why did he pretend to care about me? ***Why***?" Nat asked, angry.

Eva looked down at Nat. "I don't think that he was pretending with you Natalie-"

"That's all boys are after in me Eva. They are not interested in who you are. They just want what's under your dress. Why bother being pretty, smart, or a good person, if that's all boys think you are anyway. I'm so stupid to believe-"

"No more of that kind of talk, you understand me? You are not stupid! You are a beautiful, intelligent, strong young woman, and no man would intentionally give up a woman like that. Not you. It would have to be a mistake to do so," Eva firmly asserted,. "Either that or he doesn't deserve you." Nothing consoled as Nat could not stop crying, and Eva felt herself beginning to get upset.

It was then that the General walked in and surprised them both with his presence. As Nat looked up at his grave face, his unwavering, stoicism calmed her. Eva rose to her feet and stepped back. Without fully understanding what was going on with Nat, the General stepped forward and offered his strength. His little girl was hurting badly.

Nat took it, walking into his arms and crying on his strong shoulders.

"It's okay sweetie. Dad's here. You're going to be okay," he soothed.

"It hurts Dad," Nat continued to cry. The General stood still. He was her rock, and he would stay, however long it took, until she was all right.

"Natalie?"

"Yes?"

"He is the one who is missing out, not you." Nat stopped crying. As the General looked into his daughter's watery hazel eyes, he had heard every word she had said from outside the bedroom door. "If he can't see how perfect you are and lucky he would be to have you, he is not worth your time. There is someone worthy, but it is not him."

Natalie felt elevated, her spirit lifted up by her father.

"You are so beautiful," he smiled, wiping the tears off her cheek. "Eva and I both realize how lucky we are to have the opportunity to raise such a beautiful girl."

Nat began to feel so much better. Her father's love was saving her from this pain that spiraled her into a very dark place.

"I love you Nat," he said, kissing her forehead tenderly.

"I love you too Dad," Nat whispered, hugging him again.

"I know," he said, not letting her go. Nat was totally protected within her father's arms. Eva gave a sigh of relief, while crying silently to herself. The General had finally revealed to Nat, not only what she needed to hear, but how he felt about her.

Finally.

Eva knew it and Nat knew at that moment that she would recover from this heartbreak. That she would be all right.

The General would see to that.

It would be a few days before Nat would return to school. A broken heart takes time to mend. That is why when Chris sat down next to her in the cafeteria, Nat refused to give him any more attention than he deserved. Swallowing her peanut butter and jelly sandwich down with difficulty, Nat was determined to disguise her feelings. The sooner she cut him off, the sooner she could move on.

"Hey Nat...."

Nat continued chewing on the last bite of her sandwich, before reaching for her glass of milk.

Chris knew then that she knew. He felt his face become flushed. What was he going to do? What could he say? No doubt she would be angry with him.

He could just walk. Give her some time to cool off. Maybe if he acted like nothing was different between them, Nat would see it that way too.

"I haven't seen you all week. How are you doing?" Nat refused to budge one inch. "How's the milk?" he sheepishly asked, visibly upset, and trying to get some sort of response from her. His questions were met only with an icy silence.

"Are you still running every day?"

Silence.

"I'd like to come out again, and run. Like we were doing, working on...If you want me to-" Chris said reaching his hand out to touch Natalie's shoulder, but she swiftly withdrew, repulsed from his touch. Chris felt her shudder and it sent a chill through him. An overwhelming disgust of the person next to her made Nat want to break away.

"Hi Chris," the voice of the enemy cooed. Embarrassed, Natalie found herself looking up at Betty, who was unable to contain her triumphant grin. She had *won* Chris, and her smug eyes could not help but gloat. She had won him that night in her car, when she removed her blouse and bra as Chris was turning to go. Betty had finally offered herself to him, after so many years and it was an opportunity Chris could not give up. At the time, Nat was the furthest from his mind. Only when he was done and opened his eyes, did he realize how he wanted Betty's eyes to be Nat's.

That he had made a horrible mistake.

Again Nat felt the full extent of his betrayal. The pain swelled within her, so much so that she had to look at him one last time. For closure, she had to see him for who he truly was.

A mask, with one lie compiled upon another lie, upon other lies. Nat had him unveiled, and Chris was now undone in her presence, showing who he truly was.

Selfish, immature, and dishonest were qualities that his actions and behavior testified. Chris had betrayed their friendship on so many levels, playing games with her the whole time. Deceiving and lying to her, insulting her intelligence and very being. Nat knew that the only stupid thing she did was to trust him. How he 'smoothly' wormed his slimy way into her heart under the guise of friendship to play around with her for awhile, long enough for Betty, the girl he really wanted, to become jealous and come after him.

Nat had been just a pawn.

Perhaps trying to 'get' both of them, without the other knowing, only made him more of a pig to her. Why should Nat be any different? She was so foolish to believe that she was unique or special to him.

Looking at his pathetic shape, Nat saw in that moment that she was and had always been too good for Chris Woods. Initially believing them to be equals in mind and spirit, there proved to be a huge discrepancy on her perspective.

It was time to move on and patiently wait for the "one" again. Someone who had maturity and depth. Chris had nothing to offer her, not even an apology.

"Chris, I'll meet you at my locker," Betty overtly flirted, walking away.

Chris nodded awkwardly, as Betty and her friends left.

"You know, I don't understand why you are acting this way?" Chris said defensively. "What's your problem?"

"You."

Nat's tone was scary in its coldness, but the good thing was Chris had got her to talk to him. "What?"

How he pretended like he didn't even know. It was like asking her to the prom never happened. Nat couldn't be bothered to explain it to him.

"It's not like you said we were going out."

Trying to crawl his way out of this on a technicality, irresponsible as always, another strike pierced through his lack of character. Chris was and always will be a coward, which is why he wore his mask in the first place. Chris knew that if anyone truly saw him for what he was, no one would be interested in sticking around. His ugliness would come oozing out, a realization that had been a blessing in disguise. To think she had actually *considered* giving up her dream of being in the military for a possible life with someone so unworthy of her loyalty, friendship, and love.

"You better be running along. Betty is waiting," Nat dismissed him.

Nat was surprised at how easy it was to let him go. Go ahead and move on to Betty. You'll realize what it was you gave up once you are stuck with her for a while, Nat thought to herself. Then again, being both superficial, you may both get along quite nicely, suiting one another!

"Fine. Be that way," Chris said walking away annoyed at the fact that Nat was being so hard on him. It's not like he killed anybody...he just fooled around. Chris had reasoned that he and Nat would have to be 'going out' to call it anything else. It was a way of justifying his behavior because he had not been sleeping well since that night.

"Bye," Nat smiled with finality, as she let him know who had the upper hand. She had just let him go, as this would be the last time she would ever talk to him.

Nat just needed time to cool off before she would come back to him, Chris thought to himself. He would make Nat realize that he was a good catch eventually.

Nat felt a relief come over her. It was done, and although she still felt injured by him, time would make that go away. Particularly if she kept away from him.

His painful influence would only slow her down.

That afternoon Nat was not sitting in her usual spot for Math class. Chris watched her walk right past him over to a desk that was well across the room. Fine, be that way, he thought, turning his back to her.

Only thing was that each day had turned into many, which turned into weeks.

How long would this go on? Nat still refused to acknowledge him.

Why wouldn't she just look at him? How he wanted to just reach over and pull Nat's desk to his so that they could be buddies again. Tell her one of his jokes and Natalie would cackle in laughter. To have him look her way at him again, the way she used to. With a beautiful, warm smile and sparkling eyes that seemed only for him. Natalie had a way of making him feel respected. That when he was with her, he was the only man in the room. Even if there was a huge group of people, they didn't need to talk or be with anyone else when they were in each other's company.

They were perfect together. How beautiful she still looked to him.

Mr. Ruddier began his lecture as he did every other day, but on this particular day, Chris could not help but feel out of place. Even with his friends huddled in desks around him, he felt alone. As if a piece of himself was missing, and the hole was becoming larger with every passing day. Natalie glanced over quickly to see how Chris was reacting to her lack of 'affection.' Slumped down and looking irritable and depressed, Nat smiled smugly.

Good. For a boy who was incapable of loving anyone else but himself, she was happy to see him miserable. Nat knew she had to forgive sometime soon, more for her sake than his, but she just needed more time to sort out her feelings.

Secretly resuming her training, Nat worked out in places that were not her usual spots. This way Chris would have no part in her life, and no doubt, that was bothering him. It felt good to discard the great Chris Woods, giving him a taste of his own medicine. Even if he was sorry, even if he did secretly love her, even if he did break up with Betty right now just to be with her, Nat would never accept him back.

That is why in the hallway, when Chris saw his friend Michael ask Nat out on a date, he became filled with jealousy. After gym class in the boys locker room, when the others started to tease Michael about Nat, Chris tried hard to ignore them. Only when Michael laughed and said, "Yeah, maybe Nat will show me a real good time," did Chris wheel around and physically charge him.

Smashing Michael hard against the lockers, Chris beat on him yelling, "Don't you talk about her that way!" It would be Principal Burns who would intercede to break up the fight.

The result was a three day suspension for Chris.

The fact that Michael could not take Nat out on a date because of Chris only infuriated Nat more.

"Stay out of my life!" she screamed at Chris the day he returned to school, before storming off. Needless to say, Michael, nor the rest of the guys approached Nat from that day on. The guys had figured that Chris was over her, having Betty, but obviously not. As such, Nat still had no date for the prom, but this would not prevent her from going. Nat had another escort waiting for her that night.

When Nat came down her staircase that evening to leave for the prom, both Eva and the General had never seen such a sight. The General had gone in with Eva to Saint John to buy the most expensive, beautiful dress he could find for Nat, and she did look beautiful. Dressed in a white, satin gown, that made her look so elegant and graceful, Nat was no longer the awkward girl of the past. A young woman, her dark, black hair, pale complexion, and ruby lips, made her look like a princess. Nat was as glamorous as any movie star out there.

Looking up at her proud father standing before her, the General was also dressed in his very best uniform. Not knowing quite what to say, he smiled gently and simply said, "You look beautiful Princess." With that, he opened their front door and reached out for Nat to take his arm. Nat did so, happy because she made her Dad so proud. Escorting his daughter out, over twenty-five male soldiers waited patiently by their military vehicles talking. They too were dressed in their best, ready to lead the military procession to the Hampton School Prom. When Natalie came out, the men fell silent.

Walking down the front porch steps, the men stared out of admiration and respect. Never had any of them seen Nat in this light before. Nat radiated a warmth, glow, and beauty that was all her own. Many smiled at her, hoping to catch her eye!

"Can one of you men, please open the door for my daughter," the General said chuckling. The men all jumped to the door, yet it was Private Rudy who got to it first. Nat took his hand and stepped into the army jeep. Closing the door, Rudy beamed at her and said, "You look beautiful Nat."

"Thanks," she smiled back at him, a little embarrassed by all the attention she was causing. The General stepped into the driver's seat, and yelled, "Let's move 'em out boys!"

The men quickly disassembled to jump into their assigned vehicles, and the procession was off. Nat waved goodbye to Eva, who was standing by the porch door waving her off. Feeling wonderful, Nat couldn't help but think about Chris, who was always at the back of her mind. She wondered if he would notice her tonight.

Not that it mattered.

He probably looked so handsome.

Looking up at the sky, it was a perfectly clear, black night. The stars were shining bright, and the warm air made her feel at that moment in time, that tonight would be pure perfection, unsurpassed by any other.

As the jeeps roared up, couples standing alongside the school's front steps, began backing up when they saw all the men. Some hurried back inside to the gymnasium where the prom was being held, unsure of what was going on. Approved by the Principal, so long as there were no guns or armor, the staff knew that Nat would be escorted by her father. They just had no idea that twenty-five other men would be accompanying them!

As the men assembled themselves, aligning into perfect formation, the procession began. Up the stairs they went, as Nat took her father's arm and followed behind.

The gym doors to the dance abruptly opened, as the soldiers in formation lines of two marched in with pride and grace. Taking over the floor, their entrance covered to the very centre of the room. Students backed away to watch and whisper amongst themselves as to what was going on. Chris, handsomely wearing a black tuxedo and white pleated shirt, curiously put aside his punch glass, and stepped forward to get a closer look.

"Company halt!" the Sergeant commanded, to which all the men obeyed and stopped. "Break!" With that, the two lines split, their new V formation leading to the General and Nat at its pointed end.

With her father's lead, Nat's white dress sparkled in the dim lit room. Her ruby colored lipstick highlighted a breathtaking smile, and as the two made their way in, Nat was shaking. She was getting the entrance of a lifetime and she loved it!

It was then that Chris saw her, gliding into the room as if out of this world, and it was as if all women before her vanished into insignificance. Every other woman in the room knew that none of them stood a chance. Nat's beauty surpassed them all, and no valiant efforts to do up their makeup, hair, and wear fancy, expensive dresses could compete. Nat was radiant, an ethereal apparition in motion.

How she looked like an angel, Chris thought.

Feeling such a strong connection to a girl he hardly knew, yet did know intimately, Chris had seen her vulnerability and she had seen his many flaws. Now everyone was beginning to see what he had all along, even if he had not been aware of it back then when they were friends.

That Nat was a life force who touched people without ever needing to do anything but just be. Nat moved people with her astounding beauty alone.

Now everyone knew the fact as it was beyond contestation, and all Chris could do was stand by with no other desire but to go to her. How he wanted to be Nat's chosen one that she adored, like she used to. Those eyes, playful when their guard was down, look my way. Have your beauty look my way again! Fix your gaze upon me, and awaken me as only you can because I don't want any other.

Chris felt his jaw drop, as Nat was absolutely stunning.

As his heart raced and his knees weakened, all Chris could do was stare. Nat walked into the middle of the room with her father, with such ease, confidence, and warmth, he realized that he was still in love with her.

Betty had only grown annoying the more time he spent with her, which is why Chris determined she had to go. Chris had dumped her more than two weeks ago, hoping with no luck, that Nat would come back.

"Good evening. I am General Shaw, Natalie's father. I apologize for any confusion, but my daughter needed to be properly escorted to her prom. My men cannot leave unless I know she is in good hands."

Chris had nothing to lose, and everything to gain. Stepping forward to take Nat's hand if she would have him, Chris started his walk across the auditorium floor. Many girls stared in disbelief, but it was the guys who smiled on in support.

Nat could not believe her eyes as Chris slowly walked towards her. He looked so handsome in his new suit and hair slicked back. Feeling vulnerable, Chris straightened his posture and offered his hand. If she rejected him now, it would be for everyone to see this time.

"May I have this dance?" Chris asked. The General turned to Natalie, who could only look down as she had to compose herself. Nat's feelings for him were still there for some reason. Still strong. Something inside told her to take a chance. This would be the last time she would see him.

Nat nodded.

"So be it," the General accepted, placing Nat's hand into Chris'.

"Thank you sir. It is an honor."

The General walked away respectfully. It was his daughter's night, not his own. Yet, he could not help but stop to glance back one last time at his daughter who had begun to slow dance with Chris. This young man may very well replace him and the thought made his heart ache. Why did she have to grow up so fast?

He would soon be on his own again, and he was going to miss her. The General could take comfort in one thought though.

He would always remain the constant in Nat's life.

The General had seen all that he needed to see. Nat would be fine without him. Exiting, the marching procession of men followed him out.

"You look beautiful," Chris said shaking.

"Thank you. You look handsome too," Nat said looking down.

"You are the most beautiful girl here, and I am not just saying that," Chris smiled. Nat continued to look away. "Nat, I want you to know something-" Chris began but Nat cut him off.

"Chris, let's forget about the past," Nat awkwardly interjected. "We were good friends at one time. I would like to keep it at that. No hard feelings."

"Friends?" Chris repeated.

"Yes…Good friends. You are going off to school, and I know you are going to do well. People are drawn to you Chris, and you know how to bring people together. That's a gift. Don't sell yourself short. Consider coaching or teaching. Be true to yourself and never mind what people think."

"How do you do that?"

"What?"

"See things about me that I don't?"

Nat felt a lump sting in her throat. "I see it because it's there, even if you don't know it. That's why you have friends, even a friend like me, who's there to tell you these things. A friend will always tell you the truth, even if it's painful. I think you are a good person Chris…That it has been an honor knowing you."

Chris was stunned. Nat was amazing because she was and always has been up front and direct with him. Strong and honest, which was something he had not always been for her.

Nat had forgiven him.

"Just between you and me, I got in!" Nat told him excitedly. "I told my father too. We had a big fight, but he knows that when I make up my mind, that's it. I'm not a child anymore, and he respects that. I leave in two months for basic training. I'm going Chris and I'm never looking back. I am going to see everything, because the world is mine."

Chris felt his heart sink.

"We'll both be making a difference Chris. Dreams do come true!"

At that moment Chris realized that he could never keep someone like Nat down. Although he wanted to for his own selfish reasons, a simple life was never in the cards for Nat. She could never be an average girl. It was something he both loved but tried changing about her. He would have to let her go, because she needed to be free to follow her dreams. Even if that meant down the road she would probably find someone else who was better. Someone who could give her the world and more. Nat had and would be continuing to move on without him and Chris felt himself withdraw from her.

"Thank you for the dance," Nat said. "Friends?" Nat smiled, offering her right hand. Chris swallowed hard his pride, masking his feelings.

"Friends," he smiled back, shaking her hand. "Good luck. Take care of yourself. You're going to scare the shit out of those guys," Chris acknowledged, a fondness in his tone. Nat nodded knowingly.

"Goodbye."

With that, Nat walked away, and Chris let her without a fight. Over to Anna and her date, Robbie, who were waiting for her, Nat had come alone, but as usual, she was just fine.

Chris stood very still for a moment before retreating back to his table of friends. Guys patted him on the back, but Chris did not feel that triumphant. He had won his friend back but overall lost something much greater. As he glanced over at Nat one last time, Chris resolved that he had to move on too. There would be other girls. It was like Nat said. He had so much to look forward to. No more trying for something that as Nat affirmed 'was not meant to be.'

Later that evening, as Nat left the school doors to walk home under the light of the moon that lit her path, she could not help but look back at the school one last time. Nat felt a genuine uneasiness about her future, knowing that her life would be changing. Never again would she be in high school, as her years were now done. How funny that she ached for adult challenges but felt very much like a little girl inside.

Was she ready for the big world out there? Would she be able to handle the pressure? Would she cross the ocean to see how others lived? Would she find the answers that she sought? More importantly, would she finally find a place where she truly belonged? Where the restlessness and anxiety would dissipate and there would be peace?

Would redemption find her?

10

The army facilities at Sussex Military Camp, with its fifty-five year old barracks, consisted of the standard wooden "H" huts. In other words, these buildings were unkempt, large, fishing shacks. As Nat walked up St. George Street with her backpack in tow, many of the men stared at her as she walked past the front gates. The news had spread fast about the mistake that was made. That the army had unknowingly accepted the application of a woman under the pretense, that by her very name, she was a man.

"What the hell are you telling me!?" Major-General Samson angrily said, standing up from behind his desk. "That we've accepted a damn woman!? On MY base!?"

"Yes sir," Officer Hicks confirmed, maintaining his stance.

"Well, fucking get rid of her!" he ordered, turning to his right hand man, Lieutenant-Sergeant William Peters.

"It's not that simple sir," Peters responded.

"Do I look stupid to you?"

"No sir."

"Then it is simple. Why is this even being discussed with me? I have far more important things to do with my time, than be talking about some *girl.*"

"Legally, there are no laws forbidding women from applying to the Canadian Armed Forces."

"So? That can be changed very fast, which it will!"

"Yes sir, but since we have already accepted her application, and sent documented confirmation of her acceptance, the military's attempt to overturn this decision after the fact, could become not only a legal, but very public matter."

"She's a GIIIIRL!!!" the General scoffed, "What?" Reaching for her file still resting on his desk unopened, he scanned its contents briefly. "Eighteen years old, supposedly a damn orphan for Christ sake! What is she going to do? Take on the damn military-I highly doubt that."

"No sir, you are correct. She probably won't, but her Father will."

"Then he's a stupid man."

"Look at her *name*, sir. Natalie Roberts *Shaw*."

After a moment. "General Shaw?"

"*Thee* one General Shaw," Lt. Peters stressed.

General Samson slumped back in his chair, deflated. "I didn't even know he had a child, adopted or not." Lt. Peters nodded. Nat indeed was the daughter of a great and well-respected General, whose political status three years earlier had elevated him to one of the highest, most coveted positions in the country. Selected under Prime Minister Mackenzie's approval, Lieutenant-General Shaw was the sole military representative and authority for Eastern Canada. Acting as Commander, the General oversaw and headed all military operations for the entire Atlantic coast for the Armed Forces and its military supplies.

"What the hell am I going to do?" Searching, the answer seemed obvious. General Shaw was a highly educated, very powerful, influential man, both politically and militarily. Within the community, his star was too bright to touch, let alone battle against. To challenge such a man could ruin a career.

"I will be the laughing stock of the entire military. Any ambition I have, ruined." Under his leadership, General Samson had been appointed to train the 1st Brigade group to be a part of the 3rd Canadian Infantry Division, with the goal of deployment aimed for December.

"Sir?" Peters called, waiting for further instruction.

As the General brainstormed, an idea finally came to him. "Let this girl come then…"

"Sir?"

"She won't last a day, let alone a week. After she quits, we'll have the requirements changed in writing, and there will be no further 'mistakes.' Tell me Lieutenant, who is her Drill-Sergeant?"

"Hadley, sir."

"I want him switched."

"Yes sir. With whom, sir?"

"Rossi."

"Yes sir," Peters nodded in agreement. If the General wanted to guarantee her removal, the toughest son of a bitch on any base, Rossi, seemed the perfect choice to do so. At the age of thirty-eight, with no family and fifteen years of service under his belt, Rossi was a man whose confrontational personality kept him from rising through the ranks. Uneducated and uncouth, Rossi was the kind of man to be avoided, which is why the General stuck him at the back corner of the base. Un-political in ambition, Rossi would not give a shit that she was Shaw's daughter.

"That will get rid of her," he laughed, the men chuckling with him in agreement. "Rossi will finally make himself useful. Damn, stupid whop...Dismissed."

As Nat kept her focus on the main hall that was now only a few yards away, she followed her father's directions to get there. It was down the road, at Nat's request, did the General stop his jeep to drop her off. This was something that Nat wanted to do on her own. Not a time for tears, the General offered the best military advice he could.

"Whatever happens, don't take anything personal. You'll hear everything, but let it go in one ear and out the other. Let nothing stick, understand?"

Nat nodded, trying her best to calm her fears.

"Watch your back, as the boys and your officers can and probably will be as nasty as they want," he further instructed. "Expect to be alone, because no one will want you there, but I know that when you show them what you can do, you will command their respect. Don't expect it from anyone at the beginning. You have to earn it, and that takes time."

"Yes."

"I know you don't want me to interfere, so I won't." What Nat did not know was that a good friend of his on the base would be keeping watch over her, to report back to him on how she was doing. "Don't take anyone's bullshit. If you do, you'll never win their respect."

"I'll be fine Dad."

Reaching the door, Nat knew that her moment had come. The moment she had been dreaming about for so long.

Becoming a soldier.

This was it. If Nat walked through that door, there was no coming back. She could never quit, no matter how bad it got.

Was she ready for this?

Yes.

Nat had known for awhile that her calling lie behind a door she had been waiting to open. If she had any faith in herself, in God, she could open it. Nat's heart began to pound, as she felt herself a woman, dangling from a cliff. Clinging onto a sturdy branch that was all too familiar, her only choice was to hang on or by letting go, leave behind the life she knew before, to fall into the unknown where she would experience an adventure that was completely new. A new path that would infinitely lead to a higher place of belonging.

That is, if she had the guts to let go.

That's when Nat reached for the door and took the fall. Frightening, the chill of it all was undeniable. Every man stared at her as she stepped into the room, their looks ambivalent and unwelcoming.

Finally.

"You lost missy? The latrine is that way for cleaning," barked Albert Pierre in his thick, French accent. Growing up in Edmundston, Albert had come to Moncton because no training camp, despite talks, were available in his town. Although other camps were being slated to open soon in the areas of Woodstock, St. George, and Petersville, he couldn't wait that long. Turning to take a good, hard look, Nat knew instinctively that Albert was vying for an alpha position within the group. An assumption based on how the men were crowded behind him, their laughter following his instigative lead. At a height of 6'1, he certainly was a big boy, Nat assessed. Weighing probably close to two hundred pounds, Albert's menacing presence would demand Nat's vigilant attention. Examining him closely, Nat observed a grayness in his eyes, that represented a soul both clouded and lost. Nat would have to confront him head on, or there would be no end to his cackling.

"No. Private Natalie Shaw," Nat firmly spoke. As she quickly scanned the room to visually read the others, no one really stood out aside from Albert. His strong personality could greatly influence any group, and Nat determined right there that he would prove to be her greatest adversary. Equally apparent to Nat was how she was the one under the microscope.

Approaching slyly, Albert invaded Nat's personal space in an effort to intimidate. "Where's your dress Private?" he whispered, eyeing her physique up and down. "If you are going to be accompanying us for our training, I expect to see some gams," Albert smiled, stroking her right cheek with his index finger. Once more, the group of men laughed. "Yeah, we heard you were coming, right boys?" he called, as the men nodded in agreement. "You wanna play with the big boys, we can show you how to play," Albert smiled coyly.

Such a pretty girl. Certainly she would be in awe of his strength and confidence.

"I'm here to begin training," Nat responded, unflinching.

"I can train you all right. How about you see me tonight?"

The room was filled with many 'ews' and 'aws'.

There.

Now that would send her out of the room crying. Even if she was pretty, the girl was still mixed up. She had no business being here with the men. Women were good for one thing and one thing only. The sooner this girl realize her place, like his mother, the better. If a woman needed straightening out, the man would see to it. His father had done it on several occasions, and his mother was a better woman for it.

All the men waited to see what would happen next.

"What's your name?" Nat asked coolly. "You do have a name, don't you?"

"Albert."

This was it, everyone suspected, believing that Nat was going to break down.

"Albert, don't ever stand this close to me again," Nat warned.

"Oooohhhh, whatcha gonna do about it?" Albert laughed, mockingly scared.

"If you do, I'll take my knife out, cut your balls off, and shove them down your fucking throat as an appetizer, so that I don't have the misfortune of having you *think* that you can *ever*…approach…me…again…Are we clear, big boy?"

Albert was stunned.

"I thought so. Nice meeting you," Nat said, walking away from him to sit down at the nearest, available desk for orientation. The guys were humorously surprised. Not bad, a few of them thought. It was funny to see a woman tell Albert off.

What a bitch, Albert thought, his face flushing with anger. No woman had the right to talk to him that way, humiliating him. Yet, Albert could not think of an adequate response back. With his mouth agape, nothing came out. Nat felt his glare pierce through her, but she focused her concentration on keeping neutral and numb. Nat had to keep her wits about her and not get emotional. With eyes forward, so as to avoid any further conflict within the group, Nat had done as her Dad had instructed. No bullshit from anyone, otherwise they think it's okay.

Just as Albert had recovered and attempted to speak out against Nat, he was halted by Sergeant Rossi's entrance into the room.

"Sit down gentlemen, let's go," he barked, unfazed by Nat's presence. Walking briskly to the podium, the men took to their seats. A short man, no taller than Nat at 5'7, his small, Italian frame was ironic considering his temperament in contrast. "I am Sergeant-Major Antonio Rossi, but when addressed, you shit bags will call me Drill-Sergeant. You don't ever say my fucking name, understand?"

"Yes Drill-Sergeant," everyone yelled back, including Nat. "What I say, goes, and that is non-negotiable. Last person who had a problem with me, thinking he was too 'big' to take shit from me, I told him to take his best shot if he had a problem following my orders. That six foot five tree came falling down, after I snapped his arm like a twig and broke his nose, all within the time frame of ten seconds. I anticipate that by having told you such valuable information, none of you will be as stupid to *not* listen to me."

"Yes Drill-Sergeant!"

Although a bit harsh and downright scary, Nat liked this man. His no-nonsense personality reminded her a bit of her Dad. Rossi was tough, disciplined, and forthright, and Nat sensed was a bit of an outsider himself.

"You will have twelve weeks of basic training, that will be rigorous and backbreaking, if you have the stomach to take it. Remember gentlemen, we are preparing you for war, so that means knowing your rifle, yourself, your unit, and above all, how to fight. We'll see soon enough what you ladies know. At ten hundred hours, I expect you all in full uniform, outside your barracks, which is two buildings south, standing in formation. No time for breakfast, as I won't look at anyone who has not gone to barber, and organized their cot and locker box first. You have approximately one hour to complete this. I warn you now not to be late or you'll see yourself running the base before you even begin this morning's training."

The boys were silent.

"Dismissed," he yelled, walking out without acknowledging anyone. Everyone stampeded to the door, sprinting for the barracks to accomplish all that they had to do before Sergeant Rossi got hold of them.

When an hour had passed, Nat stood in formation, her hair cut as short as a man's. It was a shock that she hadn't fully had time to absorb yet, as everything was happening so fast in her race to prepare. Dressed in full attire, Nat wore the standard Skeleton Order, WE'37 uniform. As Sergeant Rossi passed by the men one by one, harshly correcting their stance, uniform, and overall meek demeanors, similar to Nat, he was also reading his men to see what kind of regiment he had. Stepping in front of Nat aggressively, Sergeant Rossi examined her uniform and stance. With the exception of the British web anklets that would be arriving later, all components of her uniform were accounted for and perfectly placed. One waist belt with two braces on either side, two basic pouches, each containing a twenty round cartridge, one bayonet frog, large pack, water bottle carrier, Haversack, and two shoulder straps with supports. All she needed now was a Ross Marks II rifle left over from the Great War, and the whole world, Rossi thought shaking his head, would be definitely going to hell.

Whatever hole this girl came out of, Sergeant Rossi determined he would be hell bent on sending her back. In the meantime, there was nothing out of place, as Nat knew that her father had taught her well. Purposely trying to intimidate, Rossi gave a dead stare into her eyes, searching for any visible weakness that he could exploit and break, which inevitably would send her home packing.

With an unanimated, steadfast expression, Nat stared resiliently back, confident and self-possessed. Nat refused to let this man, or anyone else rattle her, and indeed Rossi noted right there and then that nothing seemed shaky about her. In comparison to the other men, they were far more cowardly and awkward looking in his opinion. Boys that he would have to bust his ass to turn into men.

That would be enough for now.

Beginning with basic commands, Sergeant Rossi taught his latest recruits how to march, so that he could work next on their endurance. Hiking all day, Nat was famished by the time she made it to the mess hall with the others. Standing in line, dinner was potatoes and pork chops, and that suited her fine. Walking over to sit down with her comrades, every single man would eventually stand up and leave her, taking their trays with them to another table. As they left one by one, Nat felt the sting of what they were doing. It resurfaced a feeling that was all too familiar.

Nat was on her own.

Again.

As all eyes in the room fell upon her to see her reaction, Nat reached calmly for her necklace. Running her fingertip along the crucifixion cross resting on her chest, she could feel Jesus comfort her. Nat was on her own, but not alone.

Never alone.

Determined not to let her feelings show, Nat ate her food silently, defying the others by merely remaining present. As the men eventually resumed to eating their meals, Sergeant Rossi watched her.

There was something different about her, besides being a woman, that he could not quite put his finger on. Something hidden, unique only to her, which meant that her reaction could never be calculated. How easy she would be to target and to dismiss, all the while possessing a will to survive that could possibly surpass any other man in the regiment.

Apparent to all was the threat that Nat represented, and how she made everyone uncomfortable. It would be a struggle those first two weeks. It was as if everything Nat had ever known to be true about this world, and believed about herself was under attack from all fronts. Challenged and confronted daily with what seemed a barrage of insults, Nat was shaken from her continuing isolation. Whenever she went to the mess hall for her meal, Nat would go sit down at the one empty table the men had left for her, since she knew that if she sat by anyone, they would just walk away anyhow. It was like the time she spent Christmas at her foster home. Everyone would get a present, courtesy of the town church, but the old woman saw to it that Nat didn't get anything. As Nat watched them open up their presents in front of her, it was if she was invisible.

How the army food bothered many of the men, but Nat ate her food without complaint. Porridge or 'slop' had been served at her foster mother's every morning. Day after day, sometimes three times a day, so the army slop didn't bother her any. Nat knew what it was like to live and endure with very little. It was something that did not go unnoticed by Sergeant Rossi.

The first day of practice fire, Nat thought for sure she would win over some of the guys. Amazing would be a word to describe her shooting skills, as the men stood by, astounded at how fast and accurate her shooting was. Not only that, but how quickly she could disassemble and reassemble her Lee-Enfield .303, Marks III rifle. Within thirty seconds flat, Nat had set a new company record!

"Hunting," Nat answered proudly, a bit cocky. "It's fun."

A few men smiled back, but all still refused to acknowledge her presence as anything legitimate. Quiet followers the men remained, desiring to keep their status quo sooner than risk being an outsider to the group. Although Nat's athleticism stood out, it proved to be a detriment anyhow as Nat was showing up many of the guys, and the effect made her even more of a target for their growing hostility.

Apparent to all was that this girl was simply not going to quit.

As the inner confidence that Nat had always possessed dwindled away, a new reality began to creep into her consciousness. It spoke to her in a quiet, doubtful tone. If kicked down, for the first time in her life, would she be able to get back up? No longer was her sights on being the best in the regiment. Now, Nat just wanted to pass so as to 'survive' training.

Nat was beginning to feel her vulnerability at a deeper level, and being new to her, she hated its exposure. Tested daily to the limit by the coarse conditions of training that threw everything at her, Nat was becoming increasingly angry and agitated at the men. Granted, Sergeant Rossi never bothered her, but Nat was always in line, accelerating at every exercise performed by the regiment. Where the Sergeant made others cry, or run, Nat wanted to start evening the score. When Sergeant Rossi hit some of the men for being what he called, "stupid shits," Nat wished it could be her.

Not a choice this time around, Nat was becoming increasingly cold from a loneliness that gnawed away at her. It was only at night, when her heart was no longer being attacked, that it opened in desperation. How Nat's heart yearned to have someone offer something that could keep her from drowning. Someone to be her lifeline and offer his strength, when hers was low.

How could she be so weak?

Why was love always in the back of her mind, more than anything else?

Why did she still feel this constant need to be loved?
Was love even something worth fighting for?

To be comforted within the arms of a man who loved
her with a passion so great, where all her aches, bruises,
and physical pains would dissipate within his embrace,
would be amazing. How all suffering would be worth it,
if that meant that the outcome was someone who loved
her for her, actively pursuing and rescuing her.

Pursuing her to the greatest depths of her heart.

'I want to be known, but no one cares to know me,'
Nat prayed silently to God. How I wait to have a man
pursue me for whom I am, inside, beyond the surface.

Lying in her cot, Nat stared up at the ceiling, unable
to sleep again. At these times when Nat reflected, it was
then that he would always come back to her.

Chris.

They were good friends at one point. How she missed
that friendship now. Struggles seemed easier to bear when
he was around, and the days seemed easier to get through,
when he was in her thoughts.

Nat wondered if her pride had been the only factor
influencing her decision to cut off all ties with him. Why
was she so quick to refuse forgiveness? Was her pride still a
factor in her inability to admit that she had possibly made
a mistake coming here?

Could Nat walk away from all this, if she knew love
was waiting for her beyond this military base?

Enough thoughts for one evening…It was time to sleep
and rest, as she would need her strength for tomorrow.

Tomorrow would come, with its greatest challenge to
Nat yet. Under Raymond's prodding, Albert would start

taunting Nat again, and his merciless tone would draw blood.

"Hey bitch. That's what you are, right? A female dog?"

Sergeant Rossi had stepped a hundred yards away to converse with two other commanding officers about the next exercise, as the regiment stood at attention, waiting quietly.

"Hey Natalie, what are you doing here, anyway? What? You can't talk?"

Nat ignored Albert as she always did, despite her growing rage and pent up hatred for him and his buddy Raymond.

However, as Albert pushed her from behind, he would step over the line. Nat trying to turn to prevent the fall, landed flat on her back in the mud. Enraged, Nat jumped to her feet, only to be punched in the face by Albert. This time she went flying face first into the mud. That is when Albert went after Nat without constraint, kicking Nat in the stomach while she was down, that made her roll over in pain. As Nat attempted to get up, someone in the crowd seemed to be pushing her around from behind, knocking her off balance. The group had joined in and their cheering caught Rossi's attention.

"Only when the Sergeant is around can you handle yourself, eh? How are you going to make it in a field? When are you going to learn that a woman has no place being here! You embarrass us all," Albert yelled angrily, punching Nat in the face one last time, as she was down on the ground.

How his yelling was reminiscent of a woman Nat knew long ago.

"Where the hell are you? Natalie?" her drunk foster mother hissed for her that fateful night. The old woman's footsteps kicked up dust under the floorboards where Nat was hiding, as she stomped on by. The rainstorm had commenced its fury that cold, October evening in 1931, as Little Nat waited.

The cold rain began to fall on the men, washing away the blood from Nat's face.

"What the hell is going on here!? Break it up! Get back!!!" Rossi yelled, as the regiment abruptly ended their cheering, realigning their formation.

Raising up her head slowly, Nat's eyes stared straight ahead, her gaze casting an altered expression. Lost of all animation, a darkness had entered again, taking hold of her.

Completely.

It had come back.

Out it gazed as the lightning of that fateful evening flashed in Nat's mind. Rising up to her feet, the voice of Sergeant Rossi talking to the men had been drowned out by the thunder she could hear, rumbling within her own dark heart. If one were to look closer, stare deep into Nat's eyes, as they fixated past the Sergeant, onto Albert, only then would one would see her…

In the darkness.

Little Nat, standing in the rain. How it had pelted on her hard that night.

Cold. Very cold.

Alone.

If one were to wait in the darkness, and wait for the lightning flash, would they be able to see fully, Little Nat standing, her dress soaked in blood.

This time, Nat's darkness was coming for Albert.

As Nat started towards Albert, it was Billy who first noticed how scary she looked.

What the hell is she doing? She's heading straight for him! Billy thought.

Pushing Sergeant Rossi out of the way from behind, Nat lunged at Albert's throat.

Instantly the men resumed their cheer.

"Jesus Christ!" Rossi yelled, yanking her back. "Stay where you are! All of you!!! I'm not done yet," he ordered, dragging Nat away by the collar. More like straighten her out as he pushed her against a nearby tree, pinning her with his arm.

" You trying to get yourself killed!? Huh!"

Nat stared past the Sergeant, refusing to let Albert out of her sight.

"Are you so stupid to not see that if you fight him, I won't be able to protect you? Not that I want to. You're on your own-"

That statement caught Nat's attention. " Who says I need your protection?" How foolish they all were, Nat thought to herself. The men had no idea what she was capable of.

Sergeant Rossi was about to respond but felt himself unable.

"I'm bounded by your 'protection.' I can't fight back. No wonder no one thinks I can fight. Give me just one opportunity to prove it."

"Pick your battles! Christ sake, Albert outweighs you by seventy pounds!"

"He's slow, and stupid," Nat scowled.

"Fighting is for the war, not here Goddammit! A regiment is a united front on the field. You are not working as a unit, Nat. Maybe you shouldn't be here-"

"Unit? What unit!? There's no team. Albert is the one who does not function as a unit. Maybe he shouldn't be here, you ever think about that!? Why is it always ME who is the problem? I'm a soldier if you just let me prove it. There will be no more fights to break up after this. I'll be the new Alpha," Nat vowed.

"Alpha my ass-" Rossi scoffed.

"I wasn't finished. I want a fight, with one rule only. Absolutely no interference. To the survivor."

"Your blood is not going to be on my hands," Rossi cautioned.

"There will be blood, but it won't be mine. If that French bastard wins, I'm gone," Nat yelled so that the men could hear her. There were unanimous cheers. "Yet, if I win, the only fighting from this point on will be on the battlefield. I never would have guessed you, Drill Sergeant, to be afraid of a little blood."

Sergeant Rossi wasn't impressed, but there was something in her conviction, the sheer belief she had in herself, that made him start to believe in her too. Nat was so confident over odds that seemed illogical and non-strategic on her part. Forget dignity and honor. Rossi was just trying to save her life.

"I know how to fight. Let me show you my God-given talent." Nat's direct, icy demeanor and calm confidence made him slowly release his grip. "You can time me on how fast I put this guy in the ground, without a gun."

"Private Pierre," Rossi called, not taking his eyes off Nat. He wanted to see if she would flinch.

"Yes Sergeant," Albert grinned, stepping forward.

"You will settle your differences today. No one is officially watching. This is a fight to the 'survivor.' It is between two people, no interference. There are no other rules regarding how you may fight, only that you cannot kill each other. Do you accept these terms?"

"If it will make her leave, absolutely."

Nat did not flinch. There was no doubt escaping from her eyes. "Very well then," Rossi said, letting her go.

"Yeah, but that means looking me in the eye when you fight me you piece of shit," Nat scowled, heading back."Without your buddies," she continued, trying to get Albert roused a bit.

"I don't need anyone's help to get rid of you. You're not even a girl. I don't know what the hell you are," Albert sputtered in retaliation.

"Everyone back up and give proper space," Sergeant Rossi instructed, himself stepping back. Billy hesitated. Could Nat really do this?

How he hoped she could.

"You trying to turn me on Nat?" Albert snickered, as Nat unbuttoned her uniform, exposing her white undershirt. The guys were stunned to see how muscular her arms were.

"I don't want your blood dirtying my uniform," Nat coldly replied, getting herself mentally into fight mode. Albert started laughing at her, but Nat was no longer flustered. No longer talking to him, he was not human to her anymore.

No mercy. Not for a man who never showed any mercy himself towards others. Not for a boy who had been a bully most of his life.

How he was about to pay today for all his sins.

"This is a joke. You're going to fight me? I'm six foot two, you're five feet of a whole lotta nothing," Albert laughed.

Turning her back on him for a moment, Nat took a breath as she looked up.

It was a similar breath she took when she looked up that October night, before lifting the floorboard's secret door to see what her foster mother was doing. Across the living room, the woman's back was turned, and she was screaming at Mary to tell her where Nat was. Little Nat's eyes were no longer afraid. Anger had taken its grip. Waiting for the opportune moment, Nat waited patiently to strike.

It was with the same look in her eyes that Nat turned around to face Albert, growling low, "You want me? Come and get me."

As Little Nat watched her foster mother slap Mary across the head so hard that the little girl hit the floor, she heard herself whisper, "You want me? Here I am."

As Albert started towards her, fists raised, Nat lunged at him, and it was at that moment that Little Nat sprang from her secret cage from under the floor to grab the lamp and smash it over the old woman's head.

Albert swung, but Nat ducked and hit him so fast and hard with her right fist, that she felt his rib break. Stunning him momentarily, Nat wheeled around from behind to kick him hard in the groin.

Just as her foster mother had collapsed onto the floor like a bag of bricks, so too did Albert fall to his knees.

"Mistake number one," Nat quoted her fight instructor. "Never underestimate your enemy you bastard," Nat said, proceeding to give Albert a right and left jab to his back ribs. "Cracked five ribs there I think," she goaded. "Aaaw, whatcha' gonna do? Poor baby. Your mommie and your brothers aren't here to protect you now," Nat circling him.

"You know what this is?" Nat said, punching him in the face. "Huh?" she hissed venomously.

"Fuck-"

"Wrong answer," she said, punching him again in the face, breaking his nose this time.

"Judgment Day you no good shit." As Nat grabbed him by the hair, Albert was forced to look at her. "You're mine today. Prepare to lose your wind you bastard," Nat said, swinging a punch right into his lung cavity. Horrified, Albert began gasping for air as the pain induced by Nat put him into a state of mental and physical shock.

How her foster mother had the same, similar look when she finally saw that it was Little Nat who had struck her from behind, and was now towering over her.

Nat then bit into Albert's right ear, as he screamed in agony.

As her fight instructor taught her, the assault should always begin first with an assault on the mind. Do something so terrifying and completely unnatural, that your opponent loses all confidence. He will be afraid because you are the one that he has never encountered.

Little Nat smashed the lamp again on her foster mother as she started to get back up, screaming, "You leave her alone! Leave her ALONE!!!" Smash again.

Releasing her bite, Nat rose up with Albert's blood all over her mouth. Holding onto his ear, he couldn't believe it was still there. His ear was completely bitten through, but still intact. Albert's eyes conveyed his terror, as he realized that he had better fight or be dead.

"You crazy bitch!" he yelled, charging at her, but Nat grabbed hold of his extended right arm, turned and broke it within a heartbeat. Albert screamed out in pain, but this would only be the beginning.

If only he knew when to stop.

A fool.

The men in the regiment stepped away, amazed and horrified at what they were seeing, but Billy was smiling. Both fear and wonder had captured their full attention. Nat was scary to watch, because her fighting skills were not only unmatched by anyone else in the regiment, but more so, because she was fearless, merciless, and tactful. When she grabbed Albert by the hair, dragging him over to the tree, the few men that stood defiantly in her way, found themselves slowly stepping aside once Nat stared them down.

It would be no interference.

To the survivor.

Albert was on his own.

After all, it was his battle to fight.

As Nat proceeded to smash Albert's face against the tree, knocking out some of his teeth, she flung him backwards onto the ground satisfied. Moaning in agony and fear, Albert crawled towards his comrades to try and get their help, but no one would intervene on his behalf.

"Where do you think you're going?" Nat patronized, turning Albert around to head lock him under her arm. Running full speed, she rammed Albert's head against the tree again, and it was this time that he dropped instantly. "Come on, get up," Nat yelled, taking Private John's rifle out of his hands, to throw it on the ground for Albert to pick up. "You coward! Get up or I swear by God I'll fucking finish you!!!" Nat yelled.

Albert reluctantly picked up the rifle. His life was at stake.

Nat waited. As Albert screamed, running towards her with every ounce of strength he had left, Little Nat had reached that night for the kitchen knife that the old woman had dropped on the floor when she was hit. As her foster mother lunged for her, Little Nat turned around to face her head on.

Nat would step aside at the last minute, take hold of Albert's rifle, and proceed to use the butt end to heave him in the stomach, the back, and finally, chest area. "THAT'S THE BEST YOU GOT!!??" Nat yelled.

No answer.

Nat hit him again with the butt end of the rifle, this time with an uppercut to the face. Albert staggered backwards, half conscious.

Little Nat stood stunned, staring resiliently back at a woman whose hands had begun to clutch her throat. Slowly her grip loosened as her arms fell down to her side. It was Little Nat who was holding her up now. Disbelief was the old woman's expression, as she looked down to see her dress stained with her own blood, the blade's tip protruding out of her own back.

It had gone right through.

Terrified, Little Nat clung onto the butcher's blade, as it was her only lifeline. The woman slowly raised her head back up, fear evident in her eyes.

"You…" The blood dripped from her mouth as she spoke. "Deeevil!" she hissed.

"You're not my mother," Nat cried, using all her strength to push the woman away from her. Back she fell, swooping hard onto the floor with such force, that it rendered her immobile. With her breathing getting heavier, Nat also felt hers. For the first time, the old woman was helpless, but would come back if Nat did not stop her…She would still continue to hurt people if she lived. Little Nat's fear changed and metamorphosed into something she had never experienced before. She felt a strength rise within her that felt powerful, like reclaiming something stolen from her.

As Nat took hold of the rifle's barrel side, winding back for her final blow, Albert was a sitting duck.

The old woman began to stir, moaning in pain, and Nat knew she had to act quickly, for her time was now. Nat was in her element, and she savored being in control of her own life…Her own destiny. Nat was in a place where there was no longer any pity, any attempting to forgive, to show mercy for someone so unmerciful. Nat stepped forward, her eyes mirroring a reflective darkness, so cold, that she was lost in it.

Winding back her rifle like a baseball bat, Nat swung and struck Albert with such force, that he swung round twice before stumbling over his own legs to lie flat on his back, his jaws completely broken. Just as the old woman's blood at one time had been on her clothes, now that blood was Albert's. As Nat took Albert's left leg, down came her rifle's butt end to pop out his kneecap. It was a gruesome, terrifying sight to witness. Albert was nothing to Nat anymore. Breaking Albert's collar bone next with the rifle, Michael had to step in.

"You think you could get rid of me? No one can. Only God and he tells me that it's not my time yet," she hissed at Albert.

" Nat? "

Still in attack mode, Nat swiftly pulled the switchblade from her boot, to turn and put it to Michael's throat.

Fast she was!

Impossible to see coming.

"Nat?" Michael whispered afraid. "He's done…I mean, you beat him-can't you see that?"

"No interference," Nat whispered back coldly, refusing to drop her knife.

"You don't want to kill him."

Nat was so quiet, she was scary. How her eyes didn't flinch.

"Nat?"

"Why not? Some people deserve to die Michael. They are useless. Is that person you, Michael?" Nat said pressing the blade into his skin. "Is it worth your life to save his?"

Michael held his breath.

"Your breath? Is it worth your last breath Michael?"

"Private Shaw," a voice finally arose. It was the authoritative, commanding voice of Sergeant Rossi. "I think it best you go clean yourself up now," he instructed carefully.

Nat still felt she was in danger. Unable to move, she refused to let down her guard.

"It's all right Nat. You've won. No one is going to bother you again," Rossi tried to reason calmly with her. "Go on and clean up. The regiment will be right here, waiting for you. You've got ten minutes."

Nat slowly let her knife down, as Michael began to feel his own breath return to him again.

"I've got God on my side," Nat growled defiantly to Albert, then to the men. "Who do you all got? Huh? You got nothing but a lot of brawn and stupidity. It won't be the bullets that kill you...only your own ignorance."

The men were silent as Nat began to walk away, heading to the mess hall. Standing upright, she walked by the various regiments of men training. They all stopped what they were doing and stared, because Nat was covered in blood. Nat had survived and overcome once again. She had fought for her very life and kept it.

Again.

Stepping into the bathroom, Nat began to wash the blood off her hands. Looking into the mirror as she did so, the reflection cast was someone she no longer recognized. Someone who inevitably had become a part of her whether Nat liked her or not.

It made her sick.

Vomiting into the nearest toilet, Nat was shaken up to her core. So shaken, it made her weep uncontrollably.

Although there would be no further mention of Albert, it was safe to say that he would not be returning to complete his training. Supposedly out for many months to recuperate fully, no repercussions would later fall upon Nat as a result of the beating. It was as if the incident never happened, as the official records read, 'hurt during a combat training exercise.'

Case closed.

Spending a few days in the infirmary, when Nat did come out for the first time since the incident happened, the response and attitude of the men towards her was drastically different. As Nat walked into line at the mess hall that evening, many of the men stepped aside and let her go through first out of a newfound respect. As Nat made her way to the empty table reserved solely for her, it was Billy who would approach first, setting his tray down in front of her before sitting. Nat continued to eat as if nothing was different, despite her inner glee. One by one, the men started coming over and sitting at Nat's table, one guy actually patting her on the back as he did so. No one had to say anything, as their actions spoke volume. It would be Billy who would speak first.

"Where did you learn how to fight like that?"

Smiling, Nat explained, and the other men listened and began talking to her as well.

Nat's triumph would be short-lived though. After nearly two months into her training, Nat received a telegram from Eva, stating that he was gravely ill.

It can't be.

Deeply upset, Nat had to figure a way out of the barracks. Just for a night. If I don't, he may die without me getting the chance to see him, Nat thought to herself.

No matter what it took, I have to get to him, Nat resolved.

Tomorrow night would be her escape from the base. Getting away undetected, Nat would go find him.

11

As the pickup truck roared stopped in front of St. Vincent Memorial Hospital, Nat got out and ran swiftly up the building's stairs, into the dimly lit front lobby. Empty, it was as if the place were deserted.

"Can I help you?" a woman's voice came from behind. Nat turned fast, a bit startled.

"Yes ma'am," she answered, removing her officer's cap. "I am looking for a patient, Christopher Woods. Can you tell me what room he's in?" The nurse stared at her for a moment, as if trying to figure out why a woman was dressed so much like a man.

"Are you a member of the family?"

"No," Nat answered self-consciously. "I am a friend."

"It's three o'clock in the morning. Visiting hours are long over." Nat could not help but look down disappointed. "Besides, access is strictly prohibited to family members only, as he is very ill, so I'm afraid you'll have to go young lady."

"Please...I have to see him. I can't come back tomorrow. This is it for me. Tonight is my only chance. If you could give me just ten minutes, I promise I'll go. I just-I just have to see him-please," Nat pleaded.

"I doubt he will wake. He sleeps most of the time-"

"I don't care. I just want to see him."

The nurse smiled. "You've got ten minutes. Room 112, straight down the corridor, last door to your left."

"Thank you."

As Nat turned to begin her trek down the quiet, dark hallway, a familiar feeling began to sweep over her. Although years ago, the same haunting walk felt as if it all only happened yesterday. As a little girl, Nat had walked unknowingly towards her mother's hospital room.

Would Chris share her same fate?

As Nat reached for the closed door before her, she could not help but stop momentarily, as she had to prepare herself for the worst. One thing she knew was certain. She would not cry, as that would only get Chris upset. Right now she had to be strong for him.

Slowly opening the door, Nat dreaded to learn whether he was worse than initially reported. The telegram was already two days old, and she had to take another day, to figure out how she could escape to see him. Climbing over the fence after lights out, Nat had ran down the road until she found a vehicle to 'borrow,' so as to make her way here.

Closing the door, Nat was surprised to see a mere cot in an otherwise empty room. Across the room from her lay Chris, only she could not see him. A plastic sheath surrounded his entire bed. Nat felt her heart sink. A part of her did not want to go any closer, but she had to. Resting her cap on the door knob, Nat made her way over to his bed. Whatever tears she had determined she would not show, could not be contained as she moved in.

Resting her right hand against the plastic, how much she wanted to just reach out and touch him.

"Chris?" Nat whispered in disbelief. Seeing him fully, the Chris she knew was strong and full of life. The Chris before her looked as though the life within him was all but snuffed out.

What was left of him that is.

Gaunt, pale in complexion, his lips were cracked and bleeding, his eyes the blackest she had ever seen. He had lost a lot of weight. Standing still for a moment in the eerily quiet room, Nat knew then that she could feel its presence.

Death was standing by and it reminded her so much of her mother. Nat was not prepared then to say goodbye, but she had to.

Nat was not ready now to do the same…for a friend.

How Death was waiting to take him.

Chris looked so at peace in his sleep, that it proved too peaceful to Nat's liking. She had to wake him up.

"Chris?" Nat whispered, trying to gently wake him. "Chris?"

There was nothing. This isn't fair God, she thought to herself, beginning to get upset.

"Chris, if I have to keep going, then so do you. You understand me? You hear me? Don't you quit, not on yourself and not on me."

"Chris?" Nat tried one last time, but he appeared to be asleep to this world. "Wherever you are right now," Nat spoke softly, "can I go too?"

Silence.

"Can you take me with you?"

Still.

Nothing.

This was it. The pneumonia was going to take him away, and like her mother's impending death, there was nothing Nat could do about it. Nothing but accept God's will, even when it made no sense to her.

Even when it made her angry with Him.

Why not take her instead? If God loved her, he would not hurt her like this. He would not keep taking people dearest to her, people that she cared about the most, away from her. People that Nat not only needed, but loved.

"Oh Chris," Nat whispered, desperate. "Chris, it's me. Your good friend, Nat." Chris remained fast asleep. "I'm here for you. I am sorry that I wasn't here sooner, but I didn't get word until now."

Still, Chris did not stir.

"I'm here for you now."

With his face turned away from her, Nat thought that maybe if she persisted, he might eventually respond to the sound of her voice. It was worth a try.

"I am such a fool," Nat confessed, shaking her head. "I have been trying so hard, for so long to be a soldier, that I've forgotten...Who I am, and what's really important in my life. I forgot about my best friend...I never realized that the thought of you possibly leaving could make me physically ill to my stomach. I mean, what is that all about? I don't understand why? I mean we have both moved on...

All I do know is that I have not felt this way for a long time..." Nat revealed, her voice and thoughts trailing off somewhere else. "Not since I was a child. Not since my mother's death."

There it was. The truth.

"It was so hard losing her, Chris. I think I decided that since I was now on my own, alone, that I wouldn't rely on anyone ever again. No one but myself. At a distance I would keep people. I didn't want to get close to anyone, if only to lose them. It seems like anyone I did care about would leave. God knows, I know how to scare them all away," Nat smiled, laughing at her own feeble attempts to protect herself.

"On the ride down here, all I could think about was all the good times that we had together. Not the bad, just the good. It's funny how the bad doesn't seem to really matter anymore. It was all the little things-things I never saw," Nat shook her head regretfully.

Why had she been so blind?

"Some strong girl, huh? Look at me," she laughed, wiping tears from her eyes. "Nat, all undone. I'm a mess. Since we're being so honest here, I must say that the military is a lot tougher than I thought it would be. Every day I think about walking. I've never had my butt kicked, so much...I used to want to succeed, but lately, I don't really care. I just want to pass...Seeing you today is by far, the highlight of my entire time there," Nat said, looking mournfully down at Chris.

"I've got news for you. I'm not going to give up, because if I give up," Nat said defiantly, "that means that you can give up too, and you can't. I won't let you. You're going to fight this Chris, and you know why?" Nat asked. "You're gonna fight so that we can see each other again...I miss you...I-"

Could she say the words?

"I love you Chris."

Yes.

"We're worth fighting for, so don't leave me behind. If you do," Nat warned, "I'll be so pissed at you...God, please, if you're listening, please don't take him now," Nat prayed.

Praying for death to go away. Praying that it was not his time.

"Please..."

Just then, Chris opened his eyes.

Nat was stunned. Chris was awake!

Had he heard her?

Maybe.

How much had he heard?

"Hi," Nat smiled, relieved to talk to him.

Chris looked up at her, but how different it was from the last time she had seen him. He had the most vulnerable eyes.

Nat had come back, and he was overwhelmed to see her.

"Hi," his strength barely able to utter the name that he loved speaking, "Nat...Natalie..."

"I'm here, Christopher Woods," Nat laughed delighted. "True friends are always there for one another."

"It's good to see you," he struggled, as her beauty was something to see after so many long days in the dark.

"You too."

"You okay?"

"I'm fine."

"Your hair-"

"Yes. I had to get it cut short, just like everybody else. It's not very pretty-"

"No-"

"I know," Nat nodded in agreement, slightly embarrassed. She had forgotten how shocking her hair must look. Having seen her hair always long, Chris must think it's ugly, Nat thought.

"No," Chris urged. Nat leaned in closer to hear him out.

"You're beautiful."

Nat felt her breath cease.

"Still," Chris whispered, his eyes revealing an anguish Nat had never before seen from him.

"Beautiful," he reaffirmed.

"Thanks."

"Sorry," Chris said, painfully looking away.

How the wound still hurt.

"I'm fine. No need to be sorry," Nat dismissed, turning away also.

Turning back, Chris waited for her gaze to catch his. "No...I'm sorry I let you down."

Nat could not take her eyes off of him.

"It's okay. None of that matters now."

This was it, as Chris had nothing to lose. It was his time to tell her the truth.

"So many times when I wanted you, I wished I could have just once had the guts to tell you that I wanted you...I was afraid...Afraid you wouldn't want me back... You seemed so impossible to get, and I just kept messing up. When I did finally get it, it was too late."

"Too late?"

"That the only way to win you would be if I was real. No tricks, no act, just me...Simple, right? Just be me. I finally figured it out."

Chris took a moment to catch his breath, and Nat patiently waited.

"I knew that I didn't have it. I didn't have what it takes to win someone like you. That's why I couldn't give up the act. I thought I wasn't good enough…Nat, you are the only girl I have ever been real with and you are the only real thing I know. You're my best friend."

"You're my best friend too."

"There have been other girls I've seen, talked to, went out with. Girls at university too, but the thing is that when I was with any of them, all I think about is you, and how they are not you. None of them have what you have. I couldn't even sleep. Every time a brunette walked my way, I'd always find myself looking at her, hoping it was you-" he said desperately.

Nat knew what Chris was talking about. Often Chris appeared in her thoughts and dreams, no matter how much she tried to deny her feelings for him and move on.

"Then she'd look my way and I didn't even care. I didn't care because she wasn't the one I was looking for. She wasn't the one I wanted."

Chris continued on.

"The girl I want is like no other. She may initially strike someone as simple, but there is nothing simple about her. Incredibly intelligent, sometimes too smart for her own good, she is stubborn beyond compare, and frustrating to try and understand, but how she has a beauty about her, beyond her looks. It is a beauty that is beyond any other girl I've ever met…"

Chris took a moment.

"Difficult to get close to. Always out of reach. Most guys give up trying. There are other girls, they tell themselves. Girls who are easier. Easy girls don't give us headaches, or make us so frustrated, you think you're going crazy. Easy girls don't challenge you, remaining in your mind for weeks, even months afterwards."

That is because I am waiting, Nat thought to herself. Waiting to see if someone can prove me wrong. If no one bothers staying, why should I entrust them with my heart? I am waiting to see if someone truly has what it takes to love me.

"I gave up some," Chris confessed, "but I never let go of you completely. I watched you go, only because I wanted to see you happy, even if that meant, without me.

I now know that I was hooked the moment I saw you, only I didn't know it then. I just want to be with you and you only…I still love you Natalie," Chris finished.

There it was. What if she had met someone else? What if she had moved on for good and wouldn't give him a second chance to prove himself?

To trust him would be difficult, but Nat, in her emerging maturity knew that everyone does make mistakes. Life was becoming increasingly complicated with its many angles. Evident to Nat was how much Chris' need for her matched her own deep need for him. How his challenges had always made her think twice, even if she didn't admit it, and how she was much more close-minded before she met Chris. Isolation and loneliness can do that but Chris unlocked the emerging woman within, and for that, she was grateful. Nat had grown out of her own self-made shell, and that without him, she was at risk of becoming closed off again. Chris had opened her heart in a way that no other had, and it's what she both loved and hated about him.

Chris had also made a very painful mistake, but he took responsibility by apologizing for it. Yes, he had hurt her, but the love they shared not only remained, but proved deeper from having gone through such an experience. Put to the test, it lingered and proved itself to be real and true.

Eva had once told Nat that love was not a feeling but a choice. Nat had never known what she meant, until now. 'Love feelings' were not enough to compel Nat to give Chris another chance. Only a single choice of the will would do that.

Could she forgive and take a chance on him again?

Was Chris the man to take care of her?

"You concentrate on getting better first, and I will be waiting," Nat vowed.

"Yeah?" Chris asked, a feeble smile appearing on his face.

"Yes. When I finish my training, I will see you again."

"Promise?" Chris asked, weakly raising his right hand to touch hers. It was then that Nat saw how imprisoned Chris was by this illness that held him hostage.

Would he ever be set free or would his final days be in its cage?

As both pressed their palms against the plastic, lingering each other's touch, Nat could not help but wonder if she would see him again. It made her not want to go.

"I promise," she vowed, looking at him one last time.

"I promise too."

"I have to go."

"Okay."

As Nat turned to leave, Chris kept his hand pressed against the plastic. It made Nat stop.

"I had to check," he smiled, "to see if I was dreaming. I'm not, am I?"

"No."

"You're real. You're really here?"

"Yes."

"You are my light Nat. My friend."

"Always…Even when I am not here, you will feel as if I am."

Chris knew then that it was okay to close his eyes. His heart was assured that the next time he awoke, and every time after that, Nat would always be there with him.

Waiting for him.

Talking in confidence to the nurse on duty, Nat handed over her pay checks.

"Take this money to help cover his medical expenses," Nat instructed, knowing full well that Chris' father, a man of the church, led a modest life. "I want to remain anonymous."

"Okay," the nurse promised, a little confused that Nat was entrusting her, a complete stranger, to do this special request.

"Can you do one more thing?" The nurse nodded. "Please take a portion of this money to buy Chris a single, white rose, that is fresh every day, for his windowsill, so that he may see and know that I am with him daily. That

I love him. Tell him that this flower is a reminder that I am waiting, and am with him, even when I can't be physically…Can you do that?"

The nurse nodded, very much moved. "Yes," she smiled.

"Thank you," Nat smiled back at her, having no more time for words. Nat had to hurry back before sunrise. Although she felt renewed, she had to get back to the base before she got caught.

Climbing back over the fence, Nat raced to her cot and fell asleep almost immediately. However, within an hour, she awoke to Sergeant Rossi's symphonic yelling, to 'get their lazy asses out of bed!' Despite being incredibly tired all that day in her training, Nat did not care. Feeling as light as a feather, Nat had the opportunity to see Chris undetected, and that was all that mattered to her.

As the final weeks progressed, Nat found her training, both physically and mentally lighter. The time seemed to be passing quickly, one day leading quickly into the next. So much so, that Nat could not keep track of the days of the week. The men in the regiment gave her no grief anymore as many now talked to her on a regular basis.

How Nat felt a sense of satisfaction and accomplishment over what seemed a daunting possibility that first day she stepped onto the base.

Only one last challenge remained before graduation. The Run. Spanning fifteen kilometers of wilderness, the run had to be completed within forty-five minutes while carrying seventy-five pound backpacks. Nat knew it would be difficult, but intrinsically was calm because she felt prepared. If she paced herself and established her breathing rhythm, as Chris had taught her, then Nat would be fine.

When the day finally arrived, the regiment anxiously suited up. Despite the morning's cloudy atmosphere, the men approached their final test with anticipation. When the commencing gunshot went off, many bolted across the field to the forest's trail, sprinting for a lead. Oblivious, Nat's focus was on a light jog where she could first warm up her muscles to prevent cramping, while simultaneously conserving her energy for later.

As Nat passed the various markers representing every completed kilometer, she ran by many of the men along the way who had stopped for various water breaks near the five kilometer marker. Quickening her pace, by twelve kilometers, Nat knew she had passed nearly every man along the way. All but one. Passing the 14th kilometer marker, Nat finally saw Raymond up ahead. Speeding up, she pushed hard past to catch up. Along the hill's edge they ran side by side. Raymond was struggling, but he refused to give up. Still, Nat was starting to pass him. What would happen next would be completely unexpected.

As Nat rounded along the outside edge, running the hill's edge, Raymond pushed her off, sending her tumbling down nearly forty feet of bush. Luckily, the backpack protected Nat's head as she rolled down, but nothing could prevent her from the tree that awaited at the bottom. Face first, it was her forehead that hit its trunk and it knocked her out cold. Nat lay unconscious at the bottom, completely camouflaged, as the other men eventually passed by the same sight without even a second glance.

As Sergeant Rossi stood alone at the finish line, it would not be until the final fifteen minutes that the men would finally begin to trickle in. Emerging from the forest's underbrush, they stumbled and staggered across the field to meet him at the finish line.

"Good job Jackson," Rossi congratulated his men, "Way to hustle Findlay."

As nearly all the men were in, one question began to emerge in everyone's mind. Where was Nat?

"Jackson?"

"Yes Drill-Sergeant," Billy said, standing at attention.

"Did you see Private Shaw?"

"Yes, she passed most of us by the tenth kilometer marker sir." Many of the men nodded in agreement. Sergeant Rossi addressed all the men.

"Is it true that Private Shaw passed all of you during the run?"

"Yes, Drill-Sergeant," the men responded in unison. All but one.

"You were the first one in Private," Rossi said, standing face to face with Raymond. "Did you see Private Shaw?"

"No Drill-Sergeant," Raymond lied, averting his eyes. "I never saw her sir." Billy knew Raymond was lying, and how much he wanted to call him on it, but it was not his place. Instead Billy, along with the rest of the men, turned their gaze to Sergeant Rossi, their leader, to say something.

"Sergeant Rossi!" a voice from behind bellowed, like a cannon being shot into his eardrums. How that voice made his skin crawl.

"Yes, General Samson," Rossi acknowledged with a salute, turning to face front and centre.

"What a fine morning we're having," the old man chuckled. Rossi's former Drill-Sergeant all those years ago, and current 'boss,' Rossi thought the man was nothing more but an arrogant and pompous racist. Samson had made Rossi's training and early years in the military sheer hell, all because he wanted his 'whop ass' out of the military.

"Yes sir."

Accompanied by three other officers, the General's 'minions', Rossi was not impressed. Why was he really here? What was he up to?

"Girl's not here, is she?"

That was it.

"No sir."

"Good."

It made sense. The standard regulations used for this same test prior, were drastically altered at the last minute. All in a final attempt to try and keep Nat out. If she could not finish the run in time, she would not be graduating. Nat would have to repeat the training all over again, only next time, they would not make the same mistake twice. Nat would never have her application accepted.

Sergeant Rossi turned his gaze back onto the field.

Where was she?

As Nat awoke from her brief slumber, the pain was instantaneous. Grabbing her head to stop the throbbing, Nat's hand became bloody from her wound. Feeling about her scalp, it was a small cut, maybe a stitch or two.

No big deal.

Shit.

What time was it!?

As Nat looked frantically to her watch, clearing off the mud, she saw that there was only twelve minutes left of the run.

Get up!

As Nat pushed herself up onto her feet, she crumbled to the ground just as fast. It was her right ankle. Feeling about, Nat felt no fracture. Only a sprain.

With that, Nat propelled herself up again, placing most of her body weight on her left side. Reaching to her buttocks, Nat took out her helve, entrenching the tool into the dirt, so as to pick her way back up the hill crawling to the top. Resuming her run with less than a kilometer to go, Nat's anger would see to it that she made the finish line in time.

"Seven minutes left," General Samson scoffed. "She'll never make it." As the rain began pouring down, his dour prediction seemed likely.

"Soon enough sir," Rossi commented. That's when Billy saw a tiny figure emerge onto the field. Limping, there was no mistaking that it was Nat.

"There she is!" Billy pointed, as everyone turned to look. Limping her way towards them, struggling every step of the way, Nat tripped again, this time falling face first into the mud. Seeing the finish line two hundred meters away, Nat struggled to get back up. The rain felt like it was pounding her further into the mud.

She was so close.

The pain in her ankle was becoming unbearable. If she crawled, she would never make it in time! Looking again to her watch, Nat had only six minutes left.

The officers looked on smugly, secretly celebrating. That was that. The girl was finished.

"Stay down," General Samson said.

Sergeant Rossi intensely looked at his watch. Nat had approximately five minutes and forty-five seconds to finish her run. Why was she not getting up? She was so close.

"I told you a woman could never do what a man does. Their sex is far too weak and fragile. She had no business being here," the General announced arrogantly.

Hearing every word, all regimental eyes turned to Sergeant Rossi again. Soaked from the rainfall, every man remained standing to support Nat until the very end. After all, she had earned it, but there was nothing they could do. Angry, Billy looked over at Raymond, who defiantly turned his head away to ignore his glare.

Nat could see them all, blurred within the distance. Nat was beginning to see her dream taken away from her, with no amount of will and determination to physically get her over the finishing line. Struggling to lift herself up with her arms numb from the cold, they wobbled into collapse. "Dammit," Nat began crying. "Get up, come on!" she cried, trying again, but unable.

The officers started laughing aloud again. "Look at her! Trying to get up, but can't!"

"Just rest awhile dearie!" another shouted. "We're sending in the men to come carry you off the field once your time is up!"

"Enough of this nonsense! Sergeant Rossi. Give me the watch," General Samson ordered. "This run has been completed."

"There is still five minutes and fourteen seconds left," Sergeant Rossi said, not letting go of his watch. Nat was going to show up these assholes, just as she had done every other test before, he thought to himself. Rossi felt all eyes were on him. He could not complete the test for her, but he could do the next best thing. Sprinting across the field towards her, Nat found herself looking up at Sergeant Rossi's two very large boots.

They were there to kick her butt.

"What do you think you're doing? The finish line for this test is straight ahead and you have four minutes to cross it."

"Sergeant Rossi, I can't. I've failed-I just don't have the strength to do it," Nat cried out, trying to keep herself from letting her emotions get the best of her. Sergeant Rossi bent down and looked her square in the eye.

"Block out the pain and get up now. I know you can do it. Now get up, if not for yourself, for me," he smiled at her. "You're just as good as any man here," he confided. "Even better." Nat looked up at him renewed. "Now block out the pain and get your ass up now. That's an order Private."

It was all Nat needed to move forward. Grabbing a wood stick off of the ground, she bit down, reached her right hand out into the mud, and began to raise herself up.

"That's right!" Sergeant Rossi yelled, standing. "Are you a soldier!?"

Spitting out the stick, Nat grunted in pain,"Yeess!"

"I didn't hear you!" he yelled.

"YES. Yes, I'm a SOLDIER!" she affirmed, staggering her way through the mud, heavy backpack in tow. Just block out the pain she told herself.

Nat then heard some of her peers from afar start clapping. Nat had three minutes left and Billy couldn't stand by any longer. Rushing over to Nat to run alongside her, others in the regiment followed his lead, yelling out their encouragement.

"Come on Nat. You can do it!"

"You're almost there!"

"You're gonna do it!"

"Hurry!" Billy yelled at her, breaking out into laughter, "You're gonna do it. You are gonna DO IT!!! **GO**!!!"

As the adrenaline kicked in, Nat gave it her all, pushing hard up the small hill. With the cheering, a slight smile came across Nat's face as she saw the end nearly in sight.

"How much time?" she gasped.

"Fifteen," Sergeant Rossi said, jogging right behind her. "RUN!"

"Oh shit," Nat winced, skipping as best she could, to keep the pressure off of her right foot. Then there was a sudden burst of hollering. "Where's the line?" Nat called out, still running.

"You passed it!" Sergeant Rossi yelled back. Coming to an abrupt halt, Nat fell to the ground exhausted. It was not enough to stop her peers from running over and lifting her high up above their heads. Like a rag doll Nat lay, the only possible detection of life evident being when she lifted her weary head up to give a half smile to her comrades. "Take her to the infirmary to get checked out," Rossi ordered, as the men carried her off.

It was then that Sergeant Rossi turned to his 'comrades,' as Raymond walked away fuming.

"Well, gentlemen, with five seconds left, she made it," Sergeant Rossi acknowledged. "Ah, but you never can quite tell with women though," he shrugged, walking up to face General Samson. "Women kind of remind one of Italians, now don't they?"

The men remained silent.

"Always underestimated. When beaten down, time and time again, they not only keep getting back up, they give a good kick in the balls while doing so." Looking up, the rain had ceased. "What a fine day it is," Rossi smiled. "Gentlemen," he saluted, leaving the field.

The inevitable would come, forever changing the way the military would run for generations to come. The General could not stop it now.

One thing was certain. Nat would become a soldier, and being the General's daughter, with his military and political clout, she would have to be given the opportunity to serve overseas in an infantry capacity.

There was no stopping it.

A secret.

The military would keep her a secret. With a speedy ceremony, no one would notice or recognize her presence in the Canadian Armed Forces. That would prevent any other woman from signing up ever again.

Nat would remain the military's best kept secret.

12

Charlie Smith, a reporter with Saint John, New Brunswick's, 'The Telegraph Journal,' sat behind his desk typing away, when his phone rang. Working on the next day's headline, he was annoyed at having his train of thought interrupted.

"Whoever this is, it better be good," he gruffly answered. What he would hear on the extension would be better than good. It would be shocking.

"What the hell are you talking about?" he enquired, listening intently. "There's never been a woman in our armed forces ever. Are you certain?" What became increasingly apparent as he continued to listen was there was no mistaking that this girl was real indeed.

"Well, what's her name? Natalie Bovaird Shaw.... An orphan? Now that is even better," he enthusiastically commented, beginning to write notes on his desk pad. "A General's daughter! What's his name?"

Still there was more. "She's graduating in five days? No shit? Jesus, we have a Canadian Joan of Arc happening," Charlie began babbling, envisioning the headline already. "Can you imagine the journalistic possibilities with this scene? A girl who showed up the boys, eh? No doubt the military is trying to hush this one up, but the public has the right to know. Women wanting to do their part in the war effort against the Germans sparks patriotism, and patriotism boosts volunteerism, preventing conscription. This could very well get the Canadian morale going, as a young Canadian girl heads to face the battle in Europe," Charlie asserted, exploring his journalistic subject from various possible angles.

"Okay, we're getting pictures taken, and we're getting-wait, is she mad? She's normal, right? We wouldn't want to use her as a kind of role model for women and men to get more involved if she's crazy...Valedictorian, natural athlete...Okay, I got it....And she passed all her training tests?" he finished.

"Did I ever tell you I love you? Our paper is going to sell like hot cakes! I just know it....If I want to see it, then I know the maritime public will...Do you have the place and time? Well, find out, and find out fast!" he pressed, "because I'm going to publicize the hell out of this... Anyone else know about her?"

"Get on it then...Call me back and don't forget, alright?" Charlie said, finally hanging up his phone. Removing the sheet from his typewriter, he reached across his desk to replace it with something far better. A blank sheet with the title, "Local Girl Becomes a Canadian Soldier."

Charlie knew the story was going to sell, and sell it did! Word spread fast not only within Saint John, but across the province. Little did Nat know that suiting up that last morning as a recruit in her Drill Order WE'37 uniform, that the public would be waiting for her. The morning, with its crisp air and glorious sunshine could not have been more perfect. Not a cloud in the sky, unusual for late November weather.

As their regiment began their marching descent from the base towards the city's centre, Nat felt like she was caught in a moment with the drums and horns before her.

That it was her time.

With her regiment walking up Moncton's Broad Street, Nat could hear the first roars of cheering and clapping coming from afar. Thinking that only a few would be in attendance, Nat was surprised to hear the sound of *many* people. Once the regiment came up over the hill, the sound heightened as hundreds of people stood lined up along the streets, waiting for their impending arrival. With all the publicity generated about a girl who fights like a man, all in the name of Canada, the public was intrigued. Nat had been the talk of the Maritimes, with people coming out as far as Newfoundland to get a glimpse of her. The photographers were there as well to capture who this young girl was.

What did she look like?

Why did she become a soldier?

"Pucker up fellas," Sergeant Rossi instructed to his regiment. "We are all getting the royal treatment today, thanks in part to our first female private. Enjoy the ride men. Walk proud. Show the people how we do things."

Even if it was their last day, Sergeant Rossi would still be their leader to the very end.

"YES, DRILL-SARGEANT!"

In anticipation, everyone in the regiment pulled back their shoulders, and their heads shot up all that much higher, as the public drew closer. People began pointing fingers as the regiment became visible in the distance. The question on most people's minds being, "where is she?" It was all so overwhelming to experience, making Nat smile in wonder. Despite her male attire, there was no mistaking her radiant feminine smile.

"There she is!" Nat heard a woman yell out in the crowd.

"You see Harold," one older woman scolded her husband loudly. "I told you a woman could do anything once we had the vote. Women can do anything, and do it even better than lang-blasted men!"

"About face! Don't forget to smile pretty boys," Sergeant Rossi ordered. The regiment turned and looked into the faces of the people who were waving and supporting them on. Nat felt tears come to her eyes as some people called directly out to her.

"You're doing a great job!"

"You make us proud!"

"We love you Natalie!"

People that she did not even know giving her so much love. What an unexpected, but wonderful surprise! This kind of admiration that Nat believed was impossible for any one person to receive was happening to her!

Keeping herself composed, Nat knew that she must remain focused, demonstrating maturity under such adulation. She was a soldier now, a representative of the Canadian Armed Forces.

It was then that she caught the gaze of a young girl, maybe eight or nine, looking up at her in amazement. The little girl, in a poor, torn dress, had stepped right up front to the street curb, to get a better look at Nat to see if she was real. The little girl wanted to see for herself if what the papers did say was true. As her heroine marched by, the little girl waved frantically to get Nat's attention. Unable to break with protocol by waving back, Nat reciprocated with a smile and a wink that was solely for her. Delighted, the little girl smiled back.

As the cameras continued to flash, the noise of the crowd increased as the regiment made their way to the Moncton's downtown centre. Pay attention, Nat thought to herself, and take it all in because this moment would not last.

As the faces in the crowd continued to smile back at her and her comrades, Nat's gaze followed along until she stumbled upon a lone figure immersed within the crowd unnoticed.

It was a young woman wearing a white hospital gown, her dark hair blowing gently in the wind.

Appearing ravaged from a sickness that plagued her mercilessly, it was her fragile demeanor that haunted Nat the most. How the pain of seeing her again sent a ripple through her soul.

You see me, don't you?

Are you proud of me?

With a tender face, her mother's eyes carried an incredible sadness that Nat could both see and feel deep within her heart.

Was she in pain still?

What would she say to Nat now?

Again, her mother's eyes spoke to her, whispering still.

Someday.

'Someday,' Nat whispered back with her own eyes. 'I love you mom, and I miss you.'

That is when Nat heard her mother's voice speak to her again, the noise of the crowd muted. *Someday we will see each other again.*

Was that a promise?

No answer would reach Nat though because as her eyes squinted and blinked under the sun's rays, so too did her mother disappear out of sight.

Gone.

Someday, Nat thought one last time to herself.

Forcing herself to face forward, Nat could see General Samson and his officers in the distance, quietly sitting in the main stands reserved for military personnel only. Nat knew that traditional protocol dictated that all military men present were expected to rise and salute the regiment in approval as they passed by, but no such action seemed likely today.

It was then that her Dad walked up onto these same main stands, with Eva by his side, followed by his own entourage that spread out into single line formation behind him. While General Samson and his officers sat in defiance, it would be her Dad, the General, who would lead the salute that the other men were forced to take notice. Although initially reluctant, the General's influence commanded every man to slowly rise to their feet and salute. Maintaining a cool exterior, the General could not wait to see Nat pass by. How he had been waiting for this moment.

Saluting his child, a soldier, as she walked on by.

Nat raised her hand to salute her superiors from above, but it was her Dad whom she was truly saluting. How he had introduced her to it all and taught her everything she knew. How incredibly proud she felt to have such a strong, brilliant, and honorable father whom everyone respected. He was a tough act to follow but Nat had proven herself on her own merit. Still, she would never tire of being known as the General's Daughter.

After the presentation of regimental colors had concluded, Nat and her comrades were swarmed by photographers and reporters from across the country.

"I just believe that we all have something to offer to this world, and that it is up to us to use the time we have to make our 'mark,'" Nat explained to one reporter. "I think-" she continued but was unable to finish.

"Yes, Miss Shaw?" the reporter urged, but it was too late. Nat had caught glimpse of him in the distance coming towards her and nothing else mattered.

"Excuse me," Nat smiled, not taking her eyes off of him.

"Wait, Miss Shaw-"

Nat's comrades watched to see where she was going and whom she was going to? Through the crowd they pushed to get to one another, until finally they stood face to face, only a few feet separating them.

"Hi!" Nat whispered softly, in disbelief.

"A promise is a promise."

"It is," Nat cried, running into his arms. Holding each other so tight, the men clapped teasingly, none of them aware that Nat had a steady 'beau' waiting for her.

Chris had made it!

Embarrassed, Nat turned to shush them, but none of them listened. Chris looked down at her, gently pushing her bangs aside to get a better look at her face, as Nat caressed his face.

Finally, they were able to touch one another again!

"You did it…I knew you would."

"I knew you would," Nat affirmed, making reference to his illness. Although still a little weak in recovery, Chris was strong.

"This is for you," he said, placing a ring on her finger. "It's not an engagement ring, but it is my promise. I want you to be mine, if you want me to be yours," Chris said intensely.

"Yes!" Nat nodded. Chris then took her face gently into both his hands and leaned in to kiss Nat. Like coming home, her lips were as sweet tasting as the best wine. Thirsty without her, Chris could drink from those lips forever.

"Nat!" Eva cried out, running over to embrace her own daughter. Locked deep into each other's eyes, Nat found it hard to break away, but Eva had to see her too!

"Eva!" Nat smiled, hugging her, as the General's entourage cleared their way through the crowd. Nat moved to go to him but he held out his arms and stopped her. The General had something to say first.

"I am so proud of you…I love my little girl." It was difficult for him, but the General finally said it, opening his arms to Nat who embraced him. "You did it! You are both the daughter and son I never had. You are *my* daughter."

Dad was proud of her and that meant the world to Nat.

"Chris, you are looking very well," Eva greeted, giving the boy a hug. Whether or not the General liked it, Eva knew that Chris was going to be family. It was best to start treating him that way.

"Thank you. I feel much better," Chris smiled humbly, before turning to the General. "Sir," Chris said, offering his hand to a man he wanted respect from. The General looked him over to size him up. So this is the man who would be replacing him? No longer the same cocky boy, the General could see the emerging man standing before him.

Nat waited for her Dad's approval.

The General reached out and gave a firm handshake.

"Nice to meet you again, sir."

"Likewise Mr. Woods," the General answered, as both Nat and Eva let out a simultaneous sigh of relief. "When is your deployment?"

"Two days."

"Well, let us go home for dinner to celebrate. Mr. Woods, if you would be so kind as to join us?"

"Yes sir. I would love to," Chris answered, smiling at Nat.

"Good. Shall we?" the General said, offering his arm to Eva.

"General?" Charlie Smith called out. "May we have a picture of you with your daughter?"

"Certainly. Come," the General ordered everyone in. Eva, Chris, the General's own entourage, and Nat's closest comrades who were standing by. What a picture! Within the faces of all who were in it, the moment captured their time of great joy. A time of hope and adventure towards a future that was waiting for them. How each and every one of them had completed another chapter in God's great story!

A fine dinner the Shaw family would have that evening, filled with laughter, stories, and many fond memories. Spending the next day with her Father, Nat asked permission to spend that final evening with Chris, to which her father obliged. It was four o'clock in the afternoon when Chris picked up Nat in his father's old car, but dressed in his best suit, he was as handsome as ever. Nat was dressed her best as well, with her hair cropped up, and a white dress that took his breath away.

Opening the door for her, she waved goodbye to her father and Eva who were both standing on the porch watching her go. As Chris took off down the road, heading out of town, the General and Eva turned to one another. No words were necessary.

A family now, they had one another, and the General would never be alone ever again. As he gently pulled Eva closer to him, the two of them smiled fondly at one another. That is when he leaned down and gave her a kiss.

"What do you say we go inside little lady?"

Eva smiled, following the General inside.

Stopping suddenly in front of a lively Irish pub in Sussex, Chris helped Nat out of the car. "Here the band plays all night long," he said excitedly, as they came in through the door, the place loud and filled with smoke. Being in the paper, Chris ensured Nat's privacy by picking a place where no one cared who you were, because they were so hammered! Chris could not have picked a more fun place to party. Sitting down at a table to hear the old Celtic tunes being played by the local band, a favorite, 'Mari-Mac' came on, and Chris had to dance. Grabbing

Nat by the hand, he pulled her up onto the floor. Already drunk by that time, the two of them could not stop laughing as they swung about the dance floor.

"You look like you need help," Chris slurred.

"No, you look like you need help!"

"Come here darling, and let me show you how it's done. Let me teach you the maritime way," Chris playfully said, pressing Nat close to him, so as to swing her about the room with everything he had. Not that Nat seemed to mind because he was still a good dancer, drunk or not. Besides, she was having so much fun.

> There's a sweet little lass
> And her name is Mari-Mac
> Make no mistake
> She's the girl I'm gonna attract
> A lot of other fellas
> Try to get her on her back
> But I'm thinking they will have ta' get up early…

With sweat dripping from their skin, Nat began to crave him the way she used to. Wanting him so bad, in every way that it hurt! As they twirled faster and faster, Chris swung his pelvis, dipping Nat down, before throwing her back up into his arms. That's when he mischievously slid his right hand down her backside to squeeze her bum, apologizing for nothing, as he wanted her too. Nat pretended to be shocked, but she liked it. Even with the sweat dripping off his chin, Nat found him incredibly sexy.

Chris continued playing to see how much he could get away with, Nat smiling, whispering with her eyes that she was up to his game. That Nat could equally play and keep up to him. Chris then knew that now was the time to leave. Any other plans he had for the evening would have to be scrapped. All he knew was that Nat wanted him and he wanted her.

NOW.

As their silhouette figures ran along the ocean's shore, having already taken a dip in its waters, the moon's rays lit a path to a cave that only the two of them knew. A place where no one would intrude, as it would just be the two of them now.

Chilled with anticipation, the fog kept them warm, as they hurried away from prying shadows to its secluded darkness. Starting a fire, Chris and Nat found themselves standing a few feet apart, looking into each other's eyes. Moving towards her, Nat took a breath to hide both her excitement and fear of the unknown. Reassuring, his hand touched her face, and Nat felt his warmth. As her heart began to race, so too did her body begin to tremble. Chris sensed her fear, as his body pressed up against hers.

"Are you all right?" he asked.

Nat looked down, her heart and soul ready to succumb, but anxiety loomed.

"I'm just...scared...I mean, I've never done this before....I've dreamt about it, but I don't know how...," Nat whispered, a little embarrassed.

"You know more than you know...It's inside you Nat. Just do what comes naturally. All you have to do is just let go and trust what happens," Chris earnestly answered. "Trust me."

"Kiss me," Nat responded taking a breath, knowing that Chris was going to take her breath away.

Chris kissed her with lips that were so tender and gentle, that any fears Nat had were put to rest. His passion moved her, and kissing him, Nat would not hold anything back. The intensity of their hunger for one another, suppressed for so long, had finally been set free.

Weak within his arms, Nat did her best to keep up, but his kisses were becoming aggressively swift. Fumbling to unbutton her own blouse, Chris could not wait, as he tore it open, so that he could touch her.

Off came his shirt as he took Nat's timid hand, and placed it on his chest. Nat could feel him, his heartbeat. That's when she leaned forward to kiss the nape of his neck. She wanted to not only feel him, but taste him! The tip of her tongue rolled along his skin, the woman in her, coming out.

Chris drew his head back, savoring every lingering, sensual touch. Feeling her way along every muscle of his body, Nat felt Chris tremble as he untied her bra, and took a moment to look at Nat as it slipped to the ground.

Did he like what he saw?

Chris was more than pleased, as Nat's body surpassed any fantasy he ever had. So firm and toned, every contour looked amazing. A perfect hour glass figure, Nat's round hips and large breasts made him crazy with desire for her.

Without holding back, Chris pulled her close with his right hand, and bent down to kiss Nat all over. Trying to catch her breath from the excitement and tingling that she felt, Nat felt herself dizzy from the warmth of his tongue. Surrendering to all that she felt, her head fell back as her mouth opened. No longer afraid, she moaned softly within his embrace, trusting him completely.

Reaching his hand up her inner thigh, Chris slid his finger up inside of her, caressing all that was warm and wet. Chris was unable to let go, and Nat did not want him to!

Feeling her knees buckle, Chris gently lowered her to the ground, their body heat keeping each other warm. Like a sculpture, Nat followed his lead, trusting him to do everything right. Helplessly rendered under the pressure of his touch, Nat felt everything seize within her, as a powerful wave gripped her from below. This new sensation was an ecstasy she had never before experienced. Pleasurable, it also left her weak.

Watching her reaction, Chris could no longer contain his own desire. Taking the remainder of his clothes off, both naked now, he came upon Nat, kissing her all over—breasts, neck, bellybutton, inner thighs. With eyes closed, Nat wanted it all never to end.

Excited that she was excited, Chris smiled in anticipation as he came inside of her.

Nat's eyes opened at this strange new feeling. A little painful at first, but mostly strange, Chris waited for her response.

"Don't stop," Nat said, stroking his face tenderly.

"Are you sure?" he asked, panting.

"I just feel a little out of breath. I'm okay," Nat whispered.

As Chris began to thrust, his breathing intensified along with Nat's. She was now his, and he was hers.

The pressure was building for both of them, as Nat clasped her nails into his back to keep him close. That's when he felt himself pulsating. The blood was beginning to rush in.

As he came within her, his eyes, ever watching Nat finally closed in release, as the wave that swept through his body was unstoppable. As his mouth opened, Chris collapsed exhausted within her arms.

After a moment. "Do you think this is what heaven is like?" Nat asked, caressing his hair.

"God, I hope so," he answered chuckling, panting still.

When he finally looked up, he found Nat looking deep into his eyes.

"I love you," she whispered.

"I love you too," Chris said without hesitation, stroking her cheek ever so gently. For the first time, Chris understood what it was like to *not* want to leave. His heart was hers, because all he wanted to do at this moment was stay inside of her.

As the hours passed away, Nat laid within Chris' arms throughout the night. As the fog crept past the moon's light, making it disappear in entirety behind its elusive veil, neither could sleep.

Afraid that in the blink of an eye, morning would come, and their night would end.

Whispering back and forth laughing, the two of them shared tales of their first impressions of one another. The times they shared, and how they had been waiting so long for one another.

"How beautiful are thy feet with shoes, O Prince's daughter," Chris smiled, always a smooth talker.

Nat laughed, but Chris shushed her gently as he was being quite sincere.

"The joints of thy thighs are like jewels, the work of the hands of a cunning workman," Chris spoke, mischievously sliding his hand up her inner thigh. "Thy navel is like a round goblet, which wanteth not liquor," his finger dipping into her belly button. Nat was intrigued.

"This thy stature is like to a palm tree, and thy breasts to clusters of grapes, that I will go up to the palm tree and take hold of the boughs." Nat giggled as he grabbed hold of her right breast with his whole hand.

"Thy neck is as a tower of ivory," he continued, his finger gliding along her neck. "How fair and how pleasant art thou, O love, for delights. The roof of thy mouth like the best wine, that goeth down sweetly. I am my beloved and my desire is toward her…" Chris kissed her.

"That is beautiful," Nat smiled. "Where did you read that?"

"The Bible. It's King David's son, Solomon, and his 'Song of Songs.' It is describing the love that a husband and wife share for one another…Where they delight in one another, in *all* ways. The way God intended."

"Is that your idea of a proposal," Nat giggled, but Chris stopped for a moment. The thought was not so bad.

"Maybe."

"Yes," Nat affectionately affirmed, kissing him once again.

It is the song of lovers that the two of them were singing, before they even met, let alone knew they were destined to be lovers.

It went like this:

One night as I was sleeping,
My heart awakened in a dream.

I heard the voice of my lover. He was knocking at my bedroom door. 'Open to me, my darling, my treasure, my lovely dove,' he said, 'for I have been out in the night. My head is soaked with dew, my hair with the wetness of the night.'

But I said, "I have taken off my robe. Should I get dressed again?"

My lover tried to unlatch the door and my heart thrilled within me.

I jumped up to open it.

My hands dripped with perfume, my fingers with lovely myrrh as I pulled back the bolt.

I opened to my lover…

Place me like a seal over your heart,

Or like a seal on your arm.

For love is as strong as death, and its jealousy is as enduring as the grave.

Love flashes like fire, the brightest kind of flame.

Many waters cannot quench love; neither can rivers drown it…

I am my Beloved…

As the morning came, the General and Eva stood at the train station anxiously waiting, but still, there was no sign of Nat. Just then, Chris pulled up in his car. Helping Nat out, she was dressed in full uniform, ready to go.

"Dad!" Nat called, running towards him.

"Hurry up girl. You are late. The train for Halifax is leaving in ten minutes," he scolded.

"I know, I'm sorry."

"Never mind sorry. You've got to go," the General pushed.

"I hate goodbyes," Nat confessed, "so I'll see you soon?"

"See you soon," Eva said, crying.

Giving everyone a quick hug, Nat assured once more that she would be fine overseas. Honestly excited at a new adventure that awaited her across the Atlantic, Nat knew that with her gifts, she would be coming back home. Without doubt in her mind, Nat would see them again.

Turning to Chris, Nat gave him one last, passionate kiss. It made the General uncomfortable as he looked away. It was awkward to see the two of them carry on like so, especially in public.

As the train began to move, Nat ran after it, stepping up onto its rail. As the train began to move further away, Nat put up her right hand.

"What does that mean?" Eva asked, as both Chris and the General responded back with a similar gesture.

"It means 'I love you' in sign language," the General said quietly.

Disappearing out of sight, the General wondered what Eva and Chris did not. Would their love be enough?

Would it be enough to save her from what lie ahead?

13

It all seemed so surreal when Nat stepped off the boat onto European soil for the very first time. Seasick and exhausted from the cold, wet conditions aboard her ten day journey across the Atlantic, it was still her dream finally realized. Landing in London, the British people waved to the 3rd Canadian Division's arrival as if greeting a long-lost cousin who had finally come home. Although officially independent from Britain for a decade, Canada still viewed Britain as a mother, because it was Britain that had given birth to Canada. Many Canadians, including Nat, felt a loyalty to help Britain in her hour of need.

Marching off the boats onto the docks, no one noticed Nat as different, which suited her just fine. Nat was here to do a job, just like any other man, which made her nothing special. In December, 1940, winter had fallen upon the city that was under siege. The arrival of their Canadian 'brothers' was greatly appreciated. Yet, Nat and her regiment would not see much of England after that, as they were sent immediately to the island's countryside to continue their initial training that had 'begun' in Canada. The only Europeans the Canadians would end up fighting those first eight months would be the men of the British Armed Forces through endless training exercises. It was espoused that the Canadians would be brought up to speed in terms of weaponry and military tactics before being sent in.

Initially expecting to have much in common, any conversing that occurred between the two countries those first few months could be best described as 'awkward.' Certainly Nat was treated scathingly by a few in the beginning, but her peers were quite willing to straighten the Englishmen out on her behalf. Strange, Nat found that the English talked funny, as some of them were just plain funny looking to her. Yet, how the English 'probably think the same of us,' she determined.

The Brits were expecting commonality, all too ready to embrace their fellow Englishman who would no doubt talk and think like them. Nothing could be farther from the truth, as the Newfies in particular, with their accents were very difficult to understand. Even people in New Brunswick found the Newfies hard to understand, but still.

Labeling the Canadians as loud, braggy North Americans, who drank far too much *all* the time, was a bit rude. Many brawls would break out those first few weeks. Nat and her comrades had to 'correct' the Brits mistaken attitudes, redefining themselves as merely an eager, enthusiastic group waiting for their chance to fight.

How long would the wait be?

As tensions subsided, and the two cultures worked through their differences and peculiarities to advance their training together as a united front, there was a growing impatience. The Canadians had come to fight, not simulate battle scenarios. Nat understood the significance of enhancing her technical knowledge of all military equipment, but she was frustrated.

How long would they have to wait?

It would take eight months before the Canadians would see any action. The German blitzkrieg over London had done and was still doing extensive damage to the city with its continuous aerial bombings. Walking past city dwellings, or what was left of them, Nat was disappointed to find that their platoon, along with the remaining Canadian platoons, were all being assigned to clean up duty. Piles of stone and rubble lay strewn about the streets from buildings that had been completely gutted from the explosions and fires, and their objective was to clean up the streets and any dead or wounded they came across.

As Nat began her search, she would not have to look very far. Bodies were strewn about as far as the eye could see, most often under the boulders and bricks. Getting help from Billy, they would lift it together to find a woman's head ripped open from the impact, or worse. One time Nat saw an arm reaching out from under another pile. Hurrying to dig the person out, Nat would find that the arm would be the only body part lying underneath. Blown apart from the impact, the body was simply in pieces everywhere.

A gruesome sight.

Looking at her surroundings, Nat could not help but wonder how anyone could do such a thing. These people are civilians with no chance of protecting themselves. It was all so *senseless*.

Anger was beginning to brew within her again.

God, where *are* you? Why are you letting this happen?

Day after day, for weeks on end, their detail to help 'clean' resumed.

How their Division's efforts seemed futile because it was never-ending.

It would be during October that Nat would encounter one of her worst days. Walking across a field of burnt grass, a cloud of black smoke engulfed another ruined area of London they were all about to enter. Apocalyptic in sight, the scene was a complete massacre. As a baby lay screaming beside his dead mother, others lay wounded or dead amongst the ashes. Nat intrinsically suspected that more bodies remained, yet to be dug out of the destroyed, collapsed buildings..

Never had Nat witnessed, nor imagined such destruction even in her worst nightmares. The crying of children, a sound one seldom forgets, echoed throughout her conscience.

Stopping at their designated post, the British General ordered Nat's regiment into battalion units of twenty-eight, instructing that citizens must be found first, dead or alive. Saluting, Nat headed towards the north-eastern part of the city. Grabbing a handkerchief from her pocket, Nat wrapped it tight around her face, to protect her mouth and nose from possible germs. Reaching out, her gloved hands picked up the lifeless arms of a woman who had been burned alive. So burned was she that when Billy lifted her charcoal legs, the woman's skin simply flaked off, revealing her bones. Flinching, the smell of her rotting flesh permeated, as they both hurried to throw her carcass on a wagon for cremation with the others.

"What a horrible way to die," was all Billy could say, his eyes cast downward.

"Yes," Nat said finally, turning away from the disposed body. At that particular moment, Nat longed to be anywhere else but here. "We're lucky to live in Canada," she concluded, walking away to continue on with her duties. Billy nodded in silent agreement.

As Billy walked on, Nat felt herself drawn to a child in the distance who had begun crying. A child that only she could hear, as no one else was responding to the little girl's voice. Going to this child without hesitation, Nat could barely make her out as the smoke clouded her vision. Coming closer, the child's eyes finally met hers, and there was no mistaking her identity.

In disbelief, Nat was shocked to see a girl staring back at her that she knew intimately. Bloodied from bruises which covered her arms, legs, and face, it was a painful reflection that Nat would just as soon forget.

Why had she returned?

With a despondent, weary face, Little Nat at eight years of age, was reaching out to her but Nat refused to step any closer. This was one child she was not prepared to help.

A hand reached out and touched her shoulder.

It was Billy.

"Nat? You okay?" he asked, observing her response carefully. Nat meekly turned back around to find that Little Nat had disappeared.

"Nat?"

Nat regained her composure and merely nodded, putting the handkerchief back on her face before walking away.

The image rattled her. Why was she seeing herself?

More so, why at that age? She was not that same vulnerable, scared, little girl anymore. Nat was a strong young woman now. Never again would she feel that way.

Get your bearings Nat, because with enough effort, you can make it go away. Just as you have always done.

As Billy followed behind Nat, the two continued to work side by side for the remainder of the afternoon. The rotten, burnt corpses of the dead becoming a smell as familiar to Nat as the sea water she grew up in all her life.

Amidst such suffering, Nat's heart would begin to open with it. Many things would come spilling out. The pain of her own wounds.

The suffering of her own heart.

By this point, a lot of the men in her regiment turned to drinking at the pub and getting laid to deal with their frustration over what they were seeing every day. The men just wanted to feel good for a change.

That is when Nat would think of Chris the most. When she saw some of her comrades dancing with the girls, loneliness would creep in. Nat had opportunities, as she was asked often to dance. Although tempted at times, Nat would always decline. No matter how lonely she became, all other men would only be a substitute for Chris.

Chris was the one she wanted.

In the beginning, the nights seemed peaceful. Yet, as the daylight hours became shorter, the nights would last longer. With it, the darkness grew stronger in presence. When the bombs were heard in the distance, shadows began to lurk in unseen places.

Nat suspected that they were getting closer, as if coming only for her.

As Nat slept, she found herself dreaming of walking through a house that had all of its doors closed. It was the house of her foster mother, and it was darker than even she had remembered. As Nat pushed past the cobwebs and dust-covered furniture, she drew open the covers to the dining room's window. In filtered a ray of light so warm, that it sparkled over every facet of the room. The darkness had dissipated and Nat felt safe.

Was she?

As an adult, Nat fearlessly inspected every window opening. As an adult she had more power, a developed objectivity that only time can impart.

That's when Nat noticed one door that would not be lit by virtue of natural light alone. That this door was closed and could only be opened by one person.

It was the door to Little Nat, and Nat was haunted by its sight.

Slowly walking closer, she was scared to look inside, but a calm was urging her forward. This same door had been shrouded in darkness for so long.

Compelled, Nat reached for the door knob, finding to her surprise that she had the sole power to unlock it. How strange that she had never tried opening it after all this time.

Opening the door ever so carefully, Nat's heart sank at the vision before her. Sitting alone on cold, wooden floors, Nat saw a girl she knew long ago. Abandoned but not forgotten, the child did not notice her.

At that moment, sweet little Mary entered the room. "Mary!" Nat smiled fondly.

Her only childhood friend, Mary sat down next to Little Nat, as the two read quietly alongside one another. Little Nat put her arm around her 'buddy,' a memory recalled but slightly altered.

That is when Little Nat looked up, and her sad, grave eyes were penetrating. How she wanted to reveal herself.

What Nat could not understand was why her former shadow insisted on making contact?

Why could they not remain two separate entities? A present and former self, cut off from one another?

A loud thud in the next room startled Nat.

The woman had come home.

Looking back down at the tiny figure that was her former self, Nat tried to warn the two helpless girls away from what was coming.

"Go. Get out of here, quick! She's home," she pressed, but the girls did not hear her. Anger filled Nat's heart as she stood boldly in front of the doorway to act as a barricade to a woman that she despised.

Still.

There was no stopping the past.

As Mary scurried out, Little Nat was beaten for no apparent reason, and Nat found herself having to look away.

"Think you're smart? Think you're better than me?" the old woman snarled, exhausted at her own exertion. "You ain't gonna do nothing with your life, because you're jus' a stupid orphan. I have a better chance of makin' something than you do…Since I can't, what makes you think you will? I'm gonna put this in the trash where it really belongs," the woman scowled, leaving with Nat's reading book.

In the blink of an eye, the scene had ceased and all was quiet in the house once again.

"DAMN YOU!!!" Nat screamed at the apparition, her voice echoing throughout the house.

The woman was gone and only Little Nat remained, calling out with eyes that reflected a truth Nat neither wanted to see nor feel.

Little Nat would not avert her eyes.

"I am beautiful inside," she finally spoke. "God and mommie told me so, no matter what she says."

How those eyes overwhelmed her. Astonished by her own strength and resilience, Little Nat had whispered a revelation she had been unwilling to hear all these years.

I am beautiful.

After all this time, Nat had believed the old woman's lies.

Nat's heart *was* a good one. She was not evil. She was not a bad person. All were lies.

Why did Nat have the capacity to empathize with others but not herself?

"Naaatalieeeee," a hoarse voice growled from behind, causing Little Nat to disintegrate immediately as the room went to black.

Nat turned to look behind, knowing that her inner demon had been set loose. It was what she was most afraid of if she went back. Horrified, Nat watched in terror as its entity dragged its skeletal figure towards her. Blackened from the decay, its eyes were blood red and its fanged teeth were manic.

"You thought you got rid of meee?" It spewed its venom. "No one can kill me off!" Paralyzing her, Its claws clasped around her throat and squeezed.

Breathing erratically, perspiration soaking her uniform, Nat forced herself awake.

So it began that night, and every other night after that.

Nat would no longer have peace of mind. Unable to sleep, her anxiety and insomnia grew. Fearful of It returning, Nat took brief naps during the day, under the warmth and protection of the sunlight. If her Dad or Chris were here, she would be protected by their strength, but Nat was on her own, and she was scared.

Where was God when she needed him most?

Why didn't he hear her?

As the weeks past, Nat was beginning to get a sinking feeling. That a storm was brewing all around her, and that her little boat would not be able to last past the night. Soon, she may very well be in the water. Could she keep herself afloat in its thrashing sea?

Would God save her from drowning?

Patrolling London's night streets, Nat knew that she had fallen into an abyss that kept her prisoner. With all hope fading, the magnitude of her sadness was only heightened by the prospect that she was never going to be rescued. No one was coming for her and the isolation of her pain felt like she was dying a slow death. That she had become one of the living dead.

It was at times like these that she wanted her mother. If her mother came back, she would be saved again.

How?

By being beautiful in your eyes, thus mine own, no longer would I be mired down in all this ugliness.

What happened to my beauty? Where did it go?

Like the time when Nat twirled about in her best Sunday dress outside of the church. Only five at the time, Nat had her beauty then. Nat's soul sparkled a vibrancy and innocence that glowed with her every move. As the sun cascaded down, her skirt sailed magnificently, soaring through the air with the grace of a bird. She was vulnerable, and her mother watched with beauty in her eyes…Nat was free and she was beautiful.

"Nat."

Flinching at his voice, Nat turned to find Billy looking down at her.

"Get some sleep…"

Nat pulled her rifle closer to ensure it was still there.

"You've got to sleep, you know."

"I'll sleep later," Nat resolved. Awake, Nat was in control and could keep her wits about her.

"Here." It was Billy's flask. "It'll knock you out. I'll watch your back," Billy assured.

Nat was so tired. "You'll watch?"

"Yeah," he reassured, concerned at how black her eyes were.

'Perhaps it was all getting to her,' Billy thought. Although he had never really seen Nat rattled, she was different now. Mute practically, Nat's exhaustion rested with a struggle that he did not fully understand. Certainly the war with its civilian casualties was a devastating thing to witness day in and day out, but if you shut off your emotions, do your duty, one gets used to it all. Numb, it no longer moves you anymore the way it once used to.

Nat seemed not able to separate herself.

Nat had said literally nothing these last few weeks, and it was troubling because she was breaking down before his eyes.

Taking the flask, Nat drank its shot. Burning down her throat, Nat coughed at its sting.

"It's good stuff, eh?" Billy laughed. This was the first time in a long time that he had seen Nat smile. It was then that she looked up at him.

"I needed that."

What a relief it was to know that she could depend on Billy to look out for her.

Just like a brother he was.

"How quiet everything is tonight," Billy observed, scanning his surroundings. Lying on the bricks inside another building that had been bombed into rubble by German planes, the open roof that had been blown off revealed a clear night of luminescent stars.

"If only my Dad could see me now."

"Do you wish he were here with you?" Nat asked.

"Well, I suppose he is…He died when I was twelve. He taught me everything I know. Farming, hunting, fishing, God…He served in the last war, but rarely spoke of it."

"How did he pass?" Nat asked gently.

"Got sick with scarlet fever," Billy said looking down. "Worked hard all his life. A good man, I remember that much of him. I can still picture his face inside my head, after all these years. I imagine he is watching me, seeing what I'm up to. He raised me to be a farmer. I don't know what he would have thought of me being a soldier now, like he was at one time…Who knows really?" Billy resided, pulling the blanket over his legs to keep warm, as the fire's small flames flickered.

"My mother died when I was seven," Nat confessed, not taking her eyes off the fire. "She died of cancer, in a hospital bed. I lay beside her when she died. I saw her take her last breath, and then she was gone."

Billy slowly sat up. Nat had never revealed anything personal to anyone before. He had no idea what her story was.

"I was an orphan, but I was not adopted right away by the General. After her funeral, I was sent to live with a foster family in Nova Scotia. A woman with two children, one who was deaf, I believe, from a mother who beat her. She was a drunk who beat me, daily."

How her story made sense. Nat was different from any other girl he had ever encountered, and her propensity for fighting had a foundation and origin.

"I don't remember when or exactly how I changed. I just know that I became altered at some point, and just woke up one day and decided that I had had enough. That I was done," Nat spoke painfully.

Nat felt awkward telling Billy the intimate details of her life, but she needed to tell someone. It was time. Billy possessed an integrity and compassion that made him more than trustworthy. It set him apart from the others in the regiment.

"I hated her so much Billy, that one night, when she was looking for me, I came after her from behind. I took the kitchen knife that she dropped and when she charged me, it went right through."

Billy listened intensely.

"I remember her bleeding on the floor before me, and that I felt nothing for her," Nat recalled, lost in her own recollection. "Everything inside me had gone cold. There was no pity, no remorse, not even fear anymore. Only anger…As I lifted the knife above my head, I wanted her to die. She was not going to hurt anyone ever again," Nat's voice trailed off.

"What happened Nat?" Billy asked, intensely waiting for her answer.

"I was lost Billy," Nat explained carefully. "I felt lost. In the dark."

"Yes?"

"That's when the light came."

Billy waited silently.

"The light came into my darkness."

Billy did not understand.

"I saw my mother. She was there. When I saw her I stopped everything. I no longer wanted to do it…As I lowered my knife, she disappeared…Vanished. My foster mother was struggling to breathe, so I ran to get help. I ran down the road to a neighbor's farm…"

"What happened to her Nat?" Billy's grave voice enquired, dreading her possible answer.

"She survived…" Nat said, a quiet in her voice. "I was sent to live at the orphanage. I was eight years old."

The fire was fading fast.

"I didn't kill her, but how I wanted to. Why? What child has that in them?" Nat knew that she felt ugly inside. That is why she had kept it a secret for so long, but it had finally caught up with her. "I have this anger that I can't shake free from, that returns again and again, staying with me. I have carried it for so long that I don't know what life would be like to not have it. Who would I be without it?"

"You would be Natalie," Billy answered. "Free, the way God intended for all of us."

"Free?" Nat asked a glimmer of hope in her voice. "How?"

"Repent and ask him to take it from you because you are tired of carrying it. In His grace, I believe He wants to heal you. Hand it over to Him, because our sins have already been paid for by Jesus. All we have to do is let go," Billy spoke with the power of the spirit coming through his words. Raised by Christian parents who had explained the New Testament in full during his young life, Billy had an understanding and wisdom that was beyond his years. "You didn't kill her. That's a good thing."

The thing was Nat knew she could do it. Hurt someone with the intent to kill. That it was still in her.

"Albert…"

How could God possibly forgive Nat if she could not even forgive herself?

"I think we all have that in us Nat," Billy interceded. "When the time comes, some situations will bring out the worst in us. We're seeing that now with this war. You can't escape its misery. We see it every day…Whatever you felt compelled to do at the time, you have to remember that you were just a child."

Nat wondered if she would ever see her mother again? If she were to die tomorrow, would God allow her to come up to Heaven? Had she done enough good during her life to make up for the bad?

"My Dad once told me, just before he died, that evil touches us all. None of us are free from its infliction and suffering. Born into a broken world, we will become broken by it. We will be in a constant war against the darkness, fighting for our own hearts. If we don't guard our hearts, the darkness will take over, and we've lost everything. The heart is our soul, and without it, our soul will fall. That is why we pray to God for strength of heart. After the battle for your heart has been fought, we will emerge victorious, because we will not have taken the darkness we fought with us. You're still a good person Nat. Your heart is still here, and it is good" Billy empathetically explained.

"Good person…" Nat repeated, trying to affirm for herself that she was. "You do understand," Nat smiled faintly, relieved. "Most people think that I am crazy because they don't understand and they don't want to Billy. My mother, like your father, is watching over us, and God will continue to protect us from every battle," Nat concluded. "The battle for our hearts, the key to our soul."

"Yes," Billy nodded, as Nat finally understood. It was a relief for Billy to share his beliefs with someone who understood and felt the same beliefs about God as he did.

"Thank you." Nat handed the flask back, but Billy knew Nat wasn't talking about the drink. Billy was the first to be open to Nat when she first came into the military. God had bestowed Billy with the gift to see people from a spiritual heart rather than a physical, temporal perspective.

"Get some sleep," he urged. Nat lay her head down and closed her weary eyes. As the light of the stars faded from her consciousness, Nat quickly drifted into a deep sleep that would not be wakened by the shots fired throughout the night.

Billy was on guard, so there would be no nightmares tonight.

The next evening would not feel so safe. Nat would keep her guard up no matter how exhausting, all the while, the question lingering at the back of her fatigued mind.

What if she just let go? Handed it all over to God?

Would she open herself up to being hurt and nearly destroyed again by people?

Would she die?

Suddenly the street lights went out, and a howl lingered through the night air. Something was coming, and only the full moon from above could reveal its shape. Assuming the firing stance with pistol drawn, its inhuman silhouette glided closer towards her at an astonishing speed.

Armed and ready, the creature finally stepped out of the dark.

Only a few yards away, Nat was taken back to see that it was a red fox who stood before her. Withdrawing her weapon, she breathed a sigh of relief. Foxes were known for not being troublesome, as they were very shy. Despite staring at her right now, the fox would ultimately want nothing to do with her. As Nat lowered her weapon and turned her back to begin walking away again, the fox silently slinked behind, its young, scraggly looking figure following. Nat feeling its presence turned around swiftly, stopping the animal in its tracks.

The animal looked to her with a deep sense of urgency.

"What little fella? What is it? Do you want food? I don't have any," Nat said, unsettled as she saw the fox creep timidly towards her, wanting to get closer. Nat was afraid.

Did it see her as food?

Perhaps it was so hungry that it would attack her?

As Nat carefully backed away, the fox did something that was completely uncharacteristic. The emaciated animal began to yelp to her, its calls demanding her attention.

Nat turned her back and began walking away. The animal persisted. Turning back around, Nat was frightened at the fox moving in only a few feet away from her.

"What is it? What do you want?" The fox was startled. Its beauty had captivated Nat a bit as her fear dissipated. Ravaged, the red fox radiated a strength and innocence that was mesmerizing at closer inspection. Nat was drawn to its presence.

The animal cried out again, trying to talk to Nat.

Trying to reveal something to her.

Encircling, the fox had Nat's full attention, but was she listening? Was she ready to see?

This was something new and it was too much.

"I have to go…Go. Beat it!" Nat instructed her newfound friend. The fox stopped walking, understanding her words, "I have to go."

As Nat walked away, the fox called out again, unmoving, one final time. Once a good distance, Nat turned to look back. In the middle of the street the fox remained, watching her go.

Walking away, Nat could not help but feel the presence of God all around her. Nat remembered that

God can take on any life form, at any time, if he wants to communicate with us.

Communicate with her?

Nat had been praying to God to show her what was beautiful about herself. Was there anything to love about her?

What did she look like deep inside if God were to reveal and cast her mirrored reflection? That's when Nat heard the answer whispered into her from amongst the dark.

You are the fox.

God had revealed in His mysterious way, what she had just prayed to him to see. The little fox was in rough shape, and its resiliency was never more beautiful. With golden hair, the fox's eyes spoke of a depth that even Nat was unaware of. Graceful in movement, the fox carried a dignity that was deserving of redemption.

Nat's beauty had tried to reach out, but unknown to her, Nat pulled back afraid to go any closer to something so unfamiliar.

As Nat turned around to go back, it was too late. The little fox had disappeared back into the dark.

The very next evening Nat headed out again in search of the little fox to no avail. Many more nights would follow without any luck. Seeking, the steps in her journey were becoming increasingly dark.

Would God answer her prayer again?

After many weeks, she headed out once again, unaware of what was coming for her that night. That there would be no place to hide to escape from its truth. As the wind hissed its vehemence, Nat was too tired to take notice. The fox was on her mind again. To everyone else but Billy, Nat must have appeared crazy. All she could think about was that fox and how she had to find it!

Walking alone, Nat looked up to see the street lights suddenly flicker out. The moon, covered by foreboding clouds, offered little light. Nat felt her heart race, but she persisted onwards, in a trance, obsessed by it all. Walking alone through the darkness, her determination was impenetrable.

That's when Nat heard them.

Their wailing, restless, and sinister grumbles. They had Nat in their sights, the whites of their eyes visible only to them. The skin flaked from their bones, as the evil behind their black eyes began to bleed. Nat knew at that moment, she was not alone, and that it would be another night of grappling with them. All six of them encircled.

Standing her ground, Nat would not go down without a fight.

"You stupid bitch," one hissed at her. "Why don't you just kill yourself, you worthless girl!"

Fear turned into anger. "You want me? I'm not going anywhere…Come and get me…"

All six lunged at her, and although she punched two to the ground, Nat was hit from behind, and they began to pulverize her, relentless in their attacks. Although she valiantly fought, Nat was exhausted from her struggle with her own demons. This was a battle she could not win on her own.

"God, help me…"

Just then, a piercing light shot from the sky rippled through the night air with the speed of sound. The attack had stopped, as all six of the demons turned to look behind them, blinded by the light that was coming to expose and eliminate them. With petrified eyes, the shadows screamed in terror, scurrying away, but the light caught up to them, dissolving them on the spot.

As Nat slowly stood up, she could see a vague figure of her rescuer. It was the silhouette of a man fast approaching in the night air. Floating across the street towards her, a gust of wind blew, draining all blood from her face. Instantly cold, the figure was heading straight for her! Taking out her pistol, the man seemed undeterred.

The realization began to sink in. If He wasn't afraid of her gun, then He wasn't human.

He was sweeping in.

Whatever he was, Nat knew one thing.

Run!

Putting her pistol back into its holster, Nat took off like a shot, sprinting for her very life. Too scared to look back, He pursued, his wind chilling the hairs on the back of her neck. Leaping over stones and rubble, Nat had to outrun him! Seeing the fence ahead, it was too late to turn back. Hurdling forward with a mighty jump, Nat grabbed hold of the post, to climb frantically up, pulling herself over. Jumping down, she landed on the other side.

The street lights faded to complete black.

Wanting to get up and run, Nat sat completely still when she heard His panting on the other side of the fence. Crippled by fear, Nat's hand trembled as she fumbled to take her pistol out. The light of the moon cascaded down upon her.

Flying over the fence in a burst of energy, He sailed so fast above her that Nat started firing randomly into the dark until her clip was nearly out.

"Who are you!? Show your face you coward!" Nat yelled, rising to her feet. That's when the dark figure started to come towards her. "Stop or I'll shoot!" she yelled, unflinching.

Death crept in closer. "I mean it!"

Nat fired her last two remaining shots but they went straight through, the bullet's whistle echoing long down the alleyway's narrow path. Nat's arms slowly dropped in disbelief. It was then that he came before her, stepping into the light.

Petrified, Nat looked up at a man who was beyond a giant.

"What do you want!?" she demanded fiercely, throwing her pistol away and raising her fists.

"I have come for you."

That was all Nat needed to know. Charging him immediately, Nat attacked him with every ounce of strength she had in her. A magnificent fighter, her skills were graceful in its movements, as her explosive fear left him shell-shocked. Punching and kicking him full force, Nat's blows were relentless. Barely able to keep up with her, Nat made his nose bleed instantly with her left foot kick, and that's when he let her have it. Striking the palm of His right hand into her chest, Nat flew ten feet back, slamming hard against the building wall, before falling to the ground on her stomach.

What the hell was that!?

'Breathe in, breathe out,' she told herself. Catch your breath! Get back up!

The man remained standing where he was, waiting patiently.

Nat got back up. This was her life. Get up and fight or He'll take you!

Again she charged, running towards him and this time He was ready. As they exchanged blows back and forth, both began to tire.

"Who are you!?" Nat demanded again, spitting out blood. "Reveal yourself to me!"

Still, the man wouldn't, and so they fought on. He was hurting, but not nearly as much as Nat. She wore on, exhausted, but she would not quit. As her fist came for him, He grabbed hold and crushed the bones in her hand. Nat screamed in agony, "Who are YOU!?"

The man finally spoke again. "I am the one you have been seeking."

"Liar!" Nat vehemently hissed, swinging at him with her right fist.

This time He caught her, and held on tight, not letting go.

"Let me go!" Nat screamed, struggling to shake her body free. How she just refused to give up her own pain.

"I want to set you free, if you'll let me."

"I don't even know who you are! What do you want with me?" she asked crying, slowly falling to her knees exhausted.

Broken.

"Do you trust me?"

"You broke my hand...How am I supposed to trust you!?" Nat asked, terrified. She was defenseless now, stripped of all her strengths that she relied so heavily upon. God-given abilities that can be taken away if not used for His intent.

Nat was totally vulnerable to Him.

"I have come for you, because you are most precious to me. You have been lost, carrying the weight of your pain for so long. All you do is fight to keep it. Do you want me to take it for you?"

Nat couldn't move, let alone have the strength to utter a single word. She was too was tired from such a savage fight.

Still.

Whatever it took to encounter her in a real way where they could confront one another in direct relationship, He would do. Whatever it took to release her, He would do. How much fear she carried, causing such rebellion in her heart to her own detriment. Slowly Nat raised her eyes to see for the first time, His eyes. All this time she had seen the face of her opponent, but did not recognize His face. All this time she thought she knew Him, but she didn't know His face, or recognize His character at all.

Nat was about to become acquainted with who He really was. Searching for the truth, Nat became lost in eyes that spoke so much, transcending her body and soul. He knew her intimately. In His eyes she saw not only all she had been through, but the glory and beauty that was distinctly hers. An inheritance from royalty. Nat finally understood all that He had designed her for. Nat believed in her beauty for the very first time, and realized finally where it was that she belonged.

It was to Him

Unable to take her eyes off Him, Nat wearily crawled over to His feet. No longer running away, hiding, Nat had been found again after being lost for so long.

"I know who you are…I am sorry," Nat cried, closing her eyes.

Tenderly smiling down at her, He touched her face. Cold for so long, Nat felt a warmth race through her being that only His amazing grace could give. A few drops of rain gently tapped her face as the weight she had felt and carried for so many years was finally released. Nat's broken hand, along with the rest of her body was instantly healed.

When Nat opened her eyes, she discovered that He was gone, the light sprinkle of the rain soothing as it cleansed her.

Rising up to her feet slowly, that is when Nat felt someone watching her. Slowly turning her eyes, Nat was stunned to see the fox sitting in the middle of the street again, its eyes watching her. As the rain picked up, the fox refused to go. Nat knew then that the creature was waiting for her, and this time, she would not be afraid. Alertly walking over, Nat bent down cautiously in front of the animal. The two were now face to face. Reaching out her hand, Nat timidly touched the fox's face, running her fingers through its wet, dirty coat. Finally, she had encountered her own unmistakable beauty reflected in the fox, that was both raw and very real.

It was time.

As the fox broke away, it turned to wait for Nat to follow her.

There is more to show me?

Nat rose to her feet once more and trusting completely without knowing, she followed the fox, God, who would lead the way.

As the two walked through complete darkness, the fox guided her into the wilderness, remaining a steady light to her path. Delving deeper, into the darkness of her own heart, the temperature dropped, and Nat began to see her own breath.

That is when the whispers began, echoing throughout the darkness.

"Do not go any further…It will kill you"

"You…Devil"

"Stupid orphan…"

"Ugly…"

"God doesn't care about you, because you don't matter…"

"No one could possibly love you…"

"Boys only want you for one thing…"

"You're not worth it…"

"You're not good enough…"

"You are too much to handle…"

Staying behind the protection of the fox, as the two delved deeper through the darkness, God, by her side was revealing the truth of these verses.

Lies.

Every whisper that she had been told and believed, as they still resonated within her heart, were lies.

Told and reinforced by the Enemy throughout her life, to keep her hostage. To keep her enslaved in chains within the dark. To destroy her potential and God-given destiny.

Knowing the truth now, Nat looked at the darkness all around her. No longer weighted down, Nat stood boldly and used her God-given authority to shut them up once and for all.

"LIES! You are LYING to me, and I'm not going to accept your lies as the truth NO MORE!" Nat screamed out loud, as a hush filled the darkness. "You will no longer inhabit my heart. Your reign is finished, beginning now."

With that, Nat felt the darkness go, as light began to stream in from above. That is when she heard it. The voice of a tiny cry that could now be heard since the dark no longer surrounded the center core of her being.

"Help me," a lone child cried.

"I'm coming," Nat yelled out, turning to the fox who would lead the way.

"No one is going to hurt you," Nat called, drawing the knife from her boot. "I promise," Nat instructed, her heart still pounding.

At a distant tree, a young girl lay curled up by its trunk. Nat felt her breath cease, as she refused to believe her own eyes. Fully awake, her mind was playing tricks on her.

It was Little Nat looking back at her, and she was crying.

"What is this?" Nat whispered in desperate confusion, holding back her own tears. "What's going on?" she asked the fox that was now sitting.

The child did not answer.

"Why am I here?"

The fox was there to heal an old wound, but it was up to Nat to feel rather than deny the pain. As the child continued to cry, Nat had to look away, as it was much too painful to see her former self, covered in bruises.

How she despised her vulnerability!

"Why do you refuse to see me?" Little Nat asked.

Nat could not answer.

"You learned how to protect yourself and others because of me. Don't you remember?"

"Remember what?" Nat cried in anguish, the pain too great.

"The day you decided to hide me away."

Nat did not understand.

"You locked me up in a place where no one could reach me, but you then threw away the key. You protected me, you protected yourself, and that is good. The thing is though, you never came back...Why did you leave me behind?"

Nat knew the truth.

"You made me disappear into the great depths of your heart, permanently, and in its cold, dark waters, you abandoned that part of your heart. Why was I not worth coming back to?"

Nat looked down, the aching pain taking over her entire body. "To go through that all again, to believe and hear all the lies I was told, I truly didn't think I was worth it," she whispered through her tears.

"You were. Your heart is good. It has been wounded, and needs to be healed, but your heart has always been good."

Nat felt her body collapse to the ground. "I find that hard to believe...God, I'm so tired...Tired of fighting everyone...I thought I could, but I can't save anybody, not even myself," Nat cried out in her brokenness.

"I've failed myself," she spoke, looking directly at Little Nat. "What is it that you want from me?" Nat whispered. "Death? I was happy where I was, with my mother. Why did God take her from me? I want to go back there. To go home. Before things went wrong. Go back to a simple life I had hoped I would live. The life that I truly wanted, but can't seem to have. It's like my life has never been my own to choose…

For so long I have feared death, always running, always focused on excelling so that I could prove to God that I was worthy…That I would earn my place in Heaven, before I died. To Heaven where there is no more pain, and love does not have to be earned. To be loved so completely-It's all I've ever been after.

I think I've done my time. I've earned that peace. I just want to go. Tell me why God won't let me go? Send my regiment to the battlefield, so that I can die, and leave this world that tears me apart."

"God knows…He has watched and suffered with you. That is why He came. For all of us, so that we may all find freedom, if we want it."

"I am sorry for what I have done."

"You have been forgiven. The question is can you forgive yourself?"

Nat nodded.

"Have you not suffered long enough?"

"Yes."

"It is time."

Nat exhausted, slowly moved in towards her, and the two embraced one another.

"What happened to you was not because you were a bad person. You have a good heart," Little Nat reassured, stroking Nat's hair. As Nat hugged Little Nat, she felt the fur of the fox run through her fingertips. As Nat opened her eyes, she stared in wonder at the fox who was now Little Nat. It was her true self, redeemed, the fox's renewal undeniable. With a shiny, thick coat, the fox's beauty had been fully restored to its rightful glory.

"I have a good heart." Nat finally believed it when she said it this time.

"Close your eyes," Little Nat whispered into the night air from above.

Nat did as she was told.

The rain began pouring down hard, soaking her clothes. Raising her arms to the sky, Nat embraced the rain that was cleansing her, redeeming her soul. Laughing uncontrollably, Nat felt herself as free as a bird. It was amazing!

As she opened her eyes, the rain suddenly ceased. All street lights were back on full, and Nat was back on the street, just as she had been before.

All was peaceful and quiet.

Calm.

As it should be.

As the clouds cleared, a myriad of stars sparkled down on her.

"Nat, you are as beautiful as the stars," God whispered to her. "You are beautiful to me."

"Thank you. Thank you God," Nat smiled back at her heavenly one. "I love you. This night you have offered me is amazing, just as you are, and I will never doubt you again."

14

Freedom was the strangest feeling.

Nat finally felt for the first time in months that she was going to be all right. Watching over her always, never forsaken, Nat was not alone. Crawling into her sleeping bag, Nat's eyes closed as soon as her head hit the pillow that next night. As Billy headed out in the morning with their Division, he let Nat be. Nat would sleep easy that night, well into the next day. Billy would return later that evening to find Nat still sleeping.

The next morning when Nat did finally awake, she felt much better. It was the best sleep she had felt in months. No longer were her eyes bloodshot because the nightmares had finally been put to rest. No longer on edge, everyone noticed the change. Nat went about her business much more relaxed, whatever plaguing her the last few weeks, apparently resolved.

A renewed and redeemed Nat was beginning to emerge. One who seemed more confident in herself, and more relaxed in her own skin. Nat was actually smiling, a rarity. Nat was also showing greater vulnerability when it came to talking with and helping the locals. No longer on guard, she was openly affectionate with young children in particular, demonstrating her maternal, feminine side. Nat's natural softness was coming out, and it was perplexing, because none of the guys had ever seen her like that before.

'Nat had to act like a guy to be taken seriously,' Billy thought. How an even greater respect for Nat was growing, *because* she still acted like a woman.

Not a woman trying to be a man.

Did it matter?

As long as she got the job done, female or male, different or not, did it matter?

As news spread that lonely Christmas of Pearl Harbor's bombing, and the Americans' inclusion into the Allied effort, everyone could not help but wonder if they would ever see action at all?

Were the Canadians only here because they were fine workers or were they here to fight?

Certainly the arrival of the Americans that spring, 1942, offered a refreshing change. A new breed of North American for the English to adapt to, the Americans seemed worse to the Brits than the Canadians with their 'loud' behavior.

As training continued, and tensions brewed, no one was aware that Lieutenant General A. G. L. McNaughton, Canada's Senior Officer in Britain, alongside Lieutenant General Cedar, Commander of the 1st Canadian Corps, were in talks for an invasion. With General Sir Alan Brooke, Chief of Britain's Imperial General Staff and all military strategic planning, and Chief of Britain's Southeast Command, Lieutenant General Bernard Montgomery, a planned invasion had been devised, and it was the Canadians who were being asked to lead it. An assault aimed for launch in three months time, the plan would mark the largest amphibian invasion of its kind ever.

"Our Prime Minister, Mackenzie, will not sanction this unless he is convinced that it is not only worthwhile, but its success can be guaranteed," McNaughton asserted conclusively at the end of the negotiation meeting. "Let me talk to him first."

"I understand," General Brooke responded, showing McNaughton and Crerar out. Once out of the room, the two men were able to speak plainly.

"If we pull this off," General Brooke stated candidly, once the door was closed, "which I believe we will, this raid will certainly get the Russians off our back to do something. Besides, the Canadians are at present the best trained soldiers in the world, so they are perfect to lead it."

"Yes, but inexperienced in war," General Montgomery objected.

"The last war, that little country of seven million made a name for itself, producing some of the most courageous soldiers the battlefield had ever seen. Call it naiveté, innocence, who knows? They probably had no idea what they were getting into when they showed up here with their moth-eaten, hand-me-down uniforms, and hole-infested boots. Hell, they didn't even have a military back then, but if they fought like that with obsolete weapons and little training, imagine what they could do now. They want to prove themselves standing on their own feet, no longer Britain's child. Mackenzie King is trying to be a political player in this conflict, but he's not. I'll send in five thousand Canadians, a thousand

British Commandos, and a few Army Rangers. Let the Canadians lead it."

"What if they do not have victory that day? No one has ever done this before, which means there is much room for failure, because we simply don't know."

"I believe," General Brooke started, "that the Canadians will improvise the best. If nothing else comes out of this, we'll have a clearer idea of how to do this kind of invasion better for the future. Even with some casualties, we'll receive less flack than if we sent in the Americans, or ourselves. We don't want to risk damaging political alliances…Good luck to you in Africa."

"Thank you General," Montgomery nodded, as the two men shook hands.

Soon it would be official as the men turned to their map one last time.

The target?

Dieppe, France.

"So what artillery am I going to have?" General Roberts enquired, walking down the long corridor to the briefing room where his assigned troops were gathered.

"It appears sir they are only going to give some fighter and light bombers, and eight destroyers with the four-inch guns," the Corporal read from his file brief.

"That's it? What the hell is that? I asked for battleships and heavy bombers," Roberts retorted.

"Supposedly the admiralty is short on ships and they won't risk losing one on an expedition which will not help them for their war at sea," the Corporal responded.

"Terrific. We're all fighting the same war, just not together...Ignore those comments Corporal," Roberts instructed.

"Certainly General."

"What about the Bombers? I've got Churchill's authority to bomb Dieppe if we want, right?"

"Yes General, but the Royal Air Force said the likelihood of hitting Dieppe, let alone specific targets looks small. They're willing on your command to try-"

"No," the General decided after a moment, shaking his head firmly. "I'm not going to take the chance. All they would do is bomb the hell out of the land, blocking up my streets so that our tanks can't get through. Tell them no. They will do a light hit at the beginning, that's all. You have the map on you?"

"Yes Sir."

"Very good," General Roberts responded opening the door. "Set it up for me, please."

"Yes, General."

Nat along with her comrades looked up with great anticipation as General Roberts entered the room. Training just this May at Sussex beach near Seaford, the cliffs and coastline best resembled the North Coast of France. Dieppe had been announced in late June, but had been cancelled in July due to weather. As the map of Dieppe was raised back up on the wall, Nat and many of her peers were confused.

"Good morning gentlemen, and lady," Roberts candidly began. "As you can probably see, the map of Dieppe has been placed on the wall. This mission has been postponed six times during the first week of July due to weather, and canceled shortly thereafter. Not for good though.

For those of you who are Irish, put your superstitions aside. This is not a sign, but merely a temporary glitch, and the raid of Dieppe has been resumed. Get your pencils out, because on August 18th, we will be sailing out with approximately two hundred and fifty-two ships, carrying yourselves with tanks from one of our four designated ports," he pointed. "Southampton, Shoreham, Portsmouth, and New Haven, which will be assigned later. Deputy Commander of this operation, Brigadier Churchill Mann will explain the details," General Roberts announced, stepping aside.

"The beaches of Dieppe, code-named Red and White, will be reached at approximately 4:50 a.m., August 19th, by yourselves, the Second Canadian Infantry Division. This is to ensure that the attack is a surprise, and that the dark aids your cover. Four flanks will be landing a half hour before the main frontal assault on Dieppe. On the far left, British commandos will destroy the gun battery at Berneval, code-named Yellow Beach. Landing at Puys, the Royal Canadian Regiment and a company of the Canadian Black Watch are to destroy guns on the east headland overlooking Dieppe harbor. That position will be code-named Blue Beach. On the extreme right commandos will destroy the Varengeville battery, known as Orange Beach, and the South Saskatchewan regiment and Cameron Highlanders will land at the Green Beach of Pourville.

The beach of Dieppe itself, code-named Red Beach, will be the largest and most difficult to penetrate. This mile-long beach will have the Royal Hamilton Light Infantry on the Western half, code-name White Beach-"

Nat knew that the Red Beach was where she was going. It made sense. All of her training was geared towards this moment. Nat would finally step into combat, after four years of cumulative training with Chris, her training camp back home, and her advanced training in Britain.

"The eastern half will be the Essex Scottish, and Les Fusiliers Mont-Royal," he finished.

That was Nat's battalion.

"The mission is simple. Destroy German defenses, capture German prisoners, and disable all communication and transportation sites. Questions?"

As the men queried further, asking their various questions, Nat was caught up in her own thoughts.

She was going.

Finally.

Wait until she tells her Dad! He will be so pleased.

Chris too.

She was going.

Soon.

Was she ready?

As General Roberts boarded the navy destroyer, Calpe, that early evening, August 18th, 1942, two hundred and fifty two ships, carrying 4,961 Canadians, alongside fellow British, American, and French soldiers, headed out across the Atlantic. All were lives, dependant upon a fate and destiny that only the unfolding of the next twenty-four hours would foretell.

Aboard, Nat waited restlessly throughout the night for H-Hour to come.

The Armageddon.

As the ocean tossed their boat to and fro, the men vomited throughout the hours, their faces resembling that of ghosts. Nat did not mind it too much. Holding onto the railings to keep her bearings, the rocking motion did not toss her about. Besides, she was used to the sea, fishing with her Dad on many occasions, and riding on the ferries.

'Just hang on and we'll get there soon enough,' she thought to herself. Preparing herself Nat knew that soon it would be time and she would need to be mentally ready. No fear.

As the hours passed, Nat could not help but feel that something was off and it was not her. A bad feeling persisted. Skeptical with the weather, their mission had already been delayed several times.

It seemed to be an omen.

Was it?

When the missile fire began at 3:47 in the morning, the unexpected had happened. A chance encounter as their boats met up with a small German convoy.

Completely unexpected.

Several boats ahead of Nat began firing, sending the enemy ship to its watery grave. The mission resumed its late schedule, but Nat could not help but think that the convoy had enough time to inform Dieppe before it went down.

If the element of surprise was lost, it could prove to be disastrous for the men who would arrive before her.

How foreboding the fog appeared in the dark, its humidity overwhelming as the sweat rolled down Nat's face. Closing her eyes, not to sleep but merely to rest, the ocean with its drumbeat would coax her senses. It was a beat that she was all too familiar with. Its rhythms comforted, its beat she felt in sync with. Lyrical, the beat grew stronger in her heart and she felt strengthened. It was an effortless bond.

Feeling a light touch upon her right cheek, Nat opened her eyes slowly to see the sun rising in the East. A glint of luminescent red streaked across the early morning sky, as if lit from the bottom of the ocean itself. It so caught her attention, that Nat found herself unable to look away. Despite the rolling waves, she could not take her eyes off its beauty. What a sunrise!

How it reminded Nat of home at that moment. Going out to the Kennebecasis River, where she would catch the morning's mist rising up off the waters, its gentle fog gliding across the air. How Nat had felt she had stepped into something magical each time. A beautiful fantasy world, an Eden, that was solely for her and her imagination. Taking a breath, nothing beat the smell of the water. So pure, so fresh, it revitalized her.

This time however, the sun would not be a friend. The cover of darkness was slipping away, their ships unveiled to the human eye. The Germans saw them, and as the missiles began their fire, the water exploded, rocking Nat's boat violently.

The Germans knew they were coming.

As Nat felt her adrenaline rush, she grabbed hold of her crucifixion necklace. "Look after me God. Protect my regiment," she whispered, as the sound of bombs, firing guns, and crashing waves grew louder. Sounding like thunder as her boat neared, it drowned out everything else, even Nat's prayer.

'Keep steady,' she told herself.

Steady boys.

The Royal Air Force over the East headland had completed their initial bombings to neutralize defenses as Nat's boat swarmed inland to shore. However, being the last group to arrive, its impact on the Germans who had scurried to hide, was only temporary.

As their boat arrived, there was a sudden stop as Nat's regiment hit shallow waters, throwing most of the men forward. The door flung open.

GOOOOO!

It was time to go, but Nat was not prepared for what came next. The first man out had machine fire rip across his waistline, cutting his body in half.

What the hell was that? He barely got off the boat. He didn't even take a step forward!

More followed, seeing if they could avert the machine gun fire. They couldn't. As soon as they stepped out they were shot down. One in particular, Tommy Cochrane from the Essex Scottish, when shot, looked up and cried, "Jesus, we got ta beat 'em!" With that he took a step forward and that was his last, as he collapsed face first into the water.

"**NO ONE ELSE MOVE!**" Nat ordered.

"I am the Commanding Officer here and I will be the one giving the orders! Let's go everyone!" As Lieutenant Colonel Fred Jasperson headed out, he urged his men who were alive one moment, dead the next, forward. For the few men from his battalion who would make it to the four-foot-high stone seawall, they would quickly place a long, thin explosive, the Bangalore torpedo under the barbed wire that was above the wall.

As it exploded, they rushed over the wall, only to find that the wire had been parted for three feet. The depth of the wire they would have to get through to penetrate was ten feet. As the Essex tried to cut through, the German snipers atop the cliffs above, with great advantage began their fatal fire. Only a dozen crouching men would make it through, the remaining men, Jasperson included, stuck at the seawall. Using the only walkie-talkie still working, he informed the Royal Hamilton Light Infantry that twelve of the men had made it into buildings on the other side.

Nat had to help them, but if their battalion went, they too would be stuck. Everyone turned to Nat as she scanned the boat to analyze a possible alternative.

The cliffs had the largest fire and best range of all men who tried storming the beach. If they could get near the cliff, under shelter and with the ability to move, their battalion could figure out what to do next.

"How about we jump out of the side, swimming over for cover under the Western cliff. That will protect us from most of the gunfire. We can decide there what we'll do next, but we need to make the beach first."

The men nodded. Their odds of even making it on the beach were painfully obvious to all.

"Let's pull back out to the water," Nat offered. "Anyone who can't swim?"

A few raised their hands quietly. "Well, today you're gonna learn," Nat shrugged. "Pull back."

As the boat pulled twenty meters back out into sea, Nat yelled out one last command amidst the explosive gunfire. "If we jump out together, they are less likely to hit as many of us, than if we went out one at a time. Pick a guy to jump with and stick with him. Cover each other. Do that, and I'll see you all on the beach. Remember why we are here. We have a mission to complete. Let's do this."

The men nodded.

"Are you all ready?" Nat asked. The entire squadron was ready to follow. "On my mark, jump fast….Steady boys."

Everyone was ready.

"GOOOOO!!!"

GO BOYS GO!

In pairs, the men jumped overboard, Nat with Billy. They would cover each other, through hell and back.

How bitingly cold and bitter the Atlantic ocean was. Nat could hold her breath for a long time, as she swam through the darkness of the sea's blood red waters. Despite the bullets ripping by, Nat had made her way to shore, along with many others from her battalion, who all ran like hell, zigzagging across the shore, to avert machine fire. Racing out of the water with Billy, Nat ran like the wind, despite the heaviness of her soaked clothes. The relentless machine fire trailed close behind them, as both began screaming, sprinting for their very lives. There was no time to think, just run!

Throwing herself under, Nat landed safely, the last bullet never catching up, as Billy hurdled himself in with her.

"Holy shit!" Billy exclaimed, reaching for his flask. Checking her body for possible hits, Nat had survived without a single shot wounding her. Catching her breath, Nat had to calm down. She needed time to think and couldn't do that if she was too wound up physically.

Nat was going to stay put so as to wait for more of her comrades. Taking a shot from his flask, Billy passed it over to Nat who took a sip.

Safe in the embankment, the men supported one another as they all ran for the cliff.

"Run!"

"Come on!"

"Don't stop!"

"You can do it!"

The German artillery continued its savage fire, but the men came in. The piercing screams and cries of the wounded as they lay dying permeated the musty, death-filled air. It distracted Nat's ability to focus and think.

It appeared that all platoon units were fragmented and displaced. Cut off from one another, it was impossible to organize themselves. The men, including Nat, were reluctant to leave their shelter, let alone go forward without some organized plan, or the cover and firepower of the tanks.

"Where the hell are the tanks?" Nat said aloud to herself, frustrated. Arriving late, the Calgary Regiment and its Churchill tanks found at least two hundred men in their path lying dead or wounded on the beach. Nat and her comrades watched in horror as some of the tanks got stuck in stones, while others that did move forward, halted at the seawall, unable to go any further. The remaining two, of twenty-nine, drowning in deep water.

"Look," Billy pointed out. Some of the tanks were making their way around the low ends of the wall.

"You see?"

"I see it," Nat affirmed smiling. "All right, let's follow those tanks up. They'll run over the barbed wire. It's our best chance of making it to town. Lock and load."

Everyone stocked up, checking over their ammunition.

"Ready?" Nat said. "GOOOOO!!!"

As her unit ripped out from under the cliff, many found shelter behind the tanks as the Germans fired away. A good sharpshooter, Nat took out two soldiers in the tower to help the men who were still coming in. Everything was flying their way with the sole purpose of wiping the Allied troops out in entirety. Surely they were being taken one by one.

GO Boys! GO!

Witness to a slaughter, Nat felt the wind come her way, carrying her across with such a speed that she knew that God had to be helping her.

Making it past the barbed wire, a grenade exploded, sending two men flying at Nat, striking her from behind. As Nat slammed face forward into the hill's muddy puddles, the pain and weight on her back was instant. Struggling to push off whatever dead figure lay on her back, Nat could not lift her face out of the water and breathe, so heavy was he. It would be Billy who would roll him off and grab Nat's collar, yanking her out of the water with a mighty pull. With eyes wide, Nat coughed, spitting out water, as she gasped for air. The pounding of her heart was palpitating at an accelerated rate.

"You okay," Billy asked. In a state of shock, Nat was unable to respond.

Had she been hit?

Touching her face and body to check, Nat nodded.

Body parts were all around her, blown off from the explosions. A bullet barely escaping his own head, Billy hit the ground, pulling Nat for cover. The tanks had become stuck again, like their platoon, this time in front of a concrete obstacle barricading the town.

As Nat and Billy huddled under the tank's cover, Nat looked on in horror as she saw Dieppe's tide begin to roll in. A tide that would reach an eventual height of twenty-two feet. The wounded were going to drown as they waited for reinforcements.

In that moment, Nat felt her heart rate slow. An anger slowly ignited within her heart, numbing all fear. Nat scanned the beach with new eyes. It was an impenetrable focus that strategically honed in on key military sights.

Forcing herself up, Nat ran for cover behind a nearby Allied tank that was closer to her targets. Most of the firing was coming from the cliff line.

"Nat!" Billy yelled, but soon followed suit. Together, they began picking off their German counterparts As the tide rolled in, men began coming out from their cover to pull the wounded above the high water mark.

"Nat?" a voice cried out in agony.

Nat glanced frantically to the beach line. Raising his arm up, Nat saw that it was Raymond.

The lucky bastard was still alive.

Running over to him, Billy covered with a steady fire as Nat picked up Raymond, and the two of them staggered for cover with Billy behind the tank.

"I think I'm hurt, bad," Raymond said trembling, his body going into a state of shock. Nat lifted his shirt up to look at his wound. Sure enough, he had been shot in the stomach.

"You're going to be just fine," Nat tearing a strip of her own shirt, applying it to his wound. "Give me your hand," Nat instructed, and Raymond did so. "Keep the pressure on. You have to stop the bleeding."

"Okay," Raymond said painfully, feeling as helpless as a little child. Nat threw off her helmet. "Who's left?" he yelled to Nat terrified, seeing no one else.

"You're looking at it," Billy said, replacing his ammo. "There are a few others up the hill."

"Reinforcements will come. They were supposed to be coming right behind us," Raymond assured, trying to calm his own fears. "Goddammit, this hurts." Nat knew she had to do something, or he was going to bleed to death.

"Can you run?" Nat asked, knowing there was only one place to go.

"Yeah. Why?"

"We're going to die here if we stay," Nat determined, "and I'm not leaving you behind. You can't fight so I'm taking you back. We can do this," Nat assured.

Raymond knew she was right. To go forward was suicide for him. Nat and the others could continue, but he would be left for dead.

"Are you with me?"

"I'll do whatever you say Nat. Let's do it."

At that moment, Raymond could not help but look at Nat with tears in his eyes. The woman he had loathed, sabotaged, was now saving his life. He didn't know how to say sorry to her. Especially now when the time to do so seemed so wrong, but Nat could see his regret.

"I know Raymond," she comforted. "We can do this. I'll cover you."

"Give us your ammo," Billy demanded, and Raymond complied.

"See that rock? Run there first for cover. Then we'll try for the boat." Raymond nodded. "Ready?"

"Ready," he yelled back.

Again Nat ran as fast as she could, and again she made it. With a nod, Raymond darted out across the beach, as Nat and Billy covered him from their positions. Struggling, Raymond gave it all he had, because his life depended on it. Even if he wanted to quit, he still had a chance to make it.

"Holy shit. Holy fucking shit!!!" Raymond gasped, leaping behind the rock with Nat.

"You hit?" Nat yelled.

"No. Those bastards are just crazy. They don't want to see anyone make it out of here alive!"

"Catch your breath. Next cover is the boat."

"Nat, I don't think I can-" Raymond said, exhausted and faint from losing so much blood. Just then, Reverend John Foote of the Royal Hamilton Light Infantry walked up to them.

"You hit?" he asked.

"Yes," Raymond answered.

"Let's go," the man said, bending down and lifting him up. "The boat is under the cliff."

"I'll cover you," Nat said.

As the two men ran across the beach, Raymond had made it to safety. Nat knew she could head back.

"Lord, make me fast," Nat prayed before running out.

Running past the shell fire again, the grenades made it feel more like an obstacle course.

Similar to the one she had trained on, how much her training was paying off as she hurled herself back behind the tank once more.

"Boy are you fast!" Billy exclaimed amazed.

Nat looked back and saw the men still trying to save the wounded as the tide came in stronger.

"The boats are leaving. They are retreating." As Nat looked up, she saw that Billy was right. "Why in the hell are they leaving? HEY! HEY!!!" Billy yelled, trying to get their attention to no avail.

That's when it all began to sink in. The truth of their situation and the reality of their mission. Nat looked down at the ring Chris had given her, her hope fading as she watched the boats sail away. Nat's eyes began to well with tears.

Nat was not going to see Chris again.

Dad.

Eva.

"We're gonna die," Billy said panicking.

This was it.

Or was it?

"Oh my God," Billy said defeated, "this can't be it. What the hell?"

No. This was not it.

"We can't stay here, hiding," Nat determined defiantly. "We've got to penetrate their line. If we don't do that, not only will we have failed to complete our mission, our duty Billy, but we won't see our families again. I don't know about you, but I didn't come all this way, just to die on my knees, hiding, waiting for them to come get me. If I'm gonna die, it will be standing up," Nat resolved, with great conviction, offering her hand. "Let's do this and see what we can do. Maybe we'll break through their lines and take the town, but we won't know unless we try. I think we can do it," Nat said impassioned. "I believe we can!"

"We can," Billy acknowledged finally, smiling.

"Let's do it," Nat answered with calm resolve. "Check your ammo. I'll take the right flank, you take the left."

Their Bren LMG rifles were set.

It was time.

Each took the other's hand, as both knew that a prayer was in order. Nat prayed aloud, "Lord, keep with us and protect us, for we know. Although we are about to walk through the valley of shadow and death, we fear no evil, for thou art with us. Thy rod and thy staff protect us. Always, no matter where we go."

They had each other to blaze a trail. God had brought Billy and Nat together for a reason. For this very day, everything leading up to this moment.

It would be their defining moment.

"Let's do it," Billy nodded.

Nat nodded with a smile, a tear running down her cheek. As both got into position, with a heavy breath, Nat turned to Billy one last time.

"Ready?"

"Ready," Billy shouted back, above the gunfire.

It was time.

15

Thrusting out from behind their cover, the next thirty seconds would feel like an hour's worth played out in slow motion. Sprinting closer to the German line, Nat raised her rifle to fire twice, killing two German soldiers from afar.

How far from home she was.

Hurdling over the dead, Nat flew as fast as her legs could carry her, but one leg would catch.

Tripping, Nat fell hard, losing sight of all when she did peer up. The smoke was suffocating, and she was lost in its haze. Fumbling about, Nat staggered to her feet and searched for her bearings.

It was then that her eyes met up with Billy's. Without saying a word, they smiled at one another for a brief second, relieved beyond measure to see that the other was still alive.

It was with her guard down that Nat bolted backwards, the bullet ripping through her right shoulder.

"NAAAAAT!!!" Billy yelled out.

Lying flat on her back, Nat did not feel like she was shot. Only that something had pinched her.

Maybe the bullet had escaped her?

A bit stunned, Nat kept her head down. Hiding behind a large rock boulder, Billy was too far away to do anything, so she would have to stop the bleeding herself. As Nat began searching for the wound, touching the right side of her stomach, fumbling her way up her right arm, to eventually her right shoulder, Nat was unable to feel anything.

Something was wrong though. Ripping open her uniform with the remaining strength she had, Nat discovered that her white undershirt was soaked with blood. Rolling her neck over to her right, she could feel the entire right side of her upper body begin to go numb.

Why didn't it hurt or was it going to very soon? What was she going to do?

God, this can't be it.

I can't be dying here.

No.

Looking above at a gray sky that was filled with smoke, Nat tried thinking her way to a safe place. Don't panic because if one panics, fear takes over.

Think.

If Nat remained still, without medical care she could bleed to death, possibly in as little as fifteen minutes.

Nat could risk running for cover at the expense of being shot at again, but without her right arm, Nat would not be able to fire her rifle anymore.

What was left of her arm that is.

Hopefully some of the others made it.

This can't be it.

A quiet desperation began to take over, as Nat had begun to realize…no matter how much she tried to figure a way to get out of this, there wasn't one. Nat was trapped.

No escape.

As the thought sank in more, real fear began to set in. Nat had always been able to get her way out of anything. What if she couldn't this time? What if she couldn't find a way?

That is when Nat began to cry, silently to herself. "God," she said, turning her hope heavenward, "help me, please...I know you're there."

The pounding of machine gun fire raged on.

"I don't want to die."

The sky was mournful.

"I'm scared God. Please, I beg you, please help me..."

Bombs exploded and the crackle of men screaming filled the morning air. All of its thunder drowning out her words.

All sounds were beginning to fade for Nat as well.

That's when it came, dropping down from out of the sky. A beautiful, piercing vision of white descending, its wings sweeping the dusty clouds aside as it flew towards Nat. From a bird's eye, Nat was the tiny one this time, her small figure lying stranded below on the battlefield.

Nat saw her. In the distance, courageously journeying through death and destruction, she was coming to bring her hope. To be by her side.

As the bird flew closer, Nat knew that it was God who had sent her Little Nat. God had answered her prayer. Little Nat had returned to help her fly when she needed it most.

I am never alone. We are never alone. By my side forever. Nat could hear a voice whisper, as Little Nat continued to encircle around her from above.

Fly. Come fly with me.

Fly, Nat thought to herself. Could she really fly? Was she trapped or did she truly have the power to set herself free from all this through God's grace?

I want out God, her thoughts louder. I want freedom.

"The Lord is my shepherd...I shall not want..." Nat recited, rolling over onto the left side of her body. Taking a deep breath, she used her left arm to painfully push herself up.

"He maketh me to lie down in green pastures; He leadeth me beside the still waters," Nat spoke resiliently, grappling for her rifle. Not that she would need it where she was going, but she was a soldier still.

I will not die in a cage, trapped.

Let go of the fear.

Stumbling onto her feet, Nat rose up, and was shocked next at the vision she saw before her. No longer standing on the battlefield, Nat had entered a whole new realm that was amazing to behold, the ugly remnants of war completely gone.

Vanished.

Now standing at the tallest peak, Nat looked around to see if it was all real. Squinting, she realized it was indeed the Bay of Fundy cliffs!

Standing tall on its glorious mountain top looking at the world from above, Nat had new eyes. Its panoramic view consumed her very being. It was by far, the most beautiful, most breathtaking place on earth! That's when Little Nat from above, flew above and past her, surpassing the cliff's edge. Look at her go, Nat thought.

Could Nat do it?

Could she really jump? Could she really let go of her fear and just trust?

Believe.

The love that filled her was amazing.

As Nat took her first step towards the cliff's edge, so too did she on the battlefield.

"Thy rod and thy staff, they comfort me," she recited smiling, following Little Nat who was leading from above. The battlefield was not so scary anymore. "You prepare a table before me in the presence of my enemies, anointing my head with oil, and my cup runneth over."

Breaking out, Nat picked up her pace on the cliff as she gleefully started running to its edge.

"Surely goodness and mercy shall follow me all the days of my life, and I will dwell in the house of the Lord forever," she finished, beginning to charge forward on the battlefield with every ounce of energy and strength she had left.

"I love you God," Nat resigned, dropping her rifle and lifting up her arms to fly. Nat was running with Little Nat again, just like he had done when she was an orphan. Just as the pitter patter of her small feet were surprisingly fast that sunny day on the playground as she tried to keep up with her furry friend back then, Nat was running underneath the bird again, this time on the battlefield.

One last time.

Leaping from the cliff, Nat no longer struggled as she fell. No longer would she try to reach out and grab a branch of some sort to hang onto. It was time to let go of all she knew. To let go of everything and take the fall.

Believe.

Trust.

God would carry her all the way home.

As dead weight, Nat fell down far, arms open wide, as if embracing the sky. That is when everything slowed, and Nat felt herself become as light as a feather.

Opening her eyes, Nat could not help but smile as she screamed with girlish delight.

Nat was simply beside herself!

I'm flying! I'm really flying!!!

With arms open, Nat soared through the air behind Little Nat, and the freedom overwhelmed her.

On the battlefield, like the orphanage, the gates were no longer closed to her. Running effortlessly, Nat pushed the gates wide open, finally free.

Let me show you more, the bird whispered. The pace quickened over lakes, rivers, and valleys that were so stunning, that Nat was in awe. What beauty! Running towards the enemy line, the Germans could see her in the distance coming.

"I'll go with you anywhere Little Nat," Nat whispered, closing her eyes in surrender.

With their rifles raised to firing position, the Commanding Officer yelled out the order to fire.

Freedom.

As the bullets simultaneously rippled through the morning air, Nat convulsed under the sheer force of machine fire. Flying violently backwards, Nat's temporal flight had come to an abrupt end.

"NOOOOO!!!" Billy screamed.

Nat's body was convulsing on the ground.

"NAAAAT!"

As Nat looked up to the sky, she saw the dove still there.

Waiting.

Nat was going to be all right.

Racing from his cover nearly ten yards away, Billy aggressively made a rush for Nat, escaping the gun fire that trailed behind him. Slinging Nat over his shoulder, Billy ran safely back to his cover.

Setting her down, Nat started coughing out the blood in her throat that was choking her.

"Don't worry," she heard Billy say. "I've got ya'."

Good old Billy. A good friend.

"Nat?" he yelled, seeing her begin to fall in and out of consciousness. "Stay with me!" he ordered. "NAT!?"

Nat's breathing was becoming steadily irregular, as she struggled to stay alive. Resting her back up against the rock, Billy looked into her anguished eyes. The pain was starting to set in. Lifting up her bloody undershirt to see how badly she had been hit, Billy was horrified by what he saw.

Nat's stomach was literally disemboweled.

"Oh God Nat," he whispered in agony. Pressing his hands against her wounds, to slow the bleeding, Nat moaned and cried out in pain. Billy didn't know what to do. The blood was draining through his fingertips, escaping everywhere. "Nat! Stay with me!" he commanded. He didn't know what else to say. Nat sensed he was scared because Billy wouldn't look at her.

"I'm okay Billy," Nat forced, shivering uncontrollably. She was so cold. "If you…get out," she whispered, blood oozing out of her mouth. "Give this to Chris," Nat said, her eyes making reference to her necklace. It carried her promise ring.

"Tell him…that I love him…always will."

"My Dad too..."

Billy held onto her hand. It was all he could do. Keep wiping away the blood that was all over her face. His hands were covered in it.

"Shhh," he comforted.

That's when Billy heard something. Turning quick, it was the sound of footsteps. Were the Germans coming for him?

Just then over a hundred Allied troops came running out from the smoke and fog, abandoning their cover. The reinforcements had come!

"Nat, they're here! Holy Christ, they're here! We're going to make it! I'm gonna get someone quick who can help you...I'll be right back! Promise!" Billy yelled excitedly, leaving Nat behind so as to signal the oncoming troops. As the Allied troops charged the German line, the Germans began their fire. The high-pitched screams of men being bludgeoned and shot continue to pierce the morning air.

Yet, Nat could hardly hear them anymore. Their cries were being drowned out by her struggle to keep breathing. To speak one last time.

"Lord, unto thee-do I lift up my soul," she whispered crying, the pain relentless. "I trust in thee," she panted. The remainder of the prayer she kept to herself, lacking the strength to utter another word.

'Let me not be ashamed,

Remember not the sins of my youth, nor my transgressions...

According to your mercy remember me for my goodness' sake God.'

Little Nat glided down to rest on a nearby boulder rock, nearly thirty yards away from Nat.

Only now was Nat beginning to understand with the last few breaths she had left what her purpose had been in the time she had been given. At the time of her mother's death, Nat did not fully know why, but now everything was clear.

The General, the only Dad she had ever known, needed her. Just as he had saved her that day in the orphanage, God had sent Nat to save him.

With her love...

How Little Nat's life had been *all* about love.

As memories from Nat's short life began flashing before her eyes, various scenes began to flicker. Blinking, Nat saw that the dove on the boulder rock was now a woman sitting down at that same spot. Dressed in white, the woman was watching Nat, waiting for her.

The morning Nat was born, when her mother pushed her out and held her for the first time.

An unconditional love.

Struggling through her first walk as a baby. How her mother's arms reached to catch her from falling. How her mother held her, with a love that was protective, nurturing, and comforting.

The day her mother died in the hospital bed where she lay next to her ailing body...I love you mommie.

Reading a book to Mary...

Little Nat's arrival...

That first day she met her Dad, the General, as a little girl. "You're big," she commented aloud to his chuckle. "That's the army, girl." How strong and wise he looked.

Despite his fallibility, he had been a perfect father. Nat's strength. How he meant everything to her....

Eva's wisdom and guidance...

Then that day she met her soul mate, Chris. How handsome and charming he was from the very beginning, the two of them unaware, that it was destiny...

How Chris made her laugh and cry, but that was okay. It was all worth it.

The fun times they had together, playing football. That first day he began 'training' her. They were great friends...Prom night when he danced so close, Nat could feel his heartbeat...A love that warmed and soothed her, like a quiet fire that would never burn out.

Not even with the passage of time.

The first and only time they made love.

It was her life, and it was all about love.

Nat could not stop crying because she knew that soon she would forget this life that had been hers. How desperately she fought to keep breathing so as to hold on. Hold on to all the wonderful memories she had of people who meant everything to her.

Thank you Sister Marie.

It is so hard to let go of you all. I can't believe this is it, Nat whispered, struggling to hold on.

Look after Dad, Chris...Remember me when I am gone. Remember me because I will no longer remember you.

Let go, a voice gently whispered to her.

Let go of your life, for it is time to pass.

"I can't."

Regrets? "

If I had to do it all over again, I wouldn't change a thing. "I've had a great life. I love you…I love you all," Nat whispered, hoping that by saying the words aloud, they would carry. Everyone she knew would hear her and know this deep down inside, because her whisper would reach their hearts. They would know, remember and feel it long after she was gone.

I love you.

Bleeding to death, Nat's pulse was dying, her entire body numb to the touch. There was not very much pain anymore, as her weary eyes glanced over the men fighting all around her.

This is only the beginning, the voice whispered.

That is when the young woman rose up from the rock and began walking over towards Nat.

As Nat's breathing slowed, the woman walked on unnoticed by those fighting and dying all around her. It was as if she wasn't there at all, invisible to this world.

Little Nat had come for her. By God's authority, Nat was His and the woman would claim God's beloved child.

What warmth is this that touches my face?

As Nat lifted her head, she became seized by a light that illuminated her entire vision. It was just the two of them now. With eyes wide open, Nat was entranced by the woman who stood looking down upon her fragile body that had been ripped apart from the guns.

"Mom?" Nat whispered, blood gurgling out of her mouth. "I'm so glad to see you again," Nat smiled up at her, crying.

With an extended hand, Elsie whispered into her daughter's being.

It's time to go home...

No longer able to speak, Nat reached out her trembling, blood drenched hand, so as to touch her mothers. Finally, they were touching again! As Elsie raised Nat up, they both smiled upon one another, overcome by an overwhelming joy that Nat had never before experienced. Reunited at last, Nat no longer had blood all over her.

On the other side, Nat was clean, and there was no more pain.

That is when Elsie motioned Nat to look behind her. No longer on the battlefield, Nat recognized the sight before her immediately. Cornerbrook, Newfoundland! Darting away from her mother momentarily, Nat ran towards the town to see for sure if she really was home.

"Can we go back to Hampton too?" Nat asked excitedly.

"We can go anywhere we want," Elsie answered, walking up to her daughter. Smiling down, Elsie offered her hand. A little girl's hand took hers back. Looking up at her mother, a seven year old Little Nat smiled a toothy grin. Walking home together, this time it would be for good.

"Nat!" a voice quietly echoed from behind her, but Nat could no longer hear.

"Nat?" Billy called out to her, returning to the rock. "NAT, we're gonna make it! There are a few boats coming back. You hear me? Nat? Nat?"

Something was wrong. With her head resting on her chest, Nat was no longer answering him.

"Nat?" Billy asked again, slowly raising her head up. It was then that he knew. Nat's eyes were permanently open.

"Nat! Shit, Nat!" Billy yelled, grabbing her limp body and shaking her. "Wake up Nat! NAATT!!! God No! Nat?"

He had left her to die alone."I'm sorry Nat."

It was no use. As he let go, Nat's dead body slumped down onto the ground.

A promise was a promise. As Billy bent over, reaching for her necklace, he had let his guard down with dire consequences. With his head exposed, a great pain ripped through Billy's throat. Stunned, he looked down to see blood squirt and gush all over Nat's limp body that was lying dead in front of him. Wanting to speak, to scream, Billy was unable. Grabbing a hold of his throat to stop the bleeding, he felt himself getting tired. Darkness overwhelming his eyesight, Billy's eyes closed within seconds, his lifeless body collapsing onto Nat's.

16

When the smoke had settled, the German soldiers combed the beach side to collect the bodies of the dead for mass trench burial. There were many, as bodies stretched along the bloody shoreline of the beach were videotaped by a German soldier as proof of Germany's victory and unequivocal power. The footage would certainly be a boost for soldier morale back home.

Other German soldiers turning over the bodies, handkerchiefs over their faces, checked for valuables. As Billy was raised off of Nat to be inspected, a German Private caught sight of Nat's promise ring and pocketed it. Whisked away, a German Lieutenant did a double take on Nat. Bending down, he took a closer look, inspecting her I.D. dog key. Knowing some English, he read her name aloud.

"Natalie Bovaird Shaw."

Noticing the Canadian flag emblem on her uniform, he was taken back. Even Canadian women fight for their country.

"I have never killed a woman, nor have I seen one dressed in uniform before, Natalie," he spoke in his native tongue. "You were a brave girl. You look my daughter's age. It would have been interesting to have seen your face as we fought you, but this does not exist in combat any more. Days of old. Machines look after that now, as we see the faces of our enemies only in death," he said, closing her eyes. "One of us must prevail. That is the way of war," he spoke respectfully.

"What do you want me to do with her, Lieutenant?"

"She was a soldier. Put her with her men," the Lieutenant answered, rising to stand.

Taking her lifeless body, the two German officers threw Nat into the 'pit.' Soon, the dirt would be thrown over her body and the dead bodies of her comrades.

Friends.

Brothers.

At rest finally, Nat was in a place where she could lie beside the ocean forever. An ocean where she once stood, looking out, dreaming about reaching the other side, only she had.

Nat had the courage to follow her heart, risk it all, and upon falling, find the greatest love she had ever known. All that it offered.

Freedom.

Peace.

Beloved.

As the dirt was thrown on her face, you could hear Nat whisper.

'I love my beloved and my beloved loves me...'

Playing cards at his home amongst four male colleagues, General Shaw gloated as he won another round. At eight o'clock that evening, he was sweeping house.

A knock came at the door.

"Eva," he yelled, "can you get that please?"

"Yes General," Eva called from the kitchen, going past the men in the dining room to answer the front door. Opening, Eva was not at all surprised to see a young officer in full uniform, standing before her.

"Yes, can I help you son?"

"Yes Ma'am, I need to speak with General Shaw?"

"Certainly. Come right in," Eva offered. "General, there's a young man here to see you," she announced in the dining room, as the officer followed suit.

"I'm General Shaw," he replied gruffly, unable to break away from his game. "What can I do for you son?"

"I'm sorry to disturb you at this hour, but I have come from the War Department General. I have a telegram for you sir," the soldier answered quietly, holding the envelope. Everyone at the table immediately stood up to leave.

Eva sensed something was gravely wrong, as the mood of the room shifted.

"We'll be going Robert," one of them said, as all motioned to Eva to bring their coats. The General could not take his eyes off of the letter. When Eva returned with coats in tow, everyone abruptly left. The General stood still, preparing himself for the worst.

"Read it to me son," he ordered, "because I don't want it." The Officer dutifully complied, reading its contents aloud.

"General Shaw," he began, "we regret to inform you that your daughter, Natalie Roberts Shaw, was killed in action, this August 19th, 1942-"

"Oh God, no," Eva gasped, her hands covering her mouth in shock. "It is noted," he continued on, "that Natalie fought courageously, saving the life of her corporal, before returning to aid her regiment in the Allied invasion. Your daughter died an honorable death."

The General stared at the letter in shock, as Eva broke down crying into his arms.

"I'm sorry General. Is there anything I can do for you?"

"No," he answered quietly with a forlorn look in his eyes. It was as if this all was not real right now. As if time was standing painfully still. "There's nothing you can do for me son except leave me alone to collect my thoughts," he said firmly. The Officer respectfully showed himself out.

Putting Eva to bed, the General went down to the kitchen to fix her some hot cocoa.

To soothe her, only he found himself standing alone at the entrance of his living room instead. Looking about the room, his eyes drifted aimlessly, devoid of all purpose. That is when he saw his favorite picture resting upon the fireplace mantel. Their first picture together. Walking over, he remembered that Nat was ten at the time…Their very first outing hunting. Wearing his clothes and hat, they were holding the rack of the deer that they had got 'together' that day. Honing in on her, the General was transfixed by her smile. Nat had the most incredible, beautiful smile on her face.

How good they looked together.

A perfect match.

That is when the General felt Nat's presence again. Someone was watching him. As he turned around, he remembered seeing her as a little girl, standing at the entranceway looking up at him. At the orphanage office, it was the very first time they ever met.

Relief flooding over him, the General smiled at Little Nat this time around, because he was no longer awkward. How she was just as he remembered her. The memory was perfect. As Little Nat remained at the doorway looking up at him, something was different this time. Nat smiled at him shyly, unmoving. The General smiled back, waiting for her to come to him. Just like she did that day in the office, walking over to him first. The General offered his hand, but Little Nat just stared back at him.

From the doorway, she finally spoke.

"Goodbye Daddy."

The horror of it all had begun to sink in, swarming his very soul. Shaken, it was the General's eyes that revealed his loss.

Nat was indeed gone, and so was that day in the orphanage. The General was indeed alone in his living room after all.

His little girl was gone.

No more hunting together. No more fishing or shooting. No more Christmases together. Never would he see her wedding day, give her away, nor see his grandchildren grow up. If he had known that last year would be their last, he never would have let her go.

Gone.

He just could not believe she was gone.

His little girl.

Murdered.

A rage was building in him and there was nothing he could do about it.

Why God? Why?

How he wanted to destroy something. Anything to help ease the pain of his grief.

"Why?" he asked, looking to the ceiling, so angry was he at God for taking Nat away from him so soon. Angry at himself for letting her do it. Angry at a fucking world that just gives out nothing but SHIIITT!

Taking the lamp, the General in a fit of rage began smashing everything in sight. Eva, incapacitated by her own pain, was unable to help him. The General was tearing the house apart.

"You stupid son of a bitch!" the General venomously spewed, cursing at God, himself, and a world that ultimately destroys anything that is good.

"WHY NOT ME!!!? Huh? Why not MEEEEE!"

"TAKE MEEEEE!" he shouted in anguish, fists raised. "So many times, I should have died, but no. You keep me here to ROT!!!"

"It should have been me," he shouted, exhausted. "Why her!? Why do you leave me here when I don't want to be here!? Why did you take her and not me?" he broke down crying.

He had to get out of here.

He had to leave.

Too many memories in this place.

Slamming the door behind him, all the General could do was think of how much he wanted Nat to come back home. He had to go off and find her somehow, but that was not going to happen this time. There would be no refuge to comfort the General that night.

Not on the worst night of his life.

Walking up the hillside that bright summer day, ironically a chill was in the air that morning. It was after all, Nat's funeral, and everyone involved felt numb. Twelve days had passed since the General had first learned of his daughter's death, and the effects showed. Drained, the General was void of all expression.

Still, he had to be strong for Eva, whom he escorted on his right arm, inviting Chris who was crying, to walk along his left. When they reached the coffin that was to be lowered, Chris felt the hand of the General upon his shoulder, which helped strengthened him. As the priest began speaking, the three stood to bow their heads, along with many other people, strangers, who had gathered to mourn her death.

After all, she was one of their own.

The General had arranged to have Elsie's burial moved to Hampton, so that her daughter could be with her forever. Buying the rights to a familial burial plot, Nat would rest eternally next to her mother's tombstone.

The voice of the priest faded as the General could not help but drift away into his own thoughts. Earlier that morning, as he put Nat's prom dress, her favorite musical box that her mother had given her, and her army graduation picture in the casket, the General reread a letter Nat had written to him shortly before her death.

Her voice he could still hear. As he stared at her coffin being lowered into the ground, Nat's enthusiastic voice spoke to him from beyond the grave.

"Hi Dad,

It's me! I am writing to let you know that I am fine, and that I have not seen any action yet, but I am sure it will be any time now! Our forces are so ready to prove ourselves again, like we did, you did, in the last war. I can't wait..."

The General smiled as he looked across the empty field. He remembers what it was like, so many years ago, when he really believed in what he was doing. The strength and vigor of his youth protecting him, keeping him alive through it all. People would fall all around him, but he would remain. These times were tortuous as he watched family, comrades, his own daughter, destroyed by the harshness of this world.

"What I have seen I know you have too Dad. Families murdered and children crying on the street because they have no one. It makes me realize how precious life is Dad. How I notice it more now, and I am thankful for all that I have.

I do miss the Maritimes. The beauty of the trees, its landscape. Everything here has either been burned or destroyed in some way that I miss seeing beauty.

I also see how everything falls into place. That we are all connected. Life is our center, not us. We all revolve around life, so as to sustain and preserve it, and God has a grand plan for all of us.

So many times, when I was in the orphanage, I did not understand why this was happening to me. How I longed to go back home, to Cornerbrook, where in this version, my mom was not dead. I would grow up, living a simple life, and I would be content, perfectly happy.

The thing is I never would have met you then…Eva…Chris. I never would have had the experiences I've had, or the memories I have grown to cherish more and more as I am out here. I would never be what God meant for me to be, so I don't think I ever would have been content. Something would always be missing…"

Lying on his own deathbed, of all the nurses to encounter that fateful, chaotic night in the military hospital, only Elsie would come to save him. That same night, Elsie would save his life twice. As he thanked her in his own, silent prayer, words could not express his gratitude enough. The General had known for a long time that something was missing in his life. It would prove to be Nat. Only by God's grace did they find one another, as Nat saved him from his own self-destructive, lonely life.

"Sometimes I feel so small in the scheme of things, but I am not. We are all important and make more of an impact than we could possibly imagine. We all matter to God, so I understand now that I must do my part to give back what life has given to me…"

As the General looked up to see around him, he knew what Nat was talking about. Always the idealist, her words made perfect sense. Life was a beautiful thing.

"All this makes me realize Dad that I want to live, more than ever. Not merely exist, for I have found a happiness in me that I have never felt before. One that can only come from knowing your purpose in this world, as God places me where I am needed, to use the gifts He has given me for His will. I could not have found this out if I had not come here, and chosen to stay. To go out every morning and be a light for others, developing my heart. When I die, I want people to say "Nat, I remember her doing this for me," or, "she used to make me laugh." I want people to remember me for what I gave to them. Not to die and have no one remember you, because you gave absolutely nothing to anyone or anything would be such a tragedy. I want to leave my 'mark.'

Dad, I always knew in the orphanage that there was a world out there that I wanted very much to be a part of. It may not be a world that I expected. It is not the world that I dreamed of initially, but a new dream has begun. I am very happy to be a part of its circle, as I am making my mark... I love you! Tell Eva I love her too, and I will see you both soon!"

Love, Nat

As the funeral service ended, Chris and the General shook hands. They were strong for each other. As the General and Eva slowly walked down the field together, one man remained standing alone, across from Chris to pay his respects. Finishing a silent prayer, this lone figure stared one last time at the coffin laid before him. A coffin which could have been for him.

"Rest in peace Nat," was all he could say to express his sincere gratitude for saving his life. As Raymond slowly left the quiet field, Nat was dead, but her memory and 'mark' lived on.

It was a mark that only the passage of time would reveal as true and profound.

Chris remained the lone one standing at her coffin that day as everyone else left, and as the decades passed, so he would remain still.

All those years later.

Standing alone at her grave.

Waiting.

After all this time.

Bending down on one knee, an elderly Mr. Woods gazed long and hard at her tombstone.

"Life has not been the same without you Nat. I am sure that you know your Dad quit the military soon after your death. I was told he walked right up to General Stevens, looked him square in the eye, and handed over his Arms. He then walked away and never looked back... He lived a good ten years after your death..."

Looking over, Chris saw the General's tombstone next to his only daughter.

"He found happiness with Eva," Chris added, glancing over at Eva's tombstone that rested next to her husband's, the General. "I would visit him Nat, but he never was quite the same after you died. We actually became very good friends throughout the years...Eva took really good care of him too. I know he is up there with you right now."

"I had heard that his death was painless. A heart attack in his sleep, so he never felt a thing, which is good...People still leave you flowers," Chris added, clearing some of the flowers to make room for his own rose. "That's because people love you. I bet you didn't know that, did you? I bet you didn't know that partly because of what you did, over fifty thousand Canadian women joined and served in the war effort after you. There was a Canadian Women's Army Corps of over twenty thousand, a Women's Naval Service of nearly seven thousand, and a Women's Air Force Division of nearly sixteen thousand…I just thought you might want to know that you made history Nat," he added with a smile, laying the white rose in front of her tombstone.

"So, here I am. One of the few left from those old days…I brought you your rose."

Chris looked at all the tombstones around him.

"No, there's not many of us left. Charlie's just up there," Chris said referring to Charlie's tombstone up the hill. "Makes me wonder when my time will come. Cheryl has passed on from leukemia, and I am sure that the two of you have met, because she was an angel too. Yes, that was five years ago," Chris said holding back his tears.

"It is not easy being one of the last ones, you know. Time has a way of just dragging on…so many memories… so many regrets."

"I miss you Nat," Chris spoke with finality. Just to say that after holding it back for so many years felt good. Not visiting for a long time, Chris had stopped visiting because it was just too painful.

"If only I had known. Maybe if I had more maturity, could I have told you sooner how I really felt…I could have had the chance to say goodbye. Yet, here I am, still talking to your tombstone, hoping to get some sort of comfort. All the while I feel bitter because you were just taken from me," Chris' voice quivered as he placed his head into his hand. "All I think about is what could have been if you had lived….I loved and still love my wife Cheryl very much…She was a wonderful wife and mother. You would have liked her. It's not that I love her any less…I've made my peace with her, because we had our whole lives together."

"I just thought that my love for you would fade over time. What surprises me most is that it hasn't… It hasn't gone away…It's so strange how love can last over sixty years…How is it that I can still feel the loss of you as if it all happened just yesterday? I don't understand why I can't put you to rest," Chris said crying. "You haunt me, and I can't let you go. That's why it has been so difficult coming to your grave sight after all these years…I should just let go, but then I would lose you entirely, and not have you at all…You know I still carry your picture in my wallet?" Chris asked, removing her picture from his wallet to show Nat. "Somehow that keeps you alive, in my mind….In my heart. You were my first love Nat….Next to my wife, you were one of the most beautiful women I have had the privilege of knowing. You helped me become the man I was meant to be. I want you to know that.

I still remember the way you looked that prom night…No other girl could even compare. Radiant. An angel in the night that sparkled when your Dad walked you in….

I wonder how you died. If it was painless and quick?….If you thought of me, like I'm thinking about you right now? Did you even have time? All the what-ifs…I hope you weren't alone when you died…I hope someone stood by you so that you weren't scared," Chris painfully whispered, tormented by so many unanswered questions.

Chris then heard a laugh he had not heard in years, coming from afar. Looking up, still very much upset, he saw nothing.

Was someone watching him?

Then he heard it again. A young girl's laugh filled the air. Chris looked to his right, then to his left but saw nothing.

Then he knew where it was coming from. One place he had yet to look was straight ahead. Slowly, his head turned back, his eyes following. Bent down, amongst the flowers, was a young girl, with black hair, a pale complexion, wearing a beautiful white, cotton dress. The girl did not seem aware of his presence as she continued picking the prettiest flowers she could find.

As Chris slowly rose to his feet, staring at this apparition in disbelief and wonder, the young girl stood up. Smelling the flowers in her hands, she slowly looked up to match his gaze, and it was Nat!

As a tear fell down his cheek, Chris gave her the biggest smile. This was Nat as he remembered her, that very first day at the Summer Fair. Recognizing him instantly, she ran down the field to embrace him. Too old to do the same, Chris merely opened up his arms to her, and Nat ran into them. The two embraced, holding each other tight.

"Hi!" Nat cried, tears in her eyes.

"Hi Nat!" Chris quietly wept. "It is so good to see you." Nat smiled at him with great love in her eyes. Chris clasped her face into both his hands and asked, "Do you know how long I've been waiting to talk to you?"

"Yes I do," Nat excitedly nodded. "That is why I am here."

"What do you mean?" Chris asked confused.

"What it is that you want me to know," Nat answered, seeing the pain in his eyes. "I have watched over you all these years Chris. You had a beautiful wife, and five great kids. You were also a fine teacher and coach. Those kids were lucky to have you. You have helped so many children, and I am so proud of you Chris. You have a wonderful life. God has been looking out for you," Nat comforted.

Chris did not know what to say. "I know," Nat said, reading his thoughts. "You have been hurting for a long time, only you did not quite know it. Old wounds will always resurface until they are healed. All these years you have wondered if maybe you brought me to my death in some way. How different life would have been........It wasn't your fault," Nat reassured.

"It wasn't?"

"It was a war that never should have happened that killed me. Not you....I wanted to be there.....It was my time. I am here to let you know that....Some people take a hundred years, but in my life, I fulfilled my purpose in twenty. It was my time."

"Thank you Nat. I needed to know that," Chris finally answered.

"I know...I also wanted to say thank you for all the roses over the years!" Nat said with a laugh.

"You're welcome," Chris smiled. "It's my way of letting you know that I think about you. That you're still my girl."

"I know and believe me, there will be a white rose waiting for you, Christopher Woods, when your time comes.....Until then, I have to go," Nat said breaking away.

"Do you really?" Chris asked.

"Yes...I love you Chris. Time doesn't change love. If anything, it only makes it stronger."

"I love you too Nat. Thank you."

Chris had finally told her how he felt.

About to leave, Nat slowly turned around. "Do you remember that song they played that first 'official' day we met one another?" Chris shook his head. "I was dancing with my father...ba, ba, da, da, da, ba, ba, da,da, da, ba, ba, da," Nat hummed, singing its melody. "The Annual Summer Fair?"

Then Chris remembered its tune. Smiling, he offered his hand. Nat smiled back at him, gave a curtsy, and took his hand. Suddenly, they both heard the lively music that had played that day, and it was as if the two were teenagers again. Laughing, they danced wonderfully together.

Then, as quickly as they had started, both stopped, mesmerized by each other's gaze. Pulling her close, Chris gave Nat a tender, soft, sweet kiss on the lips. At that particular moment in time, it was the summer of 1938, Chris was fifteen again, and Nat was the girl he was going to get!

"Bye Chris," Nat's voice quivered, her eyes looking as if she did not want to go.

"Bye," Chris said, knowing that she had to. As Nat turned around, Chris fondly watched her walk away. It was at the tree that she stopped one last time to turn around. With her right hand, she signed 'I love you', and Chris signed 'I love you' back. Nat then gave a short wave, and walked away, and as Chris watched her go, his memory of Nat faded away.

It has been said of Mr. Woods by the local townspeople, that he had lost 'reality' the day he swears he met up with the spirit of Nat. On the contrary, he had always carried her spirit with him. By visiting Nat's grave, it was a way of confronting his own pain and loss. When visiting a grave, one attempts to keep the memory of a loved one alive for many reasons. Perhaps to get that second chance to say what was never said, or to make up for time lost, that was never given. The desire being always to never forget someone who touched our lives in such a deep and profound way, that we linger still for them to return and stay forever.

As Chris lifted his cane off her tombstone, he knew he had finally found inner peace within himself. There was now closure to a very special chapter in his life. Walking away he thought, 'to love Nat had been worth it.' After all, she was a very special girl. From her he learned, among many things, that life must never be taken for granted. Cherish each day and every moment, because life is indeed a very precious thing. From a bird's eye, Little Nat watched him leave from a tree branch above.

Always watching.

Listening.

As he walked out of the cemetery, down the road, Chris had begun to fade away from memory too. What would inevitably become his last visit, Chris had left his white rose at her tombstone.

Little did he know at the time, that his rose was coming soon enough.

Continuing to walk on towards the town, so too was Chris fading from all sight…

Becoming a spirit of the past-

Gone from this world-

A memory-

Until no one remembered him at all-

It was a peaceful death.

Perched on the stone tombstone, Little Nat fluttered her wings and took flight to the sky, soaring into Heaven.

Christopher William Woods
June 1st, 1922-March 16th, 2004

"Beloved"

THE END

LaVergne, TN USA
14 April 2010
179287LV00001B/2/P